Talk Gertie To Me

Lois Winston

LOVE SPELL  NEW YORK CITY

To Rob, Chris, Scott, Jen, Jack, and Zoe
for being what matters most.

LOVE SPELL®

April 2006

Published by

Dorchester Publishing Co., Inc.
200 Madison Avenue
New York, NY 10016

ISBN 0-505-52684-0

Printed in the United States of America.

Visit us on the web at www.dorchesterpub.com.

NONE OF THE ABOVE

I motioned to my laptop dangling at his side. "You were reading my files."

To his credit, Mac flushed with guilt. At least he was man enough not to lie his way around the flagrant violation of my privacy. "Yes, well, actually, I want to talk to you about that."

I stiffened. "Talk about the height of hubris! You read my diary and then expect me to discuss it with you? I don't think so."

Mac blanched. "Your *diary?*"

"What did you think you were reading, a download of *Crime and Punishment?*"

"I thought it was e-mail correspondence you had saved to a Word file. Are you telling me that *you're* Gertie? Damn! This is too good to be true."

"What?" I grabbed for my computer, shoving his at him. "You, Mackenzie Randolph, are a pervert."

He grinned at me. "And you, Nori Stedworth, are the answer to both of our prayers." Then, instead of taking his computer and handing me mine, he placed his palms on either side of my face and kissed me.

I should have yanked myself out of his grasp. Kicked him in the shin. Slapped his face. Spit in his eye.

One of the above.

Some of the above.

All of the above.

Instead, I did none of the above. Instead, I kissed him back.

ACKNOWLEDGMENTS

Whereas it takes a village to raise a child, it takes a city to birth a book. My thanks go to the many citizens of my "city":

First and foremost, to my agent, Carolyn Grayson, for her faith in my talent and her refusal to give up on me.

To Karen Davenport, critique partner extraordinaire, I offer my undying gratitude for all she does and continues to do. And to the inventor of e-mail, who made it possible for Karen and me to communicate across an ocean as easily as if we were in the same room.

To all my friends, family, online buddies, the readers of *RT BOOKclub* magazine, and everyone else who voted for *Talk Gertie to Me* when it was known as *Resurrecting Gertie* and was a finalist in the first American Title competition. Also, thanks to Dorchester Publishing for instituting the American Title competition and choosing me as a finalist and to *Romantic Times* for hosting the competition in their magazine and on their Web site.

To all the people at Dorchester Publishing, a huge thank you for making my dream of becoming a published author come true, for shepherding my manuscript through the many stages of production, and for a truly awesome cover.

To Phyllis Towsey for coming up with the *Talk Gertie to Me* title and to all the members of both the Yahoo! Chick Lit loop and RWA's Chick Lit Writers of the World for rising to the challenge when I needed a new title for my book.

To Priscilla Hauser for first thinking up belly button casting. You may never have gotten on Johnny Carson with your idea, but I've gotten you on Letterman, if only vicariously and via a book of fiction.

Finally, to Romance Writers of America and the various chapters I belong to (New Jersey Romance Writers, Valley Forge Romance Writers, Kiss of Death, and Chick Lit Writers of the World) for teaching me so much. This book would never have been possible without the knowledge I've gained from these organizations and the friends I've made along the way.

Talk Gertie To Me

"You're listening to WBAT—Big Apple Talk Radio. I'm Gertie, and this is *Gertie Gets Even. Go ahead, caller. You're on the air."

"Hi, Gertie."

"How can I help you?"

"All the guys I meet turn out to be snakes or skunks. What should I do?"

"And you live where, caller?"

"New Jersey."

"Ah! Well, that explains everything. As I see it, you've got two choices. You can either call an exterminator or move across the Hudson. We don't have any snakes or skunks here. Just two-timing rats. Next caller. Go ahead. You're on the air."

Chapter One

Chapter One

Well, this day was a total waste of makeup
From *The Tao of Gertie*

"Times Square. Crossroads of the world," said Reese with a flourish of her arm as we exited the subway onto Forty-second Street. "And the only place in New York where you're guaranteed not to find a New Yorker." She scowled at me. "Except us."

"You're a good friend," I told her.

"You bet I am." We headed around the corner, shouldering our way through a crowd congregating in front of a tabletop Rolex salesman. Reese nodded toward the gullible tourist handing over two crisp twenties to the sidewalk hustler. "A sucker born every minute," she said, loud enough for several heads to turn and stare at us. Subtlety wasn't Reese's strong suit.

I thought about the watch I bought for my father's birthday the first week I arrived in the city. Heat crept up my neck. "Not too long ago I was that sucker."

She elbowed me in the ribs and laughed. "But we cured you. Now you're one of us."

"Damn right." I nodded in appreciation. "Good-bye, small-town Iowa naïveté; hello, cosmopolitan New Yorker."

"So, Miss Cosmopolitan New Yorker, explain why

you dragged me to Disney World North on our lunch hour."

When I stopped walking and pointed to the restaurant on my left, she tossed back her head of multicolored dreadlocks and groaned. "This is about Dave, isn't it?"

My goofy grin said it all. I, Nori Stedworth, was in love. Head-over-heels, butterflies-in-the-stomach, heart-pounding, walking-on-clouds, song-singing *in love* with a capital L-O-V-E. For the first time in my nearly twenty-six years as a living, breathing homo sapien.

Yes, I had been in love before. At least I had thought so at the time. In hindsight, though, each of my previous relationships—all of which could be counted on one hand with a couple of fingers to spare—had fallen into either the puppy love, infatuation, or lust categories. Unfortunately, this revelation always dawned as I picked up the pieces of both my shattered heart and fractured ego. But I was older and wiser now; I'd learned from my failures. And this time I knew beyond a shadow of a doubt that it was the real thing. Love with a capital L-O-V-E.

Which explains why I had left my sanity in some subterranean cave—or at least on the subway—and now stood in front of AWE, the American Wrestling Enterprise theme restaurant.

"Tell me we're not going in there," pleaded Reese.

"I have to."

"You're not in love, girl, you're in denial. Need I remind you that you *hate* pro wrestling?"

"True." I'd rather run a marathon with ten ingrown toenails than sit through an hour of steroid-filled, muscle-bound men and women knocking each other's brains out.

"Then what are we doing here?"

I shrugged. "You know how much Dave loves pro

wrestling. He lives for his weekly fix of choreographed insanity. It's his one flaw."

"One?" Reese raised both eyebrows.

I shot her a scowl. "I don't understand why the two of you don't get along."

Reese rolled her eyes. "You want a list? Let me count the ways."

I held up a hand to stop her. Besides Dave, I had three close friends in New York: Reese, Gabe, and my dearest friend, Suz. Other than Reese and Gabe, none of them cared for each other. Whenever I tried to get everyone together, the results were disastrous.

Last February I invited all four over for a winter doldrums party. Big mistake. Finally, in desperation, I popped in a video, and for the next two hours we sat in silence, munching on popcorn, drinking wine, and watching Russell Crowe slay tigers and gladiators. After that, I gave up, resigning myself to seeing Suz without Dave, Dave without Suz, and Reese and Gabe without either Suz *or* Dave.

"Look, his birthday is coming up—his thirtieth, and he's already dropped a number of none-too-subtle hints about *Mania and Mayhem on Broadway*."

"I'm afraid to ask."

"It's The Great White Way's newest offering to the culturally challenged masses. Three hours of half-naked wrestlers prancing around the stage of the Broadhurst Theatre." Okay, I'll be the first to admit I'm a culture snob. To me, the very idea of sitting through such an evening made *Hairspray* sound like Sophocles.

"Definitely theatrical sacrilege," said Reese. "Rodgers and Hammerstein are no doubt flip-flopping in their graves."

I ignored her sarcasm. Reese didn't care much for Broadway, highbrow *or* lowbrow. Her tastes ran more in the direction of salsa and reggae.

"So you're going to swallow your pride and buy him tickets?"

I offered her a weak smile. "A woman in love will do most anything for her man, including throwing a tarp over her common sense."

She greeted that confession with another groan. "And I'm here because?"

"Moral support." With that I grabbed her hand and dragged her into the alien universe of AWE.

Having caught glimpses of wrestling on television, I expected to find myself surrounded by insult-hurling eight-year-olds and their tattooed and pierced older counterparts. I wasn't disappointed. The room was filled with raucous diners of both sexes and all ages, shouting and cheering at the overhead television monitors as they gobbled up their meals.

Body art abounded, especially on the groups of teens gathered around many of the tables. Most of the men wore jeans and muscle shirts; most of the women wore hot pants and bare midriffs.

Reese glanced around the crowded room. "I think we made a wrong turn south of Saturn."

I eyed her outfit. "You fit in better than I do." She wore black leather Escada trousers and a spaghetti-strap peach corset-style silk shirt. My Ralph Lauren taupe linen suit made me stand out like a vegetarian at a pig roast.

She frowned at the overly violent scene on one of the TV monitors. "Why are we here instead of at the box office?"

"Because this is the only place you can buy tickets, thanks to some marketing genius." In a ploy that took commercialism to new heights—or more appropriately, new lows—the producers of *Mania and Mayhem on Broadway* had chosen to make tickets available only at the AWE restaurant. Not in a separate gift shop, but right in the middle of the restaurant. That way, they could tempt die-hard fans into shelling out above and beyond the one hundred dollars a ticket for all sorts of merchandising accoutrements, not to mention a meal. Smart move, considering the producers of the show were also the owners of the restaurant.

For twenty interminable minutes we inched our way forward in the ticket line. The sights and sounds of celebrity wrestling bombarded us from every corner of the cavernous space. From giant television monitors mounted around the perimeter of the room. From mega-watt speakers blasting play-by-plays. From the raucous patrons, screaming their enthusiasm, stomping their feet, and pounding their fists into tables as they watched their favorite testosterone-filled jock pummel his opponent with a stepladder. The heavy odors of fried chicken, burgers, and fries saturated the air. I tried not to ogle the freak show atmosphere surrounding me; Reese openly ogled.

"Dave's going to owe me big-time," I muttered under my breath.

She smirked. "He's going to owe you big-time squared after you sit through an evening of warbling and waltzing wrestlers."

I grimaced at the monitor where one tattooed, muscle-bound jock had just bashed a folding chair over another tattooed, muscle-bound jock's head. "Not enough. Definitely big-time cubed."

"Whatcha want, gorgeous?"

Two tickets to the ballet? I smiled to myself. Dave hated the ballet as much as I hated pro wrestling. Payback would come on *my* birthday.

"Hey, red, you wanna stop mooning over the Boulder's tight ass and tell me whatcha want? I ain't got all day."

"Nori." Reese nudged me out of my reverie.

That's when I realized I had made my way to the head of the line, and the thick-necked guy with the nose ring and shaved head was speaking to me. "Two tickets for next Saturday night." I handed over my credit card.

"Orchestra or balcony?"

My preference would have been balcony. Last row. Obstructed view. Reluctantly, I said, "Orchestra."

"What else?"

"That's all."

He raised one pierced eyebrow and leered at me. "They're for sale, you know."

"Excuse me?"

"The Boulder."

I glanced around. "What boulder?"

"*The* Boulder. The guy you were drooling over." He nodded in the direction of a life-sized cardboard wrestler wearing a leather vest, a matching thong, and a menacing grin. Nothing else. "You can stand him up in your bedroom and eye his assets to your heart's content."

Heat surged up my neck and into my cheeks. "I was *not* eyeing his assets!"

"Sure you weren't, sweet cheeks." He winked. "I can wrap him up in brown paper for you. No one'd know."

"Just the tickets," I said, wishing I could click my heels together and disappear. Damn. There's never a pair of ruby slippers around when you need them.

"How about a T-shirt?"

"Just the tickets!"

"Key ring? Hat? Beer mug?"

"No, no, and *no!*" I had to laugh despite myself. Did I really look like someone who would sport a snarling wrestler-emblazoned baseball cap? I glanced at the lunchtime crowd and then at the Coach wallet in my hand. I didn't belong in this place. I wasn't one of *them*.

Was I the only one who saw the incongruity here? I turned back to the clerk, who despite all appearances to the contrary, obviously mistook me for a fan, and shook my head. "Just the tickets, please."

He refused to give up. "What about something for your friend?" he asked, motioning to Reese.

"No thanks," she said. "I gave up wrestling for Lent."

He shrugged and ran my card. "Enjoy the show," he said, handing me an envelope after I signed the credit slip and passed it back to him.

"Oh, yeah. Definitely."

"What some people won't do for love," said Reese as we exited the world of *Wrestlemania*.

I felt the need to defend my beloved. "Look, other than this one little Neanderthal throwback penchant, Dave Manning is everything a girl could hope for."

"Really?"

"Yes, really. He's a drop-dead gorgeous hunk with a great sense of humor."

"I'll grant you the hunk. The jury's still out on the sense of humor."

"And he has a promising career as an up-and-coming dermatologist. He's poised to take over his father's practice when Dr. Manning retires next year."

"Aha! So it's really about his money."

"No, of course not."

She elbowed me. "But it doesn't hurt, right?"

"Okay, I'll admit the money's a nice bonus, but it's more than money. Dave has class."

She screwed up her face. "You're confusing class with Upper East Side snobbery."

Even though I knew I'd never convince her, I tried to explain. "He knows how to dress."

"Big deal. My four-year-old nephew knows how to dress himself."

"Not dress himself. Dress correctly. And it *is* a big deal. At least to me."

"Okay, I guess I can understand, given the last guy you dated."

"Don't remind me." I cringed at the memory of Ethan Fried showing up in a T-shirt and cut-offs for a coworker's engagement party at the Plaza.

"Let's get down to what really counts," said Reese. "How's the sex?"

"Shh!" I glanced around to see if anyone had heard her, but the crowd passing around us remained oblivious to our conversation. Still, I couldn't contain my grin. "Let's just say on that score alone I could forgive Dave his fascination with wrestling *and* a hundred other annoying habits—"

"Aha!"

"*If* he had any."

Reese shook her head. "Love is blind."

"Not blind. Open-minded. It enables me to grin and bear my way around the wrestling."

"And what do you get in return for all your altruism?"

I exhaled in exasperation. "Honestly, Reese, you make love sound like a list of debits and credits that have to be balanced out at the end of the day. Dave loves me. That's all that counts. Besides"—I beamed at her—"with any luck, a freak tornado will descend on New York and decimate the Broadhurst Theatre prior to next Saturday night."

Reese erupted in laughter. "Talk about grasping at straws."

I shrugged. "Hey, a girl can hope, can't she?"

She glanced at her watch and changed the subject. "I'm hungry. Why don't we grab a bite to eat, then walk back to the office instead of taking the subway? There's a deli over on Sixth that makes great salads.

Things are so slow that no one will miss us if we take an extended lunch."

The tantalizing aroma of spicy chicken filled the corner where we waited for the light to change. My mouth watered; my stomach growled. I glanced behind me at the street vendor hawking chicken burritos.

"On second thought, forget the deli," said Reese, following my gaze.

Big mistake. I've never burnt the roof of my mouth on a forkful of endive and raddichio.

One bite of the steaming burrito and I swear I could feel the blisters forming on my palate. Tears streamed down my face. Through my blurred vision, I saw Reese spit out a projectile mouthful, christening a startled tourist from Albuquerque.

At least I think she hailed from Albuquerque. Could have been Alberta or Albania. A splattered mélange of chicken, hot sauce, cheese, peppers, and flatbread covered all but the first three letters of the bright blue word plastered across her T-shirt.

The woman stared in stunned horror first at her shirt, then at her husband, and finally at Reese and me. Her mouth opened and closed several times but no words came out.

Reese was too busy guzzling water to offer the woman more than a guilty shrug of apology.

The woman's husband glared at Reese, then grabbed his wife's arm and yanked her away from us. As they hurried down the street, he yelled, "I told you we should have gone to Salt Lake City, Gladys. But no, you wanted to see New York. Seen enough?"

As for me, my parents hadn't brought me up to spit on strangers. So like some hair-brained cartoon character with steam spewing from his ears, I tried to hold the food between my front teeth, keeping the poultry

11

inferno from inflicting further damage, while I struggled to untwist the cap on the bottle of water I had purchased.

I couldn't swallow. I hadn't had a chance to chew, and besides, my throat had instinctively tightened in protest and defense. No way was it allowing me to risk the same damage to my esophagus. My entire body broke out in a cold sweat. My eyeballs stung. My damp palms, hindered by the burrito I still held, kept slipping over the plastic cap of the water bottle.

I glanced over to Reese for help, but she was too busy attending to her own burnt mouth. With little alternative left, I grabbed the edge of my suit jacket and wrapped it around the neck of the bottle before giving one final jerk.

Just as the cap gave way, someone jostled me from behind, unleashing a huge glob of hot sauce that fell from the tilted burrito and landed smack in the middle of my skirt. A millisecond later, most of the contents of the bottle splashed over the blob, spreading the quarter-sized stain into a flowing pink river that looked suspiciously like a menstrual cataclysm.

A fresh wave of tears gathered behind my eyes. I had just spent two hundred hard-earned dollars on wrestling tickets. I couldn't afford a new suit, and short of a Martinizing miracle, there was no way any cleaner could salvage my dry-clean only skirt. I pulled my attention away from what used to be my best suit and gulped down the remaining water, swooshing around the mouthful until the chicken cooled enough for me to chew and swallow it.

Through watery eyes I noticed a group of pointing, staring teenage boys hovering off to the side. They snickered and laughed, shouting out the type of scatologically laced mockery I hadn't heard since my practice teaching stint at a junior high school in Sioux City. Not surprisingly, each wore an AWE T-shirt with the face of some snarling wrestling superstar plastered across the front.

A dreadful thought forced its way through my haze of pain and embarrassment. If I married Dave, would his wrestling-loving genes find their way into our child and produce an offspring who would grow up into a counterpart of one of those subhuman adolescents? It was a sobering notion. Maybe Dave's love of wrestling wasn't such a benign diversion after all.

Now, along with a scorched palate and a ruined skirt, I began worrying about my yet-to-be-conceived progeny. As the boys continued their heckling, my irritation grew exponentially. "Juvenile delinquents," I muttered.

"Witness America's future," said Reese, having regained her composure and her voice. She glared at the boys. "I'd like to mash this burrito into their smug, pimply faces."

Of the two of us, Reese generally acted first and thought last. If at all. I lived a more cautious life. "Ditto, but there are five of them and only two of us. Besides, their combined weights probably equal that of a Volkswagen Beetle. Dripping wet, you and I don't add up to much more than a moped. Not good odds." I tossed the remainder of my burrito into a nearby trash can.

With a grunt of disgust, she hurled hers in after mine. "I hate when you go Pollyanna on me, even if you are right."

Moving from rural Iowa to the Big Apple was a greater culture shock than I had expected. People were different here. Very different. I had quickly acquired the nicknames of Pollyanna, Goody Two-shoes, Rebecca of Sunnybrook Farm, and Dorothy—of the ruby slippers, not Lamour or Dandridge.

"You're so naïve," my friend Suz had said when I first met her. "Remember, you're not in Kansas anymore, Dorothy."

"Iowa," I reminded her.

"Kansas. Iowa. What's the difference?"

"Two extra letters—Iowa has four, Kansas six—and a boat ride down the Mississippi."

She shrugged. I don't think Suz has any concept of geography west of Staten Island. "Whatever," she said, "but if you want to be a true New Yorker, Nori, you have to stop being a Goody Two-shoes. It's a rat-eat-rat world out there. You have to learn to do unto others before they do unto you."

Apparently, they have a different version of the Golden Rule in Brooklyn, where Suz grew up, from the one my parents taught me back in Iowa. Shrugging off over twenty years of life in Ten Commandments, Iowa, wasn't easy. When you grow up in a town like Ten Commandments, you have to be a Goody Two-shoes—especially if you're the mayor's daughter, the minister's niece, and the great-great-granddaughter of the town's founder.

With a bit of trepidation, I turned myself over to Suz's tutelage and went from timid country bumpkin to assured city girl in less time than it takes to till an Iowa cornfield. So any reference to those old nicknames made me bristle.

"Pollyanna, huh?" I scowled at Reese. Just to prove I could be as New York as anyone, I did something that would have made Suz proud of me and given my God-fearing parents apoplexy: I flipped those obnoxious reprobates the bird.

They flipped me back.

Reese shook her head and chuckled. "Sometimes you really surprise me, Nori."

She grabbed my arm, and we dashed across the street, jumping a stream of street sludge left over from last night's downpour and ignoring the flashing DON'T WALK warning. Along with half a dozen jaywalkers, we dodged three cabs, a FedEx truck, and a stretch limo. Of the eight of us, though, I was the only one in the line of fire when the limo rounded the corner, its right tire sailing through another river of gutter goop.

I shrieked.

"What a mess," said Reese, eyeing the damage.

I wiped some wet gunk from my cheek, shivering at the thought of what sorts of toxic waste covered me, and stared down at my suit. The taupe linen now resembled a Jackson Pollock spatter painting. Reese grabbed her middle and doubled up in a fit of laughter.

I failed to see any humor in the situation. "What's so funny?"

She wiped a tear from the corner of her eye. "Picture you and Dave fifty years from now, two doddering old fools in matching porch rockers, reminiscing about what you went through for his thirtieth birthday."

I offered her a wry smile. "I wonder if he'll still be watching wrestling." Then a horrible thought—one far worse than my earlier worry of wrestling-loving offspring—surfaced, settling in the pit of my stomach like one of Aunt Florrie's lead biscuits. I grabbed her arm. "Reese, what if one of our kids wants to *be* a pro wrestler?"

"Wow, I never thought of that. Big worry, huh?" She tapped her chin with a rhinestone-studded index finger and glanced skyward. "If I were you, Nori, I'd start praying my genes are more dominant than his. Meanwhile, unless you're pregnant—" She stopped and eyed my spattered abdomen. "You aren't, are you?"

"Of course not!"

"Then I wouldn't worry about wrestling rugrats for now." She scanned me from head to toe. "You have a more pressing problem at the moment."

I followed her gaze and groaned. The linen fibers had absorbed the watery filth, transforming the Jackson Pollock-like skirt and jacket into a blurry Monet. A blurry Monet on a day when the artist was in a really bad mood and only using browns, blacks, and grays.

With Reese in tow, I dripped my way to the Marriott, the closest hotel, and took the escalator up to the ladies' room. After stripping down to my undies, we went to work, Reese on the jacket and me on the skirt. Standing at the sinks, we flushed the linen with gallons of cold water.

"This isn't working," said Reese. The combination of hot sauce, sludge, and water had turned the once taupe fabric into a muddy shade of Pepto-dismal. "I think it's ruined. And for wrestling tickets of all things. Face it, Nori, no good deed goes unpunished."

Thoughts of punishment unleashed the inbred Midwestern guilt I had banished to the far recesses of my brain. Guilt never came by itself, though. It always dragged along self-doubt, triggering the memories of all those years of Sunday school lessons and church sermons. Was this some divine retribution for turning my back on my upbringing and moving to—according to my relatives—the modern day Sodom and Gomorrah? My parents would think so. After all, didn't they always tell me that God works in mysterious ways?

I heaved a deep sigh, lifted my head, and glanced at my reflection in the mirror. "Doesn't God have anything better to do than torture me for leaving Ten Commandments?"

Reese stared at me as though I'd fried a few brain cells along with the roof of my mouth. "Where'd that come from?"

I shook my head. "I don't know. I was just thinking maybe I'm in the throes of divine retribution or something for turning my back on my family and my upbringing."

"Jeez, Nori! Get a grip. You ruined a suit. It's not the end of the world."

"Why me, though?"

"Why not?"

She had a point. I shrugged at the soggy mess in the sink. "You're right. Shit happens, huh?"

"Got a Plan B?" asked Reese, nodding at the skirt and jacket.

I scowled at my suit. "If I go back to work in those, I'll be the butt of jokes for the next six months."

"A conservative estimate, considering some of the clowns in the office."

Dave's apartment wasn't far from the Marriott. "I have some clothes over at Dave's. I can change there before returning to work."

"Better also take a shower and wash your hair."

I glanced back in the mirror. "Yuck!" Although I had washed my face immediately after entering the ladies' room, my concentration had been focused on my clothing. I hadn't noticed the muck spattered throughout my hair. On a good day, my riot of strawberry blonde curls was hard to tame. After a shower of street gunk, I now looked like I'd spent a week battling my way through Amazon rain forests.

Reese wrung out my jacket and walked over to the hand dryer. "Damn," she said, pounding the button three times in rapid succession without producing so much as a whisper of air.

I tried the other dryer. Equally dead. Tossing the skirt back in the sink, I threw my arms up in the air and cried, "Can anything else go wrong today?"

"Cheer up. I think you've depleted your bad luck allowance for the year. From now on life should be a breeze."

"Yeah, if I survive the day without catching pneumonia." The early spring day had started out warm and sunny but not warm and sunny enough for walking the streets in a dripping wet suit. I squeezed as much moisture as possible out of the garments, then squeezed myself into the cold, damp, wrinkled skirt and jacket.

We headed back downstairs and through the lower lobby, an experience bordering on supreme humiliation. As I made my way outside, I suffered the condemning glares of the hotel staff and the morbidly curious stares of several dozen patrons.

"Smile," whispered Reese, grabbing my arm and offering a huge grin to a group of Japanese businessmen.

"Easy for you to say," I whispered back between chattering teeth. "You're not the one who looks like the loser on a reality TV show." Still, I took her advice. Filling my lungs, I stuck out my chest, lifted my chin, and pasted a brave smile onto my face.

Once outside I told Reese she didn't have to come to Dave's apartment with me. "It's going to take me a while to clean up. Why don't you head back to work?"

"You sure?"

"I'll be fine. Go ahead. I may treat myself to a soak in Dave's Jacuzzi."

She looked me up and down and nodded. "I'd say you deserve it."

Jacuzzis are but one of the many sybaritic pleasures Dave has introduced me to during our eight months together. Growing up in a Norman Rockwell kind of town, surrounded by nothing but corn as far as the eye can see, kept me from experiencing much of life first-hand.

College hadn't helped to widen my horizons. Mom and Dad nixed every one of my out-of-state choices. Both my undergraduate and post-graduate degrees came from a small private college within an hour's drive of home. A small private college where the president was my father's second cousin and the dean was my mother's aunt's brother-in-law. Thanks to my well-meaning but overly protective parents, I had about as much freedom as a cloistered nun during my six years of college and graduate school.

After graduation, my parents expected me to settle down back in Ten Commandments, teach English at the local high school, and eventually marry Eugene Draymore, the town's most eligible bachelor. That's when twenty-three years of toeing the line and being a good girl came to a screeching halt, culminating in my one and only act of defiance against Mom and Dad. I turned my back on them, on Eugene, and on Ten Commandments and headed for New York.

I've never looked back.

I didn't completely sever the umbilical cord, though. Besides short trips home for Thanksgiving and Christmas, I keep in touch with my parents by phone. I'd actually prefer e-mail, but Mom refuses to use it. So, I call them Wednesday evenings after my aerobics class, and they call me every Sunday after church. I speak of my job, the friends I've made, the museums I've discovered. They talk about that morning's sermon and Eugene. In the nearly two-and-a-half years since I left Ten Commandments, Uncle Zechariah's sermons haven't changed. They're still dull as dried-up Iowa corn husks, but then again, so is Eugene, who—according to my parents—has never gotten over my rejection of him.

Poor Eugene has the personality of an undertaker, which I suppose is appropriate, considering his family owns the local funeral parlor. Although not bad-looking in a monochrome, thin-as-a-cornstalk sort of way, Ten Commandments' best catch also tends to smell of formaldehyde and other odors I'd rather not contemplate.

Predictably, my parents can't understand why I don't want to become Mrs. Eugene Draymore and provide them with a passel of pale, thin, future-mortician grandchildren. "He makes a good living," my father constantly reminds me every Sunday. "He'd take care of you."

Eugene eventually takes care of everyone in Ten Commandments. I'm one of the very few who has left the town in any manner of conveyance other than a pine box. I never tell my father this, though. Instead I say, "I can take care of myself, Dad. I have a good job."

"But what about when you want to have children?" asks my mother, listening in on the other phone. It would never occur to her that a woman might keep working after starting a family. "And how can you think of raising children in *that place?* It's not safe." Then she usually launches into a ten-minute lecture on the evils of the city.

I've given up trying to explain the twenty-first century to my parents. Instead, I simply tell her, "I'm not ready to have children yet," and then change the subject as quickly as possible. There's no point in trying to change her mind about New York. With each call she worries it will be the last time we'll speak, thanks to the ever-present stalker-rapist-murderer-bogeyman-terrorist she's convinced is lurking on every street corner in *that place.*

Besides, why would I consider Eugene when I have Dave? Formaldehyde or Jacuzzi? Preparer of the dead or lover of life's pleasures? Ten Commandments mortician or Park Avenue dermatologist? Is there really a choice here? All that aside, as I mentioned before, sex with Dave is mind-blowing, whereas Eugene's kisses—the few that I had suffered through—were coma-inducing.

I shook Eugene, my parents and Ten Commandments from my head and entered the lobby of Dave's co-op. The doorman did a double-take at the sight of me, but since he knew I had a key, he simply nodded as I headed for the elevator.

Note to self: Never take an elevator with a faulty air vent while wearing a sopping wet suit. Cold air blasted me for twenty-seven floors. By the time the doors opened and I stepped into the hall, my body was wracked by shivers. I raced toward Dave's apartment, jammed the key into the lock, swung open the door, and didn't stop running until I got to the bathroom.

Then I froze.

So did they.

I stared at Dave. Stared at Suz. Naked. Together. In the Jacuzzi. Each held half-filled flutes of champagne. In his other hand Dave held a chocolate-dipped strawberry inches from Suz's open mouth. In a daze I stepped back and took in the rest of the scene. An uncorked bottle of Dom Perignon champagne rested in an ice bucket at my feet. Next to a pile of clothes. His. Hers. A platter of chocolate-dipped strawberries sat perched on the wide tub ledge.

No one said a word. The only sounds that filled the room came from the whir of the Jacuzzi, spewing steamy bubbles around my lover and my best friend. My lover and my best friend who on a good day barely tolerated each other's existence. Or so they claimed.

So what do you do when you discover Prince Charming is a toad—warts and all—and your best friend is the combined female reincarnation of Brutus, Judas, and Benedict Arnold? With as much dignity as my disheveled hair and clothing allowed, I walked out, making certain that as I turned to leave the bathroom, my purse knocked the platter of chocolate-dipped strawberries into the tub and the toe of my shoe accidentally-on-purpose kicked over the wine bucket, spilling the champagne on Dave's Armani and Suz's Dolce and Gabbana.

I don't know how I made it back to Greenwich Village. My legs carried me without benefit of my brain. My body and mind had gone numb. From cold and betrayal. I can't remember if I walked the nearly two miles or took a cab or the subway. I don't remember anything until I rounded the corner onto Bedford Street and saw a decidedly unwelcome sight parked on the steps of my apartment building.

At first I thought I was hallucinating, given the triple-whammy I had suffered. Fate couldn't be *that* cruel.

I stared at the hallucination. The hallucination stared back at me. I tried to blink it away. Instead of disappearing, it rose and spoke. "Nori, darling. I've been waiting hours for you!"

Chapter Two

I choked back the groan that rose in my throat. That old cliché, from-bad-to-worse, didn't come close to describing the unwelcome sight confronting me. I forced a smile and cloaked my voice in delighted surprise—even if *delighted* in no way characterized my current state. "Mom? What are you doing here?"

She didn't answer. Her eyes narrowed, and her hazel gaze fixed on my suit. Then she eyed me from head to toe, the way she used to when I was eight years old. I could see her brain sprockets spinning beneath her gray-streaked circa nineteen-fifties pageboy as she puzzled through the cause of my muddy and drenched dishevelment. Had I fallen off the tractor again or gotten into another knock-down-drag-out with Kurt Zwickel?

But I was no longer eight years old, and this was New York, not Iowa. When the lightbulb in her brain finally switched on, she jumped to the only other possible conclusion. "Dear Lord, you were mugged, weren't you?" She set on me like a mother bird examining a newborn hatchling, chirping and fretting, her fingers prodding and examining every exposed inch of my flesh.

"I knew it! You never should have come to this city. I

had a feeling this would happen. My earlobes have been itching for hours. Are you all right? Did you call the police? Have you gone to the hospital?"

Some people get premonitions of disaster. Mom gets itchy earlobes. I grabbed her wrists and stepped back, holding her at arm's length. "Mom, please, I'm fine. I fell victim to a mud puddle, not a mugger."

"Oh, my poor baby! You're shivering." She placed her palm on my cheek, then my forehead. "You don't feel feverish, but you are clammy."

Among other things, I thought. But Dave and Suz were off-limit topics. I wasn't up to an I-told-you-so lecture, let alone the accompanying reminder of the wonderful potential husband I had left behind in Iowa.

"Let's get you inside." She nudged me toward the concrete steps.

"No, this way." I led her to a second flight of stairs off to the side.

She scowled at the steps. "You live in the basement?"

"It's called a garden-level apartment, Mom."

"Uh-huh."

I didn't like the sound of that *uh-huh*. But far worse than Mom's *uh-huh* was the sight of the two enormous suitcases she dragged out from behind the concrete wall that separated the two sets of steps.

My mother was as opposite from a clotheshorse as any woman could get. Her entire wardrobe consisted of five church outfits—one flowery print shirtwaist with lace collar for each Sunday of the month—and an assortment of denim jumpers, blouses, and turtlenecks. Give her a sunbonnet and apron, and she'd look like she stepped out of *Little House on the Prairie*. Except for the decorative accents she embellished on each jumper. I don't think Ma Ingalls ever painted a border of watermelons or sunflowers around the hems of her skirts.

24

"How long were you planning to visit?" I asked, mentally comparing the contents of her closet and bureau at home to the dimensions of the two suitcases at her feet.

"We'll discuss that later. First, we need to take care of you before you catch your death of cold."

A hot shower would take care of my shivering limbs. The part of me that really needed fixing wasn't going to respond to a cup of tea or any of Mom's home remedies. But as I lifted one of the suitcases and headed down the short flight of steps to my humble Greenwich Village hovel, I realized that although I had no intention of telling her what had happened, there was something comforting about having my mommy there to try to make the boo-boo better.

I just didn't want her to stay too long.

Once inside, Mom eyed the interior of my apartment the same way she had eyed me, but she remained silent. She didn't have to say anything. Her thoughts blazed from her freckled face and hovered between us, flashing like Times Square neon: My apartment would fit in the pantry of our house back in Ten Commandments. Without removing any of the canned goods. And back in Ten Commandments we didn't have bars on our windows.

"I don't have a guest room," I said, taking the other suitcase from her hand and lugging both through the door that led to my bedroom. "We'll have to share a bed." I dropped the suitcases inside the doorway. They took up most of the available floor space.

"I'm used to sharing." Her attention darted around the small room, taking a quick inventory of my meager trash-picked and Salvation Army furnishings. "My bed. My bureau. My closet. My husband."

I laughed. I couldn't help it. I wasn't really living through the worst day of my life. This was all a nightmare. I'd wake up any moment, and life would get back to normal.

"I'm glad you find this amusing, Honora."

But I wasn't dreaming. One look at my mother's grief-stricken face told me that. Something was definitely rotten in the land of Hamlet, and it wasn't the remains of the two-month old Havarti in my fridge. Dave cheating on me was one thing. But my father cheating on my mother? Impossible.

"You can't be serious, Mom. Nothing—*nothing*—on the face of this earth could convince me that my God-fearing, church-going, upstanding-pillar-of-the-community father would *ever* fool around. The earth would stop rotating on its axis first."

Mom's eyes widened in horror. Her jaw slackened. She reached out and checked me again for fever, as if she feared delirium had overtaken me. "Adultery? Good Lord! Where did you get that preposterous idea? How could you even *think* such a thing about your father?"

"But you just said . . ."

"I said I'm used to sharing my husband. With the entire town!"

"Oh." Well, that was a relief. The earth could keep spinning.

"But I'm through doing it," she continued. "I'm through being taken for granted. I'm through coming last in his life. I'm through putting everyone else first and myself last." She stamped her foot for emphasis.

I gaped at the alien who had taken over my soft-spoken mother's body. What had happened to good old yes-dearing, stand-by-your-man Mom? Where was the lady who spent her days canning prize-winning pickled beets when she wasn't covering any and all surfaces with cutesy painted kittens, geese, pigs, and teddy bears?

And what about my father? Where was he during Mom's sudden women's lib epiphany?

As if reading my mind, she asked, "When was the last time you spoke with your father?"

I thought for a moment. "He wasn't home when I called yesterday. I guess last Sunday when you called me."

Mom shook her head. "No. The church board met after the service on Sunday. Wednesday there was an emergency down at the fire station. Or the grange. Or the feed store." She waved her hand. "I can't keep them all straight anymore. There's always an emergency."

Come to think of it, I hadn't spoken with my father in at least several weeks. "He has a lot of responsibilities," I reminded her. Dad was the big fish in the little pond of Ten Commandments. He had been mayor for as long as I could remember and took his duties very seriously. The town had been founded by his great-grandfather, an extremely wealthy man who left a trust to fund the mayor's salary in perpetuity. Unlike most small-town mayors, Dad didn't need to hold down another job to support his family. He considered his position a legacy handed down by his ancestors, and he looked upon Ten Commandments and its citizens as more a matter of *noblesse oblige*.

"And what about his responsibility to me?" Mom asked. "No. It's over. I've given that man thirty years of my life, and he can't even show up for dinner. I'm tired of eating cold casseroles—alone." She glanced around my bedroom. "Today is the first day of the rest of my life, and I suppose this is as good a place to start as any."

Suddenly, it hit me. This was no visit. Mom had no intention of going home. My stomach churned. "Mom? Does Dad know you're here?"

27

She shifted position to keep from looking at me and busied herself refolding a blouse I had left on my unmade bed.

"Mom?"

Finally she sighed, scowled, and glanced my way. Guilt settled over her face. "Sort of."

"Sort of? What's that supposed to mean?"

"I don't want to discuss it, and you're to keep out of this. Promise me."

I hugged myself, rubbing my upper arms. At this point I wasn't certain whether the chill consuming me was wet suit-induced or bad news-induced. I needed to strip and get into a shower, but I remained rooted to the floor. "I promise, but I think you're making a big mistake."

"I know what I'm doing."

I seriously doubted that. After a few days away from home, Mom would come to her senses and head back to Iowa and Dad. I suspected she hadn't thought through her rash decision, just jumped on the first plane headed for New York. I was amazed she had even made it to my apartment without panicking and falling to pieces in the La Guardia terminal, given her misconceptions and unfounded fears of the city. How the hell did she expect to survive here?

I watched as she opened my closet door and surveyed the interior. She may have decided today was the first day of the rest of *her* life, but I had a gnawing suspicion it was the last day of *mine* as I knew it. *Thank you, whoever is responsible for making me the butt of a very sick cosmic joke.* All things being equal, however, I would have preferred a pie in the face.

Or another attack of street sludge.

But the prankster of the universe wasn't through wreaking havoc on my life. After a hot shower and downing the cup of tea with two aspirin my mother forced on me, I placed a call to the office to inform them I was taking the rest of the day off.

"Oh," said Jane, my immediate supervisor.

A prickly feeling edged up the back of my neck. This was no ordinary *oh*, but one of those *oh*'s that meant much more than just *oh*. "Is there a problem?" With things so slow at the office, the staff indulged in twice-daily paper airplane competitions to pass time between assignments. I couldn't imagine that I'd be missed for a few hours.

"Well, actually, we do need you to come back before five, Nori."

"Can't it wait until tomorrow? I'm really not feeling well."

"No, it definitely can't wait. No one will be here tomorrow."

Her words drop-kicked my heart into the pit of my stomach. "Jane?"

She blew her nose before responding. When she spoke, her words sounded like a lament—or a dirge. "It's over, Nori. We're folding. Our backers pulled the plug about an hour ago. No more venture capital. No more jobs. The place gets padlocked at five. Anything left goes up for auction to pay outstanding debts. There's only enough cash in the bank to cover this week's payroll." She sucked in a loud sob. "I'm sorry."

For the second time that day, my brain froze. "Let me get this straight. You're saying I'm fired? And I'm not even getting any severance pay?"

"Well, not exactly. No one's getting fired. We're all being laid-off, but there's no money for severance. You can collect unemployment, though."

Woop-de-doo. Unemployment compensation would hardly make a dent in the monthly extortion I shelled out for my basement closet in the Village, not to mention my other expenses. And now I'd have an additional expense—health insurance. With the way my luck was going today, I didn't dare risk canceling my coverage. I'd probably get hit by a bus the moment the policy expired.

"I'll be there within the hour," I told her. My hand shook as I hung up the phone. "Just when you think things can't get any worse," I muttered under my breath.

"What was that you said, dear?"

Mom was unpacking in the bedroom. "I have to go back to the office," I told her as I stood in the doorway. Her two suitcases were opened on my bed. I choked back a groan as I noticed that half of one suitcase contained a myriad of paints and assorted craft supplies. Would I come home to find my entire apartment sponge-painted and decoupaged by the reigning Queen of Crafts?

She glanced up from rearranging my dresser drawers to make room for her clothes and scowled at me. "Certainly not like that, I hope."

I glanced down at the I♥NY sweatsuit I'd slipped into after my shower. Suz had rolled her eyes, her lips twisting into a sneer, when I bought it. "Only tourists wear things like that," she said. So, not wanting to look like a tourist, I never wore the sweats out of my apartment. Even though I no longer cared what that backstabbing Judas thought, sweats weren't exactly appropriate attire for the office, anyway. Nor was the towel wrapped around my damp hair. "No, not like this," I said to my mother.

I headed for the bathroom. In the course of a few miserable hours my life had come crashing down around me, but I wouldn't succumb to the raw emotions churning in my gut. Mom would see today's calamitous events as validation of her belief that I had no business leaving home in the first place. And that angered me enough to drive away any thoughts of succumbing to a sobfest.

Chapter Three

I watched my daughter grab some clean clothes and drag herself to the bathroom. She thinks I've lost my mind, walking out on Earnest and showing up unannounced as I have. A mother doesn't spend half her life raising a child without being able to intuitively discern these things. Among others. Like the fact that I can tell there's far more than an encounter with a puddle eating at her. She might as well have one of those little comic strip thought-balloons floating over her head.

But now is not the time to press. I try to keep my mouth shut. Sometimes. For the most part. Even if she thinks I meddle too much. A mother has to know how to pick her battles and when to back off. Nori might not think so, but I've backed off more than I've wanted to over the years. Lord knows, I have the permanent teeth marks in my tongue to prove it.

Anyway, maybe I have lost my mind, packing up and running off like I did, but Marjorie Draymore shares in the blame. She prodded me along. Even helped pack my bags and drove me to the airport. Before I knew what had happened, I was on a plane bound for New York. Funny, how the plan we concocted made so much sense over coffee at her kitchen table. Now I'm not so sure.

Marjorie and I have known each other since forever.

Which is nothing special, considering everyone in Ten Commandments knows everyone else since forever. But Marjorie and I have also been best friends forever. We had hoped to be much more than that, but our stubborn offspring refuse to cooperate.

As children, Marjorie and I constantly got in and out of trouble. Not that anything we did as kids really qualified as wild or daring—just wild and daring by Ten Commandments standards. In any other town our exploits would have been considered normal adolescent pranks.

Like the time we decided to see if blondes really did have more fun. Her hair turned fire-engine red, and mine turned pumpkin orange. When we tried to correct our mistake, our hair fell out in clumps. Not only didn't we have more fun, but for months, while we waited for our hair to grow back, Ten Commandments mothers pointed us out to their children as examples of what happens when you try to improve on God's handiwork. Those same mothers had standing perm-and-rinse appointments at the Bouffant Beehive, but somehow that didn't seem to count.

As we moved from adolescence into our late teens, our exploits slowed. By our early twenties we had matured into the young ladies our parents expected us to be and eventually settled into the typical lives of Ten Commandments wives and mothers.

The old Connie and Marjorie still existed, though, buried deep within all that respectability. The only problem was that when we were girls, our schemes always entailed a twosome. Never before had I leaped into the fray while she stood on the sidelines waving good-bye.

Until now.

It all started a few weeks ago. I had been down in the dumps for months, and I couldn't shake it. At first I had blamed my malaise on the winter blahs. But winter was gone, and the blahs had stuck around like the lingering stench of hogs long after the livestock trucks pass through town on their way to the slaughterhouse.

"It's the big Five Uh-oh," said Marjorie.

I glanced across my kitchen table where the two of us were drinking coffee and nibbling on a freshly baked crumb cake. "The what?"

"I saw it on *Oprah*. You hit fifty and *bam!*" She smacked her hands together with relish, as if smashing one of those elephantine mosquitoes that makes summers in Iowa so unbearable. "All of a sudden your body becomes your worst enemy and you realize you're well on your way to old age."

"So why aren't you going through it?" After all, Marjorie and I are the same age. Almost to the day.

"Who says I'm not?"

"Hmm." That last birthday had sent me into a tailspin. There's nothing like hitting the half-century mark to depress the heck out of a woman. I took comfort in knowing I wasn't alone.

"And then," she continued, "you get your nose rubbed in it when the AARP mails you one of their welcome-to-the-wonderful-world-of-senior-citizenship letters."

I wrinkled my nose. "Yeah, good-bye, middle age; hello, rocking chair and walker." The other day I had finally slipped the AARP membership card into my wallet. After all, why pass up the chance to get a discount on something?

Anyway, that's how everything started. Then the other morning I entered the bathroom and instead of my own reflection staring back at me in the medicine cabinet mirror, I encountered Great-granny Mathilda Abernathy—excess poundage, gray hair, crow's feet, and all.

I screamed.

Great-granny's ghost screamed back at me.

Eventually, I came to my senses and the unsettling realization that I had grown into the spitting image of the ancestor whose portrait hangs in our downstairs hallway.

And that's when the epiphany walloped me smack in the middle of my face: I didn't recognize myself because I had no *self*. There was no *me* to me. I was, and had always been, defined in relation to others. Calvin and Martha's daughter. Earnest's wife. Honora's mother. For fifty years I have lived my life through others. I was nobody without them. I had no career of my own. No life of my own. I had gone from being a daughter to a wife to a mother, but I had never been a *me*.

"Maybe if I had grandchildren, I wouldn't mind looking like Great-granny Mathilda," I told Marjorie later that day—again over coffee, but this time with blueberry cobbler and in her kitchen.

She placed her fingertips on either side of her mouth and smoothed back the jowls that had started to form on her own face. "I know what you mean. Who wants to look the part without the joy of playing the role?"

"At least you have a career to keep you busy."

She snorted. "Some career! I spend my days pickling people. You spend yours pickling beets. What's the difference? At least you don't have to deal with bereaved relatives, *and* you get to eat the fruits of your labors."

"Marjorie!"

"What?" She knitted her penciled eyebrows together in puzzlement. Her feigned innocence didn't fool me.

"You have a very sick sense of humor."

She shrugged. "Comes from spending the last thirty years primping cadavers."

"And what have I done for the past thirty years?"

"Don't sell yourself short, Connie. You've been a darn good daughter, wife, and mother."

Why did that suddenly sound so pathetic? "It's not enough." For my entire adult life I had always done what was expected. Never questioned. Never challenged. Everything I did was always done for others. I positioned myself last on my list of priorities and never seemed to get around to that bottom item on the list. When had the adventuresome Connie of my youth transformed into a boring housewife? "Maybe Nori has the right idea."

"What do you mean?"

I sat back in my chair and pondered for a moment. "Maybe we shouldn't have stayed in Ten Commandments. Think about it. They say if you can remember the sixties, you weren't there."

"I remember the sixties fine," she said, as if I were accusing her of something.

"Yeah, well that pretty much sums us up, doesn't it? We're supposed to be the Woodstock Generation. But not those of us who grew up in Ten Commandments. While the rest of our generation spent the summer of sixty-nine getting stoned, running off to Canada to avoid the draft, or stripping naked and singing protest songs in Woodstock, we stood around a steamy kitchen canning succotash with our mothers."

Marjorie frowned. "To the sounds of Percy Faith, Perry Como, and Peggy Lee. The Beatles and Rolling Stones were banned in my house."

"Mine, too."

"Remember that sermon old Pastor Passeldorf preached about Mick Jagger being the Devil incarnate?"

"How could I forget? Half the town believed him. He urged our parents to scour our bedrooms for contraband LP's. I ran home and hid mine under a loose floorboard in my closet."

"I shoved mine under my mattress." She laughed so hard that a few tendrils of her perfectly coifed French twist came loose and fell against her cheek. "Not the brightest move. My dad sat down on my bed, and that was the end of John, Paul, George, and Ringo."

"So why did we stay?"

She shrugged as she tucked the dull umber hairs back in place. "We fell in love."

"And grew up and became our parents." I scowled. We changed—and not necessarily for the better—but Ten Commandments has remained pretty much as it always was. Pastor Passeldorf is long gone, but the Reverend Zechariah Stedworth isn't much of an improvement in the sermon department. The town stayed entrenched in the fifties while the rest of the country moved forward, marching to the beat of a psychedelic drummer. In the past thirty years or so, progress has come at a snail's pace. We do have the Beatles on the local easy listening station now, but the jury is still out on most of the songs by the Rolling Stones.

I, on the other hand, have been thinking quite a bit about one particular old Rolling Stones song lately. "Satisfaction." My satisfaction level has hit an all-time low. After fifty years of believing I was content with my life, I suddenly realized I'm not. Nori was gone. Earnest spent all of his days and most of his nights involved in town business. No one needed me. I was superfluous. And what did I have to look forward to? More lonely nights at home while Earnest performed his mayoral duties and no sign of grandchildren on the horizon, thanks to Nori's stubbornness when it came to Eugene.

I wanted more.

"A woman can just can so many jars of pickled beets," I told Marjorie. "After all, how many blue ribbons do I need for the same darned pickled beets?"

"Even if you beat out Leona Shakelmeyer every year?"

I couldn't hold back my grin. I did take pleasure in besting Leona annually at the county fair. I've never forgiven her for asking Earnest to the Sadie Hawkins Day Dance senior year while I was home with the chicken pox. She knew we were practically engaged. But after all this time, the victory rings hollow. I have Earnest while Leona ended up with Ralph Shakelmeyer and a pig farm. No contest there. I may have to share my husband with the entire town, but at least he doesn't come home stinking of hogs and slop.

I sighed. "Leona Shakelmeyer aside, I'm sick of putting up pickled beets. And strawberry-rhubarb preserves. And corn relish. And stewed tomatoes. And here's a little secret for you: I'm not even sure I *like* pickled beets. How's that for irony?" I placed my coffee cup on the table, sat back in my chair, and folded my arms across my chest.

"You have your painting," said Marjorie, nodding across the room at the red café curtains I had embellished with a border of black and white cows for her. "And your other crafts."

I shrugged. "I haven't picked up a paint brush in over a month."

"You need a change, Connie."

"What? Switch from cows and pigs to sheep and goats? How exciting! What I need is a vacation."

"Exactly."

"Ha! You think I'm going to be able to convince Earnest to leave town for a week? I can barely get him to sit down to dinner one or two nights out of seven."

"Yes, well, that's part of the problem, isn't it?"

"What do you mean?"

"Earnest isn't married to you, Connie. He's married to the entire town. And if you ask me, he takes his duties far too seriously and you too much for granted."

I shook my head. Marjorie voiced my own nagging suspicions. For too long I had tried to convince myself that such thoughts were selfish. As mayor, Earnest carried a tremendous burden on his shoulders. He deserved my unswerving support and didn't need to hear my petty complaints about being lonely and ignored. About too many dinners eaten by myself and too many nights going to bed alone. "No, he doesn't. He has lots of responsibilities, and he's . . . well, he's . . . you know." I searched my mind and finally shrugged. "He's Earnest."

"Yes, he's Earnest," she agreed, but she had a very smug expression on her face. Too smug.

I recognized that look of hers, the wry twist of her mouth, the glint in her eyes. "What are you cooking up, Marjorie?"

"Like you said, Connie. *You* need a vacation."

That's when, prodded by Marjorie, my flippant, off-the-cuff remark took on a life of its own. By the time we were done plotting, we had hatched a plan to shake Earnest out of his complacency, me out of my doldrums, *and* solve another more pressing problem that directly affected both of us.

I felt like a kid again—excited by the idea, terrified of the outcome. Like the time we decided to dye our dogs lavender for Easter. We had learned our lesson with our own hair but figured we were safe with Rit Dye on a Pomeranian and a Lhasa Apso. Unfortunately, they proved less than cooperative. Our purple skin eventually faded, but the purple-stained grout in my mother's bathroom is a lasting testament to a not-so-great idea gone awry.

"Why do I get the feeling I'm about to embark on a lavender-dog fiasco?"

Marjorie brushed aside my concern with a wave of her hand. "Don't worry. This is too brilliant to fail. Think you can pull it off?"

"By myself?" I shook my head. "Oh, no. You have to come with me."

"Me? How will it work if I go? Trust me. You can do this, Connie. And the timing couldn't be better. Consider it divine intervention. And think of the rewards when you succeed."

If I succeed. And it was a big *if*. But here I am in New York City of all places. And I got here all by myself.

You'd think that in itself would be a lifetime's worth of adventure for one fifty-year-old woman from Ten Commandments, Iowa, but this was only the first step in our plan. Marjorie and I had mapped out a detailed agenda.

"Take it one step at a time," she said as she waited with me at the airport security checkpoint. "Remember, you're doing this for all of us."

I pulled the list out of my purse and studied it. Doubts hacked away at my resolve. I was out of my mind. "Easy for you to say. You'll be safe at home in Ten Commandments while I'm floundering in Gomorrah."

"See a few shows while you're there." Then she shoved me through the metal detector and waved good-bye.

That was early this morning. Now, while Nori showered, I retrieved the list from the zippered compartment of my purse and unfolded it. I picked up the phone on the nightstand and punched in Marjorie's number. "Mission accomplished," I said when she picked up the phone on the second ring.

"The whole thing? How in the world . . . ?"

"Don't be ridiculous, Marjorie. Just step one. I made it to New York. I'm at Nori's apartment."

She snorted. "Honestly, Connie, that's hardly mission accomplished."

I pouted, even though I knew Marjorie couldn't see me through the phone lines. "It's a major step as far as

I'm concerned, given I've never been anywhere east of Peoria." I grabbed a pencil lying next to the phone and drew a line through the first item on the list: *Get to New York City*. One down, too many to go.

I vowed to carry out each piece of the plan step-by-step. Even if it killed me. Which it might. Unless my daughter kills me first. Which she might if she discovers the truth.

I heard Nori turn off the faucet in the shower. "Gotta go, Marj."

"Keep me posted," she said. "I want daily updates."

"Have you spoken to Earnest yet?"

"Not yet."

"Why not?"

"You know Earnest. He's up to his eyeballs in some new town crisis."

"What kind of crisis?"

"The usual. Nothing you need worry about. Relax, Connie. I'll take care of my end. You take care of things at your end. And try to enjoy yourself."

Again, easy for her to say. If this plan backfires, it will blow up in my face, not hers.

Chapter Four

When I arrived in New York nearly two-and-a-half years ago, many of the dot-coms had already gone bust. Those few that had weathered NASDAQ fickleness and venture capitalist impatience limped along, eking out a small quarterly profit to sustain their investors. DataScroungers was one such company, specializing in supplying research to the serious researcher. Our clients included investigative journalists, scientists, writers, and even doctoral thesis candidates. Our search engines cut through the morass of the web and weeded out all the urban legends, junk science, and quasi-experts, thus maximizing our clients' time and minimizing their efforts.

The work intrigued me. I was part detective, part analyst, part writer. I was able to use my skills and at the same time, broaden my mind. I loved my work and did it well. We all did. For this we were well-paid by our clients. Unfortunately, we didn't have many clients.

Which explained the twice-daily paper airplane competitions.

The long lunches.

And the dissolution of the company.

"The problem," explained Jane as I sat across from her in her office an hour later, demanding more of an explanation, "is that our client base hasn't grown enough to satisfy the bean counters who work for our investors." She drummed a pencil on a packet of papers sitting on her desk. The sight of the normally cluttered—now nearly empty—desk should have squelched any hopes I had of a minute-before-midnight reprieve.

Call me obtuse. In a take-a-deep-breath-and-throw-yourself-on-the-mercy-of-the-court final attempt, I slipped into my Nellie Forbush/Cockeyed Optimist Midwest mode. "But what about . . . ?"

She cut me off before I finished my sentence. "This will explain about unemployment compensation, CO-BRA, your 401 (k), all that stuff." Her left hand swept her frizzy chestnut bangs off her forehead while her right hand, still clutching the pencil, pushed the packet across the desk toward me.

I hesitated before picking up the top sheet. Jane sighed heavily. Apologetically. Even though we both knew none of this was her fault. She was getting laid-off along with the rest of us.

Still, some irrational side of my brain had me convinced that if I whined or complained or cajoled or pleaded enough, the situation would reverse itself. *Someone* would see the error of his ways and change his mind about shutting us down. Ignoring the evidence staring me in the face and Jane's obvious desire to cut the meeting as short as possible, I decided to pursue my case. "But I thought we were making money."

"Barely enough to cover expenses," she said. "Each quarter profits hover just this side of nonexistent. These guys are in it for the money. They don't give a flying fig about research or anything else. We could be hawking fried peanut butter and banana sandwiches over the Web, for all they care. They're only interested in a quick profit, and we're not netting one for them. At the rate we've been going, they'd earn more on some safe, guaranteed investment—like T-bills." She shook her head, inhaled a sniffle, and reached for a tissue. "I'm surprised they stuck with us as long as they did."

All evidence to the contrary, I refused to give up. "What about advertising?" Marketing had recently launched an aggressive campaign to reel in big-name advertisers, luring them with the promise of bright-colored banners, boxes, and pop-up ads on our homepage.

Her expression told me she recognized my straw-grasping and that it would get me nowhere. "We cater to too small a demographic, Nori, not to mention the wrong demographic." She scowled. "The marketing department couldn't get any of the major companies interested, and the smaller ones don't have the dollars we need."

"But . . ."

"Face it, Nori. It's over. I'm sorry." She reached across the desk and tapped the remaining sheets I still hadn't picked up. "I need you to read all that paperwork, then sign the release form."

"So that's it?"

"Afraid so. Don't forget to clear out any personal items you have in your cubicle." She stood up, signaling that I should leave. "See you on the unemployment line."

I rose and headed for the door. Before leaving, I turned back to face her. "You wouldn't happen to know of any job openings anywhere, would you?"

"In dot-coms? Forget it."

"In anything?"

"I hear the city needs police officers, fire fighters, and teachers."

Great! Forget police work. I couldn't exactly see myself packing a pistol. Guns terrified me. So did the thought of hauling dead babies out of Dumpsters and trolling for whacked Mafiosi in the East River. As for fire fighting, at barely five-three and a hundred and ten pounds, I doubted I could hold onto a pressurized hose, let alone hoist an unconscious body over my shoulders.

That left teaching, a noble profession according to my parents, but not something I had ever seriously considered. Thanks to Mom and Dad's insistence, I had taken the requisite education courses in college, but a semester of practice teaching my senior year had proved what I had always suspected: I'm not compatible with anyone under the age of twenty-one.

I headed back to my workstation to read over the paperwork and clear out my desk. Reese and Gabe were waiting for me.

"That was some long soak in Dave's hot tub," said Reese. "I don't suppose he happened to be home for lunch?" She winked and nudged me with her elbow.

I winced. Dave was home, all right, but that was one conversation I didn't want to have at the moment.

Luckily, Reese immediately switched gears. Waving her arms frenetically, she bounced up and down on the balls of her feet like some out-of-control marionette with multicolored dreadlocks. "Have you heard?"

"That we're all out on the street come five o'clock?" I saluted her with the stack of papers. "Got the documentation to prove it."

"This really sucks," said Gabe. He slouched against the wall, his hands stuffed in the pockets of his designer cargo pants, a scowl etched into a face covered with just the right amount of fashionable stubble. Lord only knew how he managed to keep it at that state day after day. And Lord only knew why I dwelled on such a thought with my world caving in around me. Must be a symptom of traumatic stress syndrome, I reasoned. Focus on the insignificant to avoid facing the cataclysmic.

"I just booked my summer vacation," whined Reese. "Two weeks at a bitchin' singles resort in St. Croix. Now what do I do?"

"Cancel," Gabe suggested.

"I can't. It was one of those nonrefundable, super-cheap Web deals."

"Screwed by the Web."

"Twice in twenty-four hours," she moaned.

"Well, as I see it," said Gabe, "the only alternative left is to go out and get stinking drunk."

"Only if you're buying," I said. "As of an hour ago, I'm on a zero budget."

"Me, too," said Reese.

Gabe withdrew his right hand from his pocket and produced a crumpled wad of bills. He stared at the fist-ful of money—mostly singles and fives from the looks of it—then shrugged. "What the hell? Beats drinking alone."

I really wasn't in the mood for a post-layoff party. "I have to pack up," I said. "And sort through all this paperwork."

"We'll wait," said Gabe.

"Yeah, take your time," added Reese. "I want to walk around for one last look, anyway."

Gabe looped his arm around Reese's shoulders. "Ever the masochist. I'll make sure she doesn't attempt any self-mutilation while she's at it," he said to me as he led her down the hall.

Reese, Gabe, and I had started at DataScroungers within days of each other. Even though we had already seen a myriad number of Internet businesses tanking, we believed DataScroungers would not only survive but thrive. Lured by a promise of stock options, we gobbled up the company propaganda about how

DataScroungers was different enough to withstand the vagaries of a shaky market and daydreamed of becoming millionaires before we turned thirty.

What we didn't know at the time was that we were being hired to replace former disenchanted employees who had been smart enough to bail out before the e-commerce slaughter reached its peak. When it hit and one Internet company after another closed its doors, we copped a bird-in-the-hand attitude. The job market had taken a hundred-and-eighty-degree turn in a few short months, and none of us anticipated having much luck elsewhere. Not in dot-coms or traditional markets. Then came September 11th, and the job market went from dismal and depressing to hopeless and nonexistent.

We rationalized staying with DataScroungers by repeating the company mantra about our business being different. We dealt in research, not commerce. We sold a service, not a product. We didn't have to worry about stockpiles of books or pet supplies or healthcare products sitting unsold in a warehouse. And because our service was so specifically targeted to a unique segment of the population, we hadn't made the mistake of spending exorbitant sums of money on sock puppets and Super Bowl commercials. Other than the cost of our office space and leased equipment, our operating expenses were minimal. Unfortunately, as previously mentioned, so was our client base, and hence, our profit margin.

Reese and Gabe were my closest friends in New York after Suz. And Dave. Funny how neither of them had ever warmed up to Suz. Or Dave. But then again, up until a few hours ago, I had thought Suz and Dave hated each other.

But I guess somewhere along the line Suz and Dave had decided to give it another try—*sans moi*. I exorcised the image of the two of them in the Jacuzzi from my head and stepped into my cubicle. I had more pressing problems at the moment. I was now jobless, not to mention I had my midlife-crisis mother waiting for me back at my apartment. My broken heart and shattered ego would have to wait.

Maybe drowning my sorrows with Reese and Gabe wasn't such a bad idea. Especially if Gabe paid. At the moment I couldn't afford to get drunk. Literally.

I tossed the packet of papers on my desk, opened the bottom drawer, and pulled out a canvas tote I kept for carting reading matter home from the office. One by one I tossed boring bits and pieces of the last two-and-a-half years of my life into the tote. A bag of emergency cosmetics. A spare package of pantyhose. A box of tampons. A sweater for those days when the air-conditioning turned the office into Antarctica. The laminated collection of Dilbert and Cathy cartoons that covered my cubicle walls. My complimentary *grande*-size DataScroungers coffee mug, DataScroungers pen, and DataScroungers paperweight. An assortment of magazines and books that had somehow made their way to the office and never back home again.

I sorted through the stack of magazines, tossing *Modern Bride*—for obvious reasons—and keeping only the most recent issues of *New York* and *Time Out*. I picked up my dog-eared copy of *Bridget Jones's Diary*. Once a favorite, I now knew I could never read the book again. Today I had become Bridget, with Dave morphing into Daniel Cleaver and Suz the nude on the roof. I chucked the book into the wastebasket.

All my personal items were now haphazardly stuffed into the canvas tote except for the three framed photographs atop my computer. I grabbed the one in the middle. Mom and Dad with their heads poking out of holes in a poorly painted plywood representation of Grant Wood's *American Gothic*.

I had taken the photo at the county fair several years ago. Neither was too happy when they realized I had positioned Mom as the farmer and Dad as the farmer's wife. At the time I feigned embarrassment over the error and retook the picture, but the original shot remained one of my favorites.

A queasy pang ricocheted around my stomach. What the hell had happened with my parents? So they weren't poster children for the Woodstock Generation, and we didn't see eye-to-eye on many—okay, most—things, but they were still my parents. Two rocks of Gibraltar that weren't supposed to quake, crack, or crumble. Except the tectonic plates had shifted, sending one of them all the way to New York. I grabbed a section of yesterday's newspaper and wrapped the photo before adding it to the tote.

I turned my attention to the next photo. Dave during an autumn weekend in the Berkshires. The most romantic weekend of my life. We stayed in an old farmhouse that the owners had converted into an elegant inn. We spent most of our time in a four-poster, on satin sheets under a down quilt, leaving the bed only for long soaks in our own private hot tub or gourmet meals served in the candle-lit dining room.

"Were you cheating on me then?" He stared back at me from the photo, his eyes hooded, his mouth twisted in a seductive, come-here-I-want-you smile. A moment after I snapped the picture, he had stripped me naked and fucked me for hours.

Angry tears gathered behind my eyes. I yanked open the back of the frame and seized the photo. Grabbing a pair of scissors from the top desk drawer, I systematically cut Dave up until there was nothing left of him except confetti scraps.

Then I reached for the last frame. Suz and me posing with a Macy's Santa last Christmas—her on one knee, me on the other—both kissing a bewhiskered cheek. I cut the photo down the center. Then I decapitated my ex-best friend before consigning her to the same confetti fate.

I scooped the pile of scraps into the wastebasket. "Where trash belongs," I muttered. I tried to convince myself that the ceremonial act offered me a sense of closure. Not that I'd be able to put their betrayal behind me so easily, but right now I needed all the help I could get.

I also needed a drink. If I downed enough margaritas, maybe I'd wake up dead and discover this entire nightmare was someone else's life.

I quickly read through the out-placement papers Jane had handed me, signed where indicated, left her copies in my outbox, stuffed my copies into my tote, and set off in search of Reese and Gabe.

Half an hour later we sat huddled around our favorite corner table at CyberSuds, the local bar of choice for DataScroungers—or more accurately, ex-DataScroungers—and other refugees from the worldwide web of dashed hopes and broken dreams. We had each already polished off the first round of our brain-numbing libations of choice: a cosmopolitan for Reese, a Honker's Ale with a shot for Gabe, and my margarita. On the rocks with salt. Which wasn't the brightest idea, considering my scorched palate, but the alcohol eventually numbed the blistering pain.

"I guess this is the last time the three of us will camp out here after work," said Gabe.

Reese nursed her second cosmo. "At eight bucks a pop, I'd think so." She sighed. "Ever get the feeling your life isn't going the way you planned it?"

Did I ever! "You don't know the half of it," I grumbled into my drink, but I wasn't sure I wanted to bare my soul about Dave and Suz yet. The pain was still too raw. I'd need a few more numbing margaritas first.

And then there was my mother. After all my stories of life back in Ten Commandments, Gabe and Reese knew Mom pretty well. If only secondhand. This was a woman who would never willingly set foot in what she deemed the Sodom and Gomorrah of America. How did I explain her sudden appearance when I still hadn't figured that one out for myself?

"Talk about annihilated prospects. I came to DataScroungers with such high hopes," I continued. "I feel like I've been ground into the pavement by a corporate bean-counting Bruno Magli heel. Pun intended."

"You and me, babe," said Gabe.

Reese smirked. "Promise her endless IPOs, but give her the shaft."

"I had it all planned," said Gabe. "Hell, I was supposed to have my first million tucked away by now. Instead, here I am nearly thirty and still sharing an apartment with two other guys."

A now unaffordable apartment, I thought, considering Gabe's trendy SoHo address. But even my below-ground-level closet would be a fond memory if I didn't find another job within the next few days.

Although I lived from paycheck to paycheck, I managed to keep my credit card debt as low as possible. I suspected Reese's and Gabe's finances were in far worse condition. Unlike my friends, my Midwest sensibility forced me to shop at Daffy's and Loehmann's, where I bought last year's trends at deep discounts. Not Reese. She lived to shop, and in a wardrobe-for-wardrobe match-up, she'd beat the *Sex and the City* foursome hands down.

And Gabe was just as bad. In a gay guy sort of way. I shuddered to think what he spent at Barney's each month.

"Damn bean counters!" Gabe slammed his fist on the glass tabletop, rattling our drinks and causing a puddle of condensation to dribble onto his pricey cargo pants. He slumped forward, resting his elbows on the table and his head in his hands. "Shit! I'm probably going to have to move to New Jersey!"

"New Jersey? I'll take New Jersey over moving back in with my mother any day," cried Reese, "but it looks like that's where I'll be headed—back up to . . ."—she paused for a moment and shuddered—"Yonkers. Yuck! Do you have any idea how long I dreamed of leaving Yonkers?"

"About as long as Nori dreamed of leaving Kansas?"

"Iowa," I muttered, knowing in his next breath he'd mimic Suz's standard geographically-challenged line.

He didn't disappoint. "Iowa. Kansas. What's the difference?"

Reese answered for me. "Two extra letters and a boat ride down the Mississippi." She scowled at Gabe. "Can we get serious here? I have zilch in my savings account, nada in my checking account, and credit card debt up the wazoo." She stuck out her right leg and glanced down at her foot. Gabe and I followed her gaze, staring at the object of Reese's apprehension. "Think Manolo Blahnik would take back a slightly worn pair of sandals?"

"About as quickly as the Monkey Bar will take back the dinner Abe and I ate last weekend," said Gabe.

"Abe?" Reese and I questioned him simultaneously. The last we'd heard, Gabe was between relationships—ever since a rather public breakup several weeks ago during intermission in the lobby of the St. James Theatre.

Max Bialystock wasn't the only man betrayed at the St. James that night, but considering Gabe had paid two hundred dollars for his and Stuart's tickets and had waited over a year to see *The Producers*, his was the far greater betrayal. Gabe returned from the men's room in time to overhear his longtime companion ask another man for his number. The ensuing scene got all three booted out of the theater. Besides, at the end of the evening Max comes out on top. Gabe didn't.

Gabe's face brightened. "Abe owns the gallery where Barry shows." Barry was one of Gabe's roommates. A photographer with a penchant for shooting Dumpsters and their contents. He was working his way from Battery Park up to the Bronx, Dumpster by Dumpster in the hopes of producing a pricey coffee table book—*Big Apple Garbage* or *Five Borough Trash*. He hadn't quite settled on the title. Which was okay, since he hadn't yet convinced a publisher of the merits of his work.

Having seen some of Barry's photos, I was surprised that a gallery would devote valuable wall space to him, but after all, this is New York, not Iowa. In Iowa, Barry's work would be consigned to a Dumpster, not on consignment at a trendy SoHo gallery.

"Abe and Gabe. That's too cute for words," said Reese.

"Don't be bitchy, darling."

Reese screwed up her face. "I think I have a right to be bitchy. I just lost my goddamn job at Data-goddamn-Scroungers." She signaled for another round, then quickly asked, "You still paying?"

Gabe nodded.

"Good. Let's order some wings. As long as I'm not paying, I'm famished." She downed the last few drops of her cosmopolitan and waved the glass in the air. "Eat, drink, and be merry, for tomorrow we go from DataScroungers to Dumpster scroungers."

Gabe removed the glass from her hand. "You're drunk, sweetheart."

Reese arched one perfectly shaped eyebrow—thanks to a weekly standing appointment at Waxworks. Back to tweezers, I thought, as she grimaced an acknowledgement of her inebriated state. She released a heavy sigh. "Barry ever think of using models in his Dumpster shots?"

Gabe stared at her as if she had suddenly sprouted purple whiskers and chartreuse spots. We both knew Reese had a thing about clean. Doctors prepping for surgery spent less time washing their hands than Reese did after a potty visit. He shook his head. "I'm having trouble picturing you atop a pile of garbage, but I'll ask him. I'm assuming you prefer recyclables to compostables?"

His sarcasm was lost amid the alcohol floating through her veins. "Hell, no. I can't eat cardboard, for God's sake! If it doesn't reek, it's safe to eat, right?"

Gabe screwed up his face. "How the hell should I know? Do I look like a street bum?"

I licked at the salt on the rim of my glass, trying to keep it from touching the roof of my mouth, and paid little attention to their banter. Under normal circumstances, I'd be joining in. Hell, under normal circumstances, I'd be holding court. Living in New York had loosened both my tongue and my inhibitions. I never kept my opinions to myself anymore. But this was not a normal evening, and the more I drank, the more morose I grew over the day's events until my entire body felt like one huge tear reservoir ready to spill its banks.

Reese was too drunk to notice, but eventually Gabe took note of my silence. "Who stole the Queen of Putting-Her-Two-Cents-In and left a mute android in her place?"

"What's she got to worry about?" asked Reese. "You're forgetting Dave, the rich-ass dermatologist. Nori can move in with him." Her face brightened.

"Hey! I've got it! You and I can sublet Nori's place. Assuming we can both get something that pays above minimum wage, we should be able to swing the rent. Of course, I may have to augment our menus from what I can scavenge during the Dumpster shoots."

That's when the dam cracked and my reservoir overflowed its banks.

I don't know how long I sat there crying my eyes out. Reese and Gabe closed ranks around me, alternately comforting me and cursing as, between gulping sobs and hiccups, I related the details of my terrible-dreadful-horrible-horrendous-appalling-disastrous-cataclysmic day.

"Dave! What a bastard!" cried Reese.

"The bitch!" growled Gabe, doing equal justice to Suz.

At least neither said I-told-you-so, but if they had, I wouldn't have blamed them. I had been too naïve, too blind, too much in love to see either Dave or Suz for the bogus, two-faced, backstabbing, deceitful, spurious, two-timing, double-crossing traitors they were.

"We need a plan," said Reese, sucking the sauce from a Buffalo wing off her fingers, then washing it down with the remains of another cosmo.

I swiped at my tears and stared at her. "A plan? For what?"

"For getting even!"

I shook my head. Nori Stedworth didn't get even. Ten Commandments, Iowa, was still too much a part of me. Uncle Zechariah Stedworth's favorite sermon came to mind. I voiced a six-word summary—much to the surprise of both myself and my companions—"Vengeance is mine, sayeth the Lord."

Their jaws simultaneously dropped, their eyes bulged.

I shrugged my shoulders and grinned sheepishly. "You can take the girl out of Iowa . . . Besides, I already doused Dave's favorite silk Armani shirt and Suz's newest Dolce and Gabbana outfit with an almost full magnum of Dom Perignon." I thought for a moment. "I think I got her Prada shoes, as well."

"Pocket change for the Prince of Facial Peels and Botox," said Gabe. "And as for the slut . . ." He waved his hand in the air, dismissing Suz like a floating dust speck. "I prefer a different quote," he continued. " 'Hell hath no fury like a woman scorned.' You need to rain fury down on those two. You need to make them sweat."

"You need to make them squirm," added Reese.

Gabe's eyes glinted. "You need to make them pay."

I glanced from one to the other. My heartache had given them a cathartic diversion from their own misfortune. I let them continue their ranting and plotting as I sipped at my drink. As much as I ached, as much as I felt like the chump of the world, Dave and Suz were not my only concern at the moment. There was my mother. What the hell was I supposed to do about her?

I slumped back in my chair and closed my eyes. I didn't need a plan. I needed a miracle. But miracles had been in short supply over the past few millennia. So, barring any form of divine intervention, what I really needed was Gertie.

Gertie. I hadn't thought about her in years, but once upon a time she was my closest friend and ally. The person to whom I poured out my doubts, my frustrations, my unhappiness, my soul. She had helped me through a lonely childhood and a difficult adolescence.

As the only daughter of the town's mayor, the niece of the town's minister, the great-great-granddaughter of the town's founder, I was held to a higher standard than my peers. Add to that my lack of height, my athletic incompetence, and my uncanny ability to always maintain a straight A average even if I didn't study, and it wasn't difficult to see why I wasn't Miss Popularity around the schoolyard.

When the gym class divided into volleyball or softball teams, I was the last kid picked. But the first to get picked *on* whenever the teacher wasn't around.

I never complained, though. At least not to anyone but Gertie. I figured out early on that snitching only made the situation worse. So instead, I held my head high—which earned me the label of "snob"; or buried my nose in a book, which added "teacher's pet" to my long list of peer-dubbed defects—and tried to ignore my tormentors. And each night after I climbed into bed, I poured my heart out to Gertie.

So what if she was a figment of my imagination?

As I sat and listened to my friends discuss the finer points of drawing and quartering Dave and Suz (too messy, and Gabe hated the sight of blood) versus boiling them in oil (where would they find a large enough vat, and what type of oil worked best? Olive? Canola? Sesame?), I wondered how Gertie would have handled today. It was time to find out.

Chapter Five

Dear Gertie,

Today sucked diplodocus eggs. Remember the time I tripped on a tree root during a Campfire Girls hike and fell face-first into a patch of poison ivy? Then, the next day I broke out with the mumps? Today was worse.

In the course of two hours, I burned the roof of my mouth on a flaming burrito, got doused with sludge, discovered Dave screwing Suz, and got the ax at work. Oh, and in case you don't think that's enough of a cosmic whammy, Mom showed up—not for a visit, but an indefinite stay.

Something's going on between her and Dad, and thanks to her showing up on my doorstep, I'm now caught in the middle of it—whatever "it" is. Not what I need right now. I don't mean to sound selfish or anything, but jeez! Don't I have enough problems at the moment without having to deal with a parental midlife crisis?

Why didn't Mom go see Uncle Zechariah? This is a minister's role, not a daughter's. Unless it's something sexual. You think? I guess Mom would feel uptight discussing something like that with her brother-in-law. But wouldn't she feel as awkward broaching the subject with her daughter? After all, she still believes I'm a virgin.

So I'm thinking, is this what I get for not doing a Feng Shui makeover of my apartment? Are my elements misaligned? Was I born under the wrong sign? Is crappy karma my destiny? Or is God getting even with me for leaving Ten Commandments? And if not, why did today ever happen?

—Nori

Dear Nori,

Call me blunt. Call me incredibly trite. But the simple truth is—shit happens. Or to put it a bit more delicately—ca-ca occurs. Take your pick. The meaning remains the same. And the only way to dispose of dumped doo-doo is to pick it up and flush it away.

As for those two jerks you misguidedly assumed were your best friend and boyfriend, you should have seen that one coming. I did.

Trust me. You're better off without either of them. In your heart you know this. If you didn't, I wouldn't, right? You're sucking diplodocus eggs now, but for the past few months you've been burying your head in the sand. Don't waste another nanosecond or a single sniffle on those two scumbags. They deserve each other.

And quit bitching about losing your job. You should have seen that one coming, as well, but we won't discuss that now because the truth is, you did, didn't you?

Anyway, you won't have trouble finding another job. It's not like you don't have the education, skills, and experience. So, go update your résumé, start making phone calls to employment agencies, and get on with your life.

Which brings me to your parents. I know you're not going to like hearing this, but you've got to swallow your pride and call your dad. Even if your mother made you promise you wouldn't interfere. Don't hand me any arguments, Nori. The sooner you do it, the

*sooner you get to the bottom of the mystery and get
the situation resolved.*

*Or do you want to share your bed with your mother
for the rest of your life?*

—*Gertie*

Gertie was right. She hadn't told me anything I didn't
already know—whether I wanted to accept it or not.
However, back when we were kids, she had never been
so in-your-face. She used to wrap me in her imaginary
arms and soothe my wounded heart, not dish out advice with attitude. In the time since we had last con-
versed, Gertie had morphed from Barney into Dr.
Laura Schlessinger.

"Earth to Nori."

"Yo, girl, you still with us?" Gabe waved his hands
in front of my face, and Reese snapped her fingers with
their long, French manicured nails an inch from my
nose.

I blinked Gertie back into Fantasyland and myself
into the here-and-now of CyberSuds. My friends
stared at me as if *I* now sported those purple whiskers
and chartreuse spots.

"You really zoned out there for a minute," said
Gabe. "Where were you?"

"Nowhere worth mentioning." I dismissed their
concern with a casual shrug and a lame grin. "Too
much tequila, that's all. Maybe we should call it a
night. I've still got to deal with my mother."

Gabe signaled the waitress. After scrutinizing the
tab, he slapped down a wad of bills *and* a credit card.

"Let me help," I offered, reaching for my purse.

"Forget it, Nori."

"Gabe, we just drank enough to add another comma
to your credit card debt!"

"Who's counting?"

"I am."

He leaned over and planted a kiss on my cheek. "I'm not. Besides, it may be a long time before we get to do this again. Don't worry about it."

So we departed CyberSuds, three of us loaded in one respect and one of us totally unloaded in another. Gabe stepped off the curb, waved one hand over his head and shoved two fingers between his lips. One ear-piercing whistle later a yellow cab pulled up to the curb.

"I thought you were out of money," I said.

He winked. "I am."

"So, why are you hailing a taxi?"

He glanced over at Reese, propped against a telephone pole. "You really think she's up for the subway?"

I assessed the situation. Reese swayed precariously on her Manolos. "I suppose not." For that matter, I wasn't so sure I'd make it home on the subway, either, and I wasn't anywhere near as wasted as Reese.

After the three of us squeezed into the back seat of the cab, I dug my wallet out from the bottom of my purse and removed a twenty, passing it across Reese to Gabe. He refused it. "Don't worry," he mouthed.

Was he crazy? Surely he wasn't thinking of stiffing the driver! *Don't worry?* How could I *not* worry? We were about to rack up at least a twelve-dollar cab fare by the time the driver made all three stops. And that didn't include a tip. How did Gabe intend to pay for it without my help?

I stared at him as though *he* had sprouted those purple whiskers and chartreuse spots, but he ignored my alarm. Leaning back against the seat, he cupped his hands behind his head, closed his eyes, and began to hum "I Won't Grow Up" from *Peter Pan*.

I clutched the bill in my fist and rolled my eyes. "You have a very twisted sense of humor," I hissed at him.

Whatever Gabe's alcohol-soaked brain had in mind,

I doubted I'd like it. My own fatalistic brain began conjuring up visions of his battered and blood-soaked body sprawled in some dark alley. I glanced over at Reese. No help there. She hummed along to an entirely different melody, too out of it to know what was going on.

My stop came first. When the taxi pulled up in front of my apartment building, I hopped out. Before the driver sped away, I tossed the twenty through the open window onto Reese's lap. Call me self-centered, but after living through the suckiest day of my life, I didn't want to spend my night down at the morgue identifying Gabe's corpse.

A minute later, I entered my apartment and was hit by a stench I knew all too well.

With a groan I tossed my purse and canvas tote onto the mail table to the left of the front door. Only the mail table was no longer where it always was, where it should be, where it had been several hours earlier. Then again, neither was any other piece of furniture in my living room. My gaze darted from one corner of the room to the next. The Mad Rearranger had struck. Mom, a devotee of every interior decorating show on cable, had never met a room she couldn't improve. Or so she claimed. Much to my annoyance, the proof of that assertion now confronted me.

I stooped to pick my purse and bag off the floor and crossed the room to deposit them on the table. The table that now resided in front of the window in place of my favorite reading chair that was currently where the end table had been. "Mom?"

"In the kitchen, dear." She stuck her head around the doorway and released a rapid-fire barrage without coming up once for air. "I've made dinner. You must be famished, Nori. It's nearly eight o'clock. Where have you been? You didn't look well earlier. Are you all right? What kind of neighborhood is this, anyway? I had to go to five stores before I found one that sold liver."

Liver! Gone was any hope the smell emanated from a neighboring apartment. I forced a smile past clenched teeth and a reflexive gag. "I'm fine." At least I *had* felt fine until the vile stench of fried liver assaulted my olfactory glands.

"Well, I'm glad to hear that. Now come have dinner so you stay that way. Afterwards we'll catch up."

Unlike other Midwestern housewives who served up offerings of tuna noodle casserole ad nauseum, Mom had to be different. She believes in the healing powers of liver. Hell, if given half a chance, she'd set up a shrine to the slimy stuff. Liver, she constantly reminded me, is loaded with iron, and according to Mom, who knows more than any doctor, most ailments are the direct result of a lack of iron. So once a week throughout my childhood she cooked liver—to shoe-leather consistency.

Only back in Iowa I had made a pact with the dog. Methuselah—so named because his wrinkled gray coat made him look ancient from the moment of his birth—hid quietly under the table every Thursday night, and Mom was never the wiser. Unfortunately, Methuselah had taken up residence in doggy heaven several years ago, and I didn't own a liver-loving mutt in Manhattan.

For a fleeting moment I considered a mad dash to the local animal shelter.

The pungent odor of liver turned my stomach on a good day. Today was far from a good day. I felt myself turning green, if it's actually possible to turn green. My body proved it was.

"I see you've been busy doing more than shopping and cooking," I said, trying not to take any deep breaths as I entered my locker-sized, poorly ventilated kitchen. I reached across the sink and pried open the window an inch. Hundreds of coats of paint over the past century or two prevented me from raising it farther.

A puzzled expression settled over Mom's face.

"Did a bit of rearranging while I was gone?"

"Oh, that!" She waved one hand in the air in an attitude of dismissal as her other hand scooped brussels sprouts into a bowl. I swallowed a groan. I hate brussels sprouts almost as much as I hate liver. "No need to thank me," she said. "My pleasure. Now we can have a nice little window garden to brighten the place. Maybe grow a few cooking herbs?"

I had no desire for a "nice little window garden." Unlike my Mrs. Greenthumbs mother, I entered this world with two black opposable digits. Plants shrivel up and die if I so much as glance in their direction. And I hadn't missed the "we" instead of "you" pronoun she used.

Gertie was right. I had no choice but to place a call to my father.

"You go ahead and eat," I told her as I dashed out of the kitchen toward my bedroom, where the only things Mom had been able to rearrange were my dresser drawers and closet. Not that she probably hadn't tried, but even Mom has her decorating limitations. The size and configuration of the room allowed for only one spot for the bed, dresser and night stand.

"What about your dinner?" she called after me.

"I ate with friends." After grabbing the portable phone off the night stand, I locked myself in the bathroom.

My father and I have maintained a somewhat strained relationship since I left Ten Commandments and moved to New York. I think he still nurses a grudge over my rejection of his choices for me. Career. Husband. In his opinion, he knows what's best for his little girl. Only I'm no longer a little girl, and he can't seem to grasp that concept.

I punched the speed dial.

"You have reached the Stedworth residence. No one is home to take your call at the present time. Please leave a message at the sound of the tone. If you are calling for Mayor Stedworth, please try City Hall at—" I disconnected before the recording gave the number. I knew it by heart.

I punched in the number at City Hall.

"Thank you for calling Ten Commandment's City Hall. Regular business hours are—"

I disconnected and punched in my father's cell phone number.

"This is Mayor Earnest Stedworth. I am unavailable to take your call at the moment—"

I hung up without leaving a message. What was I going to say? "Hi, Daddy, this is Nori. What's up?" I knew what was up. What I didn't know was why, and under the circumstances, I couldn't think of an appropriate message to leave. I'd have to wait until I could reach him without a third-party voice mail intermediary.

Besides, the subject of my phone call was presently banging on the bathroom door, and I didn't want her to know I was calling Dad behind her back.

"Nori, are you all right in there? You're not sick, are you, honey?"

"I'm fine, Mom," I singsonged. "Just getting freshened up."

"Don't forget to use mouthwash, dear."

Leave it to Mom to voice her disapproval of my drinking without coming right out and saying it. I should have ordered vodka. She wouldn't have been able to detect it on my breath. "I have *got* to find some way to send her back to Iowa. Fast," I muttered to my reflection.

"*Look at it this way,*" answered Gertie. "*If you can survive Mom, you can survive anything.*"

The operative word here being *if.*

"*That which doesn't destroy us only serves to make us stronger.*"

Cute, Gertie. I resurrected you so you can spew cliches at me? I don't think so. How about some useful advice?

"*I'll sleep on it.*"

You do that. Meanwhile, I've got to get out of here. This apartment isn't big enough for the three of us.

"*Hey, did I ask to come back into your life? You're the one who ignored me for years, remember? Now all of a sudden you need good old Gertie again, and I'm supposed to tell you only what you want to hear? Not likely.*"

I rolled my eyes at my reflection. I unleashed a monster.

"*By the way, when you go out, make sure you order decaf. I need my beauty sleep.*"

For someone who hasn't been around for years, you certainly know quite a bit about me.

"*Like you're planning to head over to Bean Around the Block?*"

And you know about Suz and Dave.

"*Hey, I'm your fantasy friend, remember? I only know what you want me to know.*"

She had a point.

I returned to the bedroom, replaced the phone, and grabbed my laptop. When I turned to leave, Mom was leaning against the doorjamb, arms hugging her rounded middle, her body blocking my exit.

Part of me hated to leave her alone again, but I wasn't sure I wanted to hear what she had to say. I suspected her desire to "catch up" was more a need to unburden. Mom had always projected the image of a content, happy wife. Had she fooled me as well as herself all these years? And if my illusions were about to be shattered, how could I help her? I had to figure out my own life before I offered my services to anyone else.

Was I being selfish? Yes. Did it bother me as I stood there reading the worry and hurt on her face? Hell, yes. We may have our fundamental differences, but I still love my mother. Only I couldn't deal with her—or much of anything else—at the moment. "I have an appointment," I told her with an apologetic shrug of my shoulders. Right. An appointment with a *grande* skinny latté in a quiet corner of Bean Around the Block.

"You're going out again?" she asked. "By yourself? At this hour?"

"It's only a little after eight, Mom."

"But it's dark. Something could happen."

I brushed my lips against her cheek. "Nothing is going to happen. It's a very safe neighborhood, and I won't be long. Only an hour or two."

With a heavy sigh she stepped aside to let me pass.

I felt like a grade-A heel as I scurried out of the apartment and down the block.

"Running away from your problems, I see," said Gertie.

Who invited you?

"You did."

I hate confrontation. You know that.

"I know. If you faced your problems instead of running from them, you wouldn't need me."

Pretty damn smug for a figment of my imagination, aren't you?

"It's your imagination. I'm not telling you anything you don't already know."

So tell me something I don't know, damn it!

"Like what?"

I don't know, Gertie! Give me a break, will you? I've had a shitty day.

"And I haven't? Did I ask to get plucked back into the melodrama of your life?"

Oh, please!

I yanked open the door of Bean Around the Block and headed for my favorite table. It was taken—by a young couple making goo-goo eyes at each other over steaming cups of cappuccino. "Figures," I muttered, searching the room for another seat and finding not an empty table in the place. The normally quiet café was filled with chattering strangers who nearly drowned out the Wynton Marsalis piece playing in the background.

"How about over there?" Gertie suggested the empty chair at a table occupied by a guy with his head bent over a laptop. *"He's cute. And I'll bet he's not a loser like Dave."*

Don't you dare start playing matchmaker, I warned her. *For all you know, he's downloading kiddy porn.*

But I headed for the hunk's table and planted myself in front of him. Okay, so Gertie knew cute. I couldn't fault her on that. But then again, under the circumstances, wouldn't Gertie define cute in the same terms I did? "Do you mind?" I asked Cute Guy, aka Tall-and-Lanky-with-a-Shaggy-Crop-of-Chestnut-Hair-that-Fell-Over-One-Eye-Guy.

He glanced up. Brown eyes. Nearly black. The color of espresso. Even better. "Not at all."

"Kind of crowded here tonight, isn't it?"

"Hmm." He dropped his gaze back to his computer screen. End of conversation.

I sat down and deposited my laptop on the table opposite his, flipped it open, and powered it up. *Cute but uninterested,* I told Gertie.

"You give up too easily."

Hey, which one of us was dumped today? In the most humiliating way possible, in case you've already forgotten.

And don't give me any crap about getting right back up on the horse. I'm dealing with a lot more than a bruised ass or twisted ankle. Besides, I have other problems. Like no job and an uninvited houseguest who's going to want to drag me back to Ten Commandments the moment she finds out I'm unemployed.

I signaled Amber, one of the two regular evening waitresses. She waved back from the table she was clearing. "Your regular, Nori?"

"Thanks, Amber. What's going on here?" I scanned the room once more, wondering what had happened to my favorite hangout. Normally a quiet refuge to read or write and sip coffee, the small café now buzzed and hummed, the din escalating until it obliterated all traces of Wynton's trumpet. "I've never seen the place so crowded."

Her face broke out in a wide grin as she abandoned her task and bounced over, her pixie cut, orange-and-red streaked blonde hair bobbing around her. "You haven't heard? We're the new 'in' spot. HBO was filming scenes for the new *Sex and the City* movie here this morning, and it's been wall-to-wall people ever since. And guess what?"

She paused for effect but didn't stop hopping up and down on the balls of her purple Nike-clad feet or flapping her arms like some deranged canary. She held her breath, waiting for me to respond.

Like a dutiful captive audience of one, I took the bait. "What?"

Amber squealed and clapped her hands together as she continued to jump up and down. "I got to be an extra! I'm going to be in the movie! So's the entire staff. Can you believe it, Nori?"

"There goes the neighborhood," muttered my table-mate.

"*He speaks,*" said Gertie.

Amber and I turned toward him. "Next thing you know," continued the Cute Guy, "there'll be a velvet rope across the entrance and some beefy-looking bouncer checking your name against the A-list."

Amber's face filled with the wide-eyed hopefulness of a teenage wannabe groupie. "You think, Mr. Randolph? That would be so cool!"

He grunted his lack of enthusiasm over the idea and went back to typing.

She frowned, either confused or too dense to comprehend his sarcasm, but then she perked up and continued her chatter. "I think we should get rid of that boring jazz music and put in a karaoke machine, don't you? Wouldn't that be awesome? We could change the name to The Karaoke Koffee Kafé, with K's instead of C's."

"Clever," muttered the Cute Guy, aka Mr. Randolph, although I was beginning to think of him as Grouchy Cute Guy.

"With a C, not a K," he added in a deadpan, not bothering to look up.

Amber ignored him. "I'll be right back with your coffee, Nori. You want another, Mr. Randolph?"

Grouchy Cute Guy scowled at his empty cup. "Sure, but make it quick before the price triples to cover the cost of new signage and the bouncer."

She stuck out her tongue as she grabbed his cup. "Just because you didn't get to be on television is no reason to take it out on me."

He continued to type. "Believe me, Amber, I have no desire to be a part of television. On or off camera. Radio prima donnas are enough of a pain in the ass." He glanced up. "Now, are you going to get me more coffee, or do I have to go down the street to Starbucks?"

"Okay, okay." She turned to me and stage whispered, "He's usually not such a creep. I think he's kicking himself for missing a chance to meet Sarah Jessica Parker."

"Right." Grouchy Cute Guy shook his head and chuckled as Amber stuck her tongue out once more before heading toward the coffee bar.

I started typing out my frustrations, listing all the wrongs that had been visited upon me over the past eight hours and trying my damnedest to put a positive spin on the events. Wallowing in self-pity wasn't going to get me anywhere.

<u>MY ROTTEN DAY</u>

- Wasted two hundred dollars on prancing wrestler tickets (for soon-to-be-apparent reasons). Down side? Out two hundred dollars. Up side? Won't have to sit through an evening of prancing wrestlers.
- Scalded roof of mouth with volcanic burrito. Down side? Hurts like hell. Up side? Blisters should heal by the time I'm forty.
- Received a street sludge shower from inconsiderate stretch limo. Down side? Ruined best suit. Up side? Managed to drip my way through Marriott lobby without dying of humiliation while wearing aforementioned ruined suit.
- Caught now ex-boyfriend naked in Jacuzzi with now ex-best girlfriend. Down side? No longer have boyfriend or best girlfriend. Up side?

There's an up side to *this*? I wracked my brain, finally coming up with:

```
    At least I didn't walk in on them
    screwing each other's brains out.
  • Found Mom in throes of mental
    meltdown on my front stoop. Down
    side? Since Mom would not walk out
    on Dad, I figure she's been
    abducted by aliens. Defective
    clone returned in her place.
    (Note: Need to contact SETI
    Program.) Up side? A first-person
    paid interview in The National
    Enquirer? Could use the money
    because . . .
  • Got canned from too-good-to-be-
    true job. Down side? It was. Up
    side? Won't have to listen to
    ranting jocks blaring from the
    radio in the next cubicle.
  • Needed Gertie. Down side? Got Dr.
    Laura. Up side????
```

"What? I should have brought your pink blanky and teddy bear?"

Go away!

"Nope. Like it or not, you're stuck with me."

Swell.

She laughed.

If they ever make a movie of my life, I told her, *I'm making sure Renée Taylor plays you.*

"What? The Nanny's mom? No way. I'm holding out for Julia Roberts."

In your dreams.

"Hey, she played Tinkerbell, didn't she? If she can play a fairy, why not a figment?"

Because you're not that sweet.

"Neither was Tinkerbell. She tried to kill off Wendy, remember?"

Do you always have to be so annoyingly right?

She laughed once more but didn't answer.

Upon her return with our coffees, Amber continued to press for her name-changing campaign. "You like The Karaoke Koffee Kafé, don't you, Nori?" She placed my latté in front of me and passed a double espresso to my table partner. "Bean Around the Block is so . . . so . . ." She chewed on her bottom lip, her brow furrowed as she searched for the word she wanted.

"Has bean?" I offered.

The Grouchy Cute Guy raised his eyebrows and grinned at me. A moment later we both burst out laughing.

I laughed so hard that skewers of pain jabbed into my sides, and yet I kept laughing. I hugged my middle, my eyes filling with tears, but I couldn't stop. As much as it hurt, it felt good to laugh. Much better than crying, and Lord knew I had good reason to cry. The evidence flashed in front of me on a green screen with a blinking cursor.

Amber stared at the two of us, her expression perplexed. She shook her head, shrugged her shoulders, and crossed the room to clear another table. Guess she didn't get the joke.

After regaining some semblance of control, I watched as my tablemate swiped at his own eyes. It wasn't often that I came across someone who found my unique brand of humor so uproarious. Dave found my snappy "pun-ish" retorts and rejoinders embarrassing, especially when spouted in public. Maybe Grouchy Cute Guy didn't deserve such a quick dismissal, given the old great-minds-think-alike axiom.

"I needed that." He chortled twice. "Oh, God, how I needed that! Thank you. You wouldn't believe the day I've had."

I tossed him an expression that told him I'd match whatever disaster had paid him a visit and raise him a debacle.

"Not you, too?"

I nodded. "Big time."

"Must be something in the air." He waved his hand. "Ladies first."

With a sigh and a shake of my head, I ticked off my own day's calamities, illustrating each one by holding up my fist and raising a finger as I went down the long list. "One: Incinerated the roof of my mouth on a molten burrito. Two: Got doused with street sewage. Three: Walked in on my cheating lover. Four: Came home to find my mother had arrived for a surprise, indefinite stay. Five: Learned the company I work for—or should say, *worked* for—has gone under, and I'm officially laid off." I tilted my chin upward in challenge. "Care to top that?"

"Ouch." He raised both hands in surrender. "No contest. You win." Then he reached his right hand across the table. "Mackenzie Randolph. Otherwise known as Mac."

I shook his hand. "Or Mr. Randolph?"

"Only to bubblegum-headed teenage waitresses."

I glanced across the room to where Amber was serving another table. "She's not so bad."

He raised his eyebrows again, as if challenging me to defend my opinion.

"For a bubblegum-headed teenage waitress," I added.

He chuckled. "Right. And you're Nori?"

"To family and friends. Honora Stedworth to the IRS, DMV, and assorted telemarketers."

As Mac and I chatted over our coffees, his grumpy façade slipped away. His day had gone better than mine, to be sure, but so had everyone else's—except maybe for some hapless individual who came home to a tax audit notice in the day's mail. Or had all four wisdom teeth extracted without the benefit of novocaine. Or accidentally backed the car over the family dog. Or all three.

"Unemployment looms on my horizon, as well," said Mac. "I stopped in here to sit in a quiet corner with a cup of coffee and sort out my options."

"And instead, found yourself in the midst of groupie central?"

He glanced around the crowded room. "This dump is normally deader than the Knicks' playoff hopes when I come in during the day. Who would have expected it to go from deserted to SRO in the span of twenty-four hours?"

"And this is only from word of mouth," I added. "What will happen after the movie comes out?"

He glared into his coffee cup. "We'll have to mortgage our souls for a decent cup of espresso."

"I doubt my soul is worth enough to sustain my designer java habit." I turned my attention back to my laptop. With a few keystrokes, I exited the program and shut down the computer. Mac was far more enjoyable company than Gertie with her newfound 'tude.

Like I asked to come?

See what I mean?

Mac nodded toward the computer. "Working on a résumé?"

I wasn't about to divulge the contents of my ramblings, so I lied. "Sort of. You?"

"Trying to come up with some sort of innovative programming to save both my job and the station. Our rev-

75

enues are plummeting. Either I conjure up some magic formula to entice back both listeners and advertisers, or I'm out the door. The custom-made shirts don't listen to excuses. They're only interested in the bottom line."

"Tell me about it. I'm living proof of corporate callousness. Which station?"

"WBAT. Big Apple Talk Radio. Ever listen to it?"

Not if I can help it. I shook my head.

"Mind my asking why not?"

What planet was he from? I rolled my eyes and answered his question without thinking twice about bruising his male ego. "Why would I? Big Apple Talk Radio? Hardly. It's more like Big Jock Rant Radio. Hardly. Ever think about the other half of the population? Those of us with double-X chromosomes? Your shows are all the same, hour after hour. The only thing that changes throughout the day is the name of the guy doing the ranting and raving and the sports figure or team he's ranting and raving about."

"For someone who doesn't listen, you sure know an awful lot about the programming."

"Not by choice. The guy in the next cubicle at work used to tune in. Short of wearing earplugs, it was impossible to avoid." I grinned at him. "I guess that's one good thing about losing my job. No more jock rants."

"So what would you listen to if you had your choice?"

"Music."

"Music?"

"Yeah, you know, that stuff made up of notes on a staff. Jazz? Classical? Rock and roll?"

He shook his head. "I wish. But I'm only the station manager. The owners want to stick with a talk format. Topical and preferably controversial."

"My condolences." I rose. I had a topical and controversial topic of my own to deal with yet tonight, and I couldn't put it off any longer.

"Leaving?" He looked disappointed.

I hesitated. I wanted to stay, but I knew I couldn't. Not tonight. "I need to tackle the problem waiting for me back at my apartment."

"Your mother?"

I grimaced. "My mother."

"Good luck." He flashed me a smile before returning to his keyboard.

"Nice smile," said Gertie.

Don't start.

"Who, me?"

As expected, Mom was waiting up, ready to pounce on me the moment I entered the apartment. "Nori! Thank God. I was getting so—"

I wrapped my arm around her shoulders, kissed her cheek, and cut her off before she finished her sentence. "Mom, why don't you make us both a cup of chamomile tea, and we'll do that catching up now."

Her eyes misted. She sniffed, smiled her thanks, and walked into the kitchen. Had she manipulated me? Of course, but she could manipulate all she wanted, as long as it led to the reason for her abrupt departure from Ten Commandments. I followed her into the kitchen like a grateful puppy dog and headed for the cabinet where I kept the tea bags.

But instead of the box of Sleepy Time Celestial Seasonings I expected to retrieve from the lowest shelf of the cabinet to the left of the sink, I found three neat rows of glasses, divided by size. The middle shelf, which normally held boxes of cereal, rice, and pasta, now housed my eclectic assortment of chipped and mismatched plates and cereal bowls.

The top shelf, accessible only with the use of a stepladder, was where I stuck things I never used. Like the set of ceramic pig canisters Mom had painted and given me last Christmas. The shelf now held assorted junk food: half a bag of chocolate-covered pretzels, a mason jar of Hershey's Hugs and Kisses, three unopened packages of Nutter Butters—Dave's favorite cookie—and a half-empty box of saltwater taffy from a trip to Atlantic City.

An hour after Dave and I had arrived down at the shore last month, I lost a filling to that damn complimentary taffy. I spent the remainder of the weekend inhaling Motrin by the handful and counting the minutes until the dentist's office opened Monday morning. Dave, who claimed he couldn't stand to see me suffer, spent the entire weekend shooting craps in the casino. Talk about blinded by love. What a naïve fool I was!

"*I'll say,*" said Gertie.

I don't even know why I brought the box home with me. Who but masochists keep souvenirs from hell? Was my subconscious trying to tell me something? If so, I ignored it until the truth slammed me in the face earlier today. Maybe I should use the taffy to create a shrine to my own stupidity.

I glanced around the kitchen—not for a suitable place to set up a shrine, but to find the new home of the tea, coffee, sugar, and flour piggies. They now smiled their little pink snouts at me from the counter to the right of the sink. Alongside half a dozen mason jars—easily a three year's supply *if* I could pawn a few jars off on Reese and Gabe—of Mom's award-winning pickled beets.

As much as I wanted to scream at my mother for her intrusiveness, I bit down on my tongue—unfortunately, hard enough to taste blood. Damn! Now I'd have a tongue ulcer on top of everything else.

But whatever had happened in Ten Commandments

to make Mom scurry halfway across the country had to be big. Forget the tongue ulcer. I couldn't lose my cool over Mom's obsessive need to reorganize anything and everything in her path. If I remembered my Psych 101 course correctly, people who constantly rearrange inanimate objects do so as a substitute for the changes they either can't make or are afraid to make in their own lives. I took a deep breath and forced a pleasant tone into my voice. "Mom? The tea bags?"

She paused in filling the teapot and motioned to piggy number one. "In the tea canister, of course."

Of course.

After removing two tea bags, I went in search of the coffee mugs, spoons, and lemon juice. Nothing was where it should be. She had even shuffled around the food in my refrigerator. I gritted my teeth. The Mad Rearranger had spent her evening attacking my kitchen. Why couldn't she plop down on the sofa and watch *Survivor* like the rest of the population?

So we sat and sipped our tea and talked. Or rather, Mom talked. I listened. But she didn't say anything more than what she had told me earlier that day. She was tired of being taken for granted. It was obvious Dad didn't love her because he never spent any time at home. She wasn't getting any younger. It was time to start a new life. Yadda-yadda-yadda. This was *not* my mother. With every sentence she spoke, she gave more credibility to my alien abduction theory.

"But why New York? You hate big cities—especially this one."

"Because you're in New York, and I don't have family anywhere else other than in and around Ten Commandments." She thrust her chin out defiantly. "I'll have to adjust. You did."

"But I wanted to live here. You don't."

"I do now."

Right. And I want to climb Mount Everest. I glanced at the clock. Still early enough to call Dad. I really needed to hear his side of things. According to her, he wouldn't even realize she had left. "I'll be right back," I said.

For the second time that night I dashed to the bedroom for the portable phone, then to the bathroom. For the second time that night I connected with nothing but voice mail and answering machines. Where the hell was my father, and why wasn't he at least answering his cell phone?

I headed back to the kitchen, more frustrated and confused than ever. Mom segued into a Eugene update. "He's not dating, you know."

No, I didn't know, and frankly I didn't care, but I kept that thought to myself.

"The two of you made such a lovely couple, Nori." She sighed.

Couple? Where in the world did she get that idea? "Mom, Eugene and I were *never* a couple."

"Of course you were, dear." She patted my hand the way you'd respond to a favorite aunt who had gone senile—as if to jog my failing memory. I gave up. What was the use? At least she now sounded like the mother I knew. If she wanted to believe that Eugene and I were once a couple, let her. They'd be hoeing hyacinths in hell before I went on another date with Eugene Draymore.

I ended the discussion of Eugene with a loud yawn. She took the hint. "Oh dear, look at the time! And you have to be up for work early."

Not really, but I certainly wasn't dipping into that can of botulism at eleven o'clock at night. Instead, I smiled and nodded in agreement.

Fifteen minutes later we settled into bed. I hadn't slept with my mother since my parents invited Eugene to visit us at a summer cabin they had rented on the

Upper Peninsula. It was my junior year of college, and I had no idea he was coming until he showed up. A most unwelcome surprise planned by my parents. He and Dad shared the room with the twin beds; Mom and I shared the double bed in the master bedroom.

That's when I learned that my dear, sweet, churchgoing mother—a woman who will give a stranger the clothes off her back—is a selfish, aggressive hog in bed. She steals the blankets and sprawls diagonally across most of the mattress, leaving me six inches if I'm lucky. Since today wasn't one of my luckier days, as already documented, I wound up with about four and a half inches on this night. And did I also mention that Mom snores like a seven-hundred-pound bull moose with adenoid problems?

If nothing else, I had to get her to go home, or I'd never get another decent night of sleep.

Chapter Six

"Nori lives in a closet," I told Marjorie the next morning after my daughter left for work. "A closet in a basement, without a spare bed for her mother. Since when is living in a basement with bars on the windows wonderful?"

"Bars?"

"Bars. Like a prison cell. I distinctly remember her gushing over this place when she called home after renting it. She failed to mention either the basement or the bars. And you wouldn't believe the constant noise of people yelling and the traffic with the horns blaring and the sirens screaming at all hours of the day and night."

Marjorie made a *tsk*ing noise with her tongue. "Were you able to sleep?"

"Sleep?" I yawned. "How in the world is a person supposed to sleep through such constant racket? I tossed and turned for hours until I finally gave up and stumbled into the bathroom about an hour before daybreak. I tried taking a shower—in a dribble of barely lukewarm water even though I had the hot faucet turned all the way up and the cold off. And forget about water pressure. There isn't any. So I dragged myself into the kitchen and made a pot of coffee. I drank the entire pot before Nori got up."

"No wonder you sound wired."

I stifled another yawn. "Honestly, Marjorie, I feel worse than I did before leaving Ten Commandments."

Marjorie sighed into the phone. "You have jet lag, that's all. And it's normal not to sleep well your first night in a strange place. You'll get used to it."

"It's more than that," I admitted.

"What do you mean?"

"All night I tried to push away my qualms about this trip and our cockamamie scheme, but the more I pushed, the more the doubts nagged at me." That's the problem with impetuous notions. They always sound so sensible and logical at the time, but then you wind up with pumpkin orange hair. Or no hair at all. Or stuck in a closet in New York City. "Maybe I should have left the old me buried in the past where she belonged. After all, I'm no longer a foolhardy adolescent."

"You're forgetting the big picture," counseled Marjorie. "Don't think about the present. Concentrate on the future."

Easy for her to say, sitting in the tranquility of her Iowa kitchen. I missed my husband. My home. My life—boring and unfulfilling though it was—back in Ten Commandments. There's something to be said about the comfort of the known and ordinary, no matter how much I had complained about those very things only a short time ago. Strains of an old Joni Mitchell song popped into my head. Something about not knowing what you've got till it's gone.

Talk about a paradox. Part of me chafed at having missed out on life while the other part of me feared experiencing it. "Maybe what I really need is a few sessions with a good therapist," I admitted.

"That will certainly set tongues wagging," said Marjorie. "Besides, you don't need a shrink. You need to knuckle down and get to work. Think of what's at stake."

I screwed up my courage. "You're right. I guess I'm experiencing a touch of cold feet." But why wouldn't I? Ten Commandments was the only home I had ever known and Earnest the only man I had ever loved. We had grown up together, and sometime between the playground of our youth and the annual school plays of our teens, we had fallen in love. Marrying Earnest had been a given since as long as I can remember. And I still loved him after all these years. Even if I did feel like I often played second fiddle—or third or thirtieth—to everyone else in town.

For one thing, no matter how late Earnest drags himself home after a night at City Hall or the Grange or wherever his duties have taken him, he always climbs into bed and spoons his familiar body against mine. We've been married nearly thirty years, and aside from the few days I spent in the hospital when Nori was born and one vacation where by necessity we had separate bedrooms, we've never slept apart. That's a lot of spooning. Last night I missed his warm belly snuggled up against my backside, the light snoring noise he makes in my ear. Sharing a bed with my daughter just isn't the same.

Besides, Nori has a habit of hogging both the bed and the blankets. I had forgotten that. We only shared a bed once, during that same vacation that Earnest and I had separate bedrooms.

Marjorie offered a bit more encouragement. "You're doing fine, Connie. Just keep following the plan. Are you all set for step two?"

I reached for my purse, pulled out the list, and scanned down to step two. *Get a makeover.* No qualms there. The only beauty salon I had ever patronized was the Bouffant Beehive on Main Street. And I looked it.

"Any suggestions?" I asked.

"Go for drastic. You've been wearing the same hairdo since forever."

"The last time I opted for drastic, I wound up with pumpkin orange hair."

"Honestly, Connie! We were eleven years old. Find a good salon and trust the experts. I guarantee you'll feel much better about yourself."

I figured I couldn't feel much worse about the way I looked. No offense to Great-granny Mathilda.

"Besides," she continued, "once Earnest sees the new you, he'll trip over his own feet rushing home every night."

For a new hairdo? I doubted it. Earnest didn't care about things like that. He probably wouldn't even notice. No, the makeover was for me. An exorcism of the ghost of a long-dead relative who had taken up residence in my body. At least that's what I hoped.

"So, tell me, Marjorie, if a newer, improved Constance Stedworth is such a surefire cure for what ails me and my marriage, how come you haven't implemented it yourself?"

"What do you mean?"

"You said you were suffering from the same blahs. I don't see you hopping on a plane and turning your life upside down to spark a fire under your husband."

"There's more than one way to ignite a blaze, Connie."

"And your way lets you do it staying home, but I had to fly to New York?"

Marjorie huffed through the phone line. "Honestly, Connie, sometimes you are so dense. Because I don't have a daughter in New York, and you do. And that daughter needs to be back in Ten Commandments with my son if either of us is ever going to have any grandchildren.

"By the way," she continued. "Leona Shakelmeyer called me last night. Her daughter is pregnant."

"Again?"

"Again."

That made six grandchildren in as many years for Leona. Two for her son and now four for her daughter, but who's counting? Leona, that's who. She rubs all those grandkids in my face whenever I see her.

As much as I looked forward to the makeover, I knew that wouldn't fix my problem. The cure lay in grandchildren. I was certain of it. Lots of them. To keep me busy.

"So hang up and get moving," said Marjorie, "or we'll be too senile and crippled with arthritis to enjoy those grandbabies. Besides, I'm eating too much coffee cake all by myself. I swear I've gained two pounds since you left yesterday."

Not that anyone would notice. Marjorie has always been thin as a rail. She eats like a teenage boy and never gains an ounce. I, on the other hand, could eat like a colicky infant and still pack on the pounds no matter how many aerobics classes I took at the community center. I suppose it's all part of God's mysterious plan. Why He had decided Marjorie could eat like a pig but I would be the one to look like a porker is beyond me, though. I can only hope that in Heaven, I'll slim down to a size six.

"All right, but you *will* start the ball rolling on your end today, right, Marjorie?"

"I'll try, Connie."

"What do you mean *try?*"

She hesitated. "There've been a few additional problems since you left."

"On top of what you mentioned yesterday afternoon? What sort of problems? What's going on?"

"Nothing for you to worry about, Connie. Only the usual town messes that crop up every once in a while. You know how it is."

Yes, I certainly did. After all, that was one of the reasons I left, wasn't it? For the mayor of Ten Commandments, an infestation of mealy bugs takes precedence over his wife.

"Anyway, I think Earnest is going to have his hands full for a few days," she continued. "Might be best if I wait until things cool down here."

I didn't like the sound of that. I wanted to be back in my own bed. In my own house. "How long? Marjorie, Earnest does know where I am, doesn't he? I don't want him worried sick over my disappearance."

"Trust me, Connie. He's not worried about your disappearance. Now, you get on with things at your end, and let me take care of things on mine."

After hanging up with Marjorie, I forced aside my lingering doubts over her words of assurance and pondered step two on the list. Yesterday, when I had ventured out in search of a supermarket, I hadn't noticed any department stores—fancy or otherwise. I hadn't even come across a Wal-Mart. Little specialty shops lined the streets around Nori's apartment. A coffee shop. A bakery. A maternity shop. A shoe store. A shop that only sold handmade truffles. Even a shop that specialized in cat accessories and gifts. I can't imagine a store like that in downtown Ten Commandments. Back home cats earn their keep as mousers. They don't lounge around in rhinestone-studded collars and fur booties.

I hesitated to walk into any street corner beauty parlor. That ruled out the place I noticed a few doors down from the supermarket. But I figured that was just as well. From what I observed through the window, they catered to a very young crowd and specialized in pumpkin orange hair. And purple. And chartreuse. I had no desire to repeat that part of my youth. I wanted a transformation, but I wasn't about to put my head in the hands of Dr. Frankenstein.

Only problem was, I had no idea where the fancy-schmancy New York salons were located. Or the fancy-schmancy anything, for that matter. I didn't remember passing anything that qualified on the cab ride from the airport yesterday. Not that it was easy to make out any one store as the cab whipped through traffic. For most of the ride, I was too busy holding on for dear life to pay attention to the scenery.

I wanted someone I could trust not to turn me into a freak. I definitely didn't want an ultra-trendy salon-to-the-stars, even if they didn't specialize in pumpkin orange hair. I do read *People* magazine occasionally when I'm at the Bouffant Beehive for a trim. I've seen photographs of New York celebrities. Half of them look like they just stuck a wet toe into an electrical outlet. The other half usually bare a striking resemblance to their designer dogs, which they always seem to have tucked under their arms or nestled in designer totes.

I figured I'd probably be safest using a department store salon. Now all I had to do was find the nearest Dilliard's, Younkers, or Von Maur, but I wasn't even certain where I was in relation to the rest of Manhattan. Nori had called her area of the city "the Village." Obviously, New York City's idea of a village and my Iowan idea of a village bore no resemblance to each other. North. South. East. West. I had no idea where to head. And after my harrowing cab ride yesterday, I wanted to walk.

Luckily, I did have someone to ask. And if I played my cards right, I'd also get to check off another item on the list. If Nori didn't have me committed first.

Chapter Seven

I woke up the next morning bruised and irritable and unable to stop yawning. Since I hadn't told Mom about my layoff, I dressed for work, left the apartment a few minutes before eight, and headed for Bean Around the Block. After a transfusion of black coffee, I tried to work on my résumé, but I found myself mulling over modern methods of torture instead. The hurt and betrayal of yesterday still seethed inside me. Forget Uncle Zechariah's sermons. I wanted revenge. I wanted to hurt Suz and Dave as much as they had hurt me.

"*In some countries they behead women for adultery,*" offered a less-than-helpful Gertie.

It's not really adultery, I reminded her. *Dave and I weren't married. Besides, I don't think the guys suffer the same fate in those countries. Especially since they make the rules.*

"*And we all know what cheats guys are,*" she added.

Precisely. Anyway, I'm thinking more in terms of ultimate humiliation.

Gertie clapped her hands together. "*Lice!*"

Now you're getting the idea. I closed my eyes and pictured Dave and Suz scratching like crazy. *But where would I get lice in Manhattan? It isn't like you can walk into a local pet shop and purchase the little buggers.*

"*True.*"

However, bait and tackle shops were a good source for worms. I still had a key to both their apartments. I could sneak in while they were at work and fill their shoes with slimy, squishy, squiggly fish food. If only I had the guts—no pun intended. *Being a coward has one advantage,* I told Gertie.

"*What's that?*"

I won't land in jail.

She shrugged. "*Once a Goody Two-shoes, always a Goody Two-shoes.*"

Perhaps, but my Goody Two-shoes image didn't keep me from compiling a long list I titled "Getting Even with Dave and Suz." By the time I typed my twenty-fifth revenge fantasy—hiring a mercenary to deposit the two of them naked in the middle of the Sahara Desert with nothing but a broken Rolex, a pair of Manolo sandals, and a half-empty bottle of Perrier between them (okay, so I was operating on no sleep and too much caffeine)—it was time for lunch. The day was half over, and I had accomplished exactly zilch.

I ordered another coffee and a tuna veggie croissant, neither of which I could afford. *I'll work on the résumé after lunch,* I told Gertie.

"*Uh-huh.*"

That's when I remembered I still hadn't spoken to my father. I also remembered, too late, that with everything that had happened over the past twenty-four hours, I had forgotten to charge my cell phone. I dug the phone out of the bottom of my purse and stared at the power display. Not much juice left. I tried Dad's cell number first. Again, no answer. I punched in his office at City Hall.

"Mayor's office. Miss Schrumm speaking."

At least I had finally reached a human being. Although dubbing Louisa Schrumm human almost stretched the imagination further than humanly possible. The beady-eyed harridan made the Wicked Witch of the West look like Glinda the Good Witch of the North.

Louisa had been Dad's secretary since before I was born. And she made sure everyone knew it—especially me.

I sugarcoated my voice with a gallon of Karo syrup. "Hello, Louisa. This is Nori. May I speak with my father, please?"

Her tone made it clear she didn't appreciate the interruption. "He's in a meeting."

I added a gallon of maple sugar to the Karo syrup. "When will the meeting be over?"

My sweet tone only annoyed her more. "He has back-to-back meetings scheduled all day. The mayor is very busy."

Really? I thought he spent his days playing jacks and Pick Up Sticks. I tamped down the urge to voice my thoughts out loud. Louisa lacked the sense of humor gene; she didn't find anything funny. To my knowledge, no one had ever seen the old bat so much as crack a smile. "This is an emergency, Louisa. I need to speak with him."

"Still as overly dramatic as ever, aren't you, Honora?" She expelled a loud breath of impatience. "Well, we have our own emergencies here in Ten Commandments, and unlike yours, ours are real."

"Tight-assed bitch," I muttered. Too bad she couldn't hear me. She had already hung up. Louisa loved the power trip of hanging up on people. This wasn't the first time she had done it to me. I consoled myself with the knowledge that at least my father wouldn't hear a Louisa-colored diatribe about the filthy mouth his daughter had developed since leaving the bosom of Ten Commandments.

With nothing else to do, I turned my attention once

again to my résumé, but I found it difficult to keep my thoughts from wandering back to the Wicked Bitch. Most everyone at DataScroungers had gotten along. Some more than others, granted, but the office had been free of people like Louisa Schrumm.

I wasn't naïve enough to believe that the Louisas of the world only worked for small-town mayors in Iowa. An unpleasant thought popped into my brain and made its way down to my stomach like a two-year-old fruitcake. What if my next boss was a Louisa clone? My lack of an emergency nest egg required that I grab the first offer I received. Unemployed beggars didn't have the luxury of being choosy.

Putting up with Louisa's insults during an occasional visit back home or a phone call was one thing. Working on a daily basis with a person like her was something else. I needed a game plan for dealing with a possible Louisa scenario. Otherwise, I knew I'd get my ass fired quicker than you could say, "We welcome you to Munchkinland." I opened a new file—"Dealing with the Office Bitch."

"Learn to kiss ass," suggested Gertie.

Along with swallow your pride and keep your big mouth shut? Welcome to life in the real world. What if at this early stage in my working life, my two-and-a-half-year stint at DataScroungers turned out to be the best job I ever held? Talk about looking ahead to a depressing future! *There's got to be a better way.*

"Maybe you're worrying for nothing. After all, if you don't get that résumé finished, you won't find a job—with or without an office bitch."

Jeez, I hate it when you're right. I closed the file and re-opened the one titled "Résumé."

Several hours later, as my stomach signaled dinnertime and Bean Around the Block filled up for the second day in a row with *Sex and the City* groupies, I sat back, sipped my fifth—or was it fiftieth?—cup of coffee, and read through what I had written. It wasn't much. *Kind of light on experience,* I muttered to Gertie.

"Enough. You got your first job with less."

I got my first job because anyone with an ounce of intelligence and a modicum of experience had enough sense to stay away from dot-coms.

Her lack of a snappy retort confirmed she agreed with my pronouncement.

The résumé complete, I shut down my computer. Now all I needed were places to send the sucker. I snatched up a copy of *The New York Times* that someone had left on a nearby table. With any hope, I'd find the answer to my prayers in the Help Wanted section.

My muscles screamed in protest as I swung my laptop strap over my shoulder. Other than an occasional trip to the restroom, I had barely moved all day. Except for my fingers as they flew across my keyboard, and they now throbbed from repetitive stress syndrome. Thoughts of a hot soak in Dave's Jacuzzi taunted me. But all I had to look forward to was my miniscule tub and an ancient hot water heater that never produced anything warmer than tepid.

Tucking the paper under my arm, I headed back to my apartment. And Mom. What wonderful surprise did she have in store for me this evening? Had she spent the day stripping and faux finishing my bedroom furniture? Lengthening my miniskirts? Baking fruitcake doorstops?

I paused outside the apartment door and sniffed. No liver. No brussels sprouts. A definite improvement over last night. I took a deep breath, unlocked the three deadbolts, and stepped inside. "Mom, I'm . . . oh, my God! What have you done?"

Mom—or at least I think it was Mom—stood in the middle of the living room. She patted her hair, twirled around, and beamed at me. "You like it?"

"Um . . ." I was speechless. My mother was nowhere in sight. In her place stood a younger, more sophisticated version of the woman who had raised me. Gone was the *Little House on the Prairie* dress. Along with the Eisenhower era, graying, mousy-brown pageboy. And the freshly scrubbed face, devoid of any traces of makeup, save a coat of lip gloss.

"I treated myself to a makeover," she said, twirling around once more. This time she swept her hand from her stylishly cut and colored hair and made-up face down across her body to indicate the—*Donna Karan black silk pantsuit?*

My mother didn't wear Donna Karan pantsuits. She didn't wear Donna Karan anything. She wore flowery cotton shirtwaists and denim jumpers that she bought at Wal-Mart.

She pointed her left toe to draw my attention to her foot. I looked down to discover she had replaced her normally sensible penny loafers with a pair of stiletto sandals that looked suspiciously like the Manolos Reese had sported yesterday. A lump the size of Cedar Rapids, Iowa, settled in the pit of my stomach. "Mom, where did you buy those sandals?"

"At the department store where I bought all my new clothes." She made a *tsk*ing sound with her tongue. "You know, Nori, this Manhattan isn't so special. For a city that's supposed to have everything, you don't have a single Dilliard's or Younkers or Von Maur."

"Those are Midwest department stores, Mom. Besides, you don't shop at Dilliard's, Younkers, or Von Maur. You shop at Wal-Mart and K-Mart. And occasionally JC Penney when you want to splurge."

She placed her hands on her hips and jutted out her

bottom lip. Her expression dumbfounded me. In all my life, I had never seen my mother pout.

Then she whined—like a five-year-old! "Well, I wanted to splurge, and your upstairs neighbor didn't know of any Penneys in the city, either."

My upstairs neighbor? "Which neighbor?"

"Hy."

Hy? In the year and a half I'd lived in my apartment, Hyman Perth—otherwise known as Oscar the Grouch—had grunted maybe a dozen words at me, none of them friendly. I only knew his name because I occasionally received some of his mail in my box. And here's my mother, a woman afraid of the big, bad city, striking up a conversation about department stores with a total stranger—and a very unfriendly one to boot? "How did you meet Oscar, I mean, Mr. Perth?" I asked.

"We met yesterday while I was waiting for you to come home."

"And you happened to strike up a conversation about department stores?"

"Don't be ridiculous, Nori. I rang his bell this morning and asked if he'd give me directions. He invited me in for a cup of tea, and we had a nice chat. Lovely man."

Unbelievable! I stared at her and shook my head. "So he recommended a store? Which one?"

"A wonderful place. Bergman something-or-other, I think." She waved her hand in the air, dismissing the need for an exact name. "I wanted a store within walking distance. Honestly, Nori, the cab drivers in this city drive as though they're at the Indianapolis Speedway. But Hy said all the best stores were too far for me to walk. He did hail a cab for me, though. Wasn't that sweet of him? And he told the driver if he scared me out of my wits, he'd report him. Took down his name and made me promise to tell him about the ride when I returned. So the trip wasn't as bad as the one from the airport, but I still don't like cabs.

"Anyway, I had the nicest salesgirl once I got to the store. Hy called ahead and made an appointment for me with my very own personal shopper. Loretta. She helped me coordinate everything, and she even made the hair and makeup appointments for me at the salon.

"Loretta also suggested I get a facial. Have you ever had one, Nori? I was exfoliated and oxygenated and hydrated like you wouldn't believe. Then, I was slathered with seaweed!" She made a face—the kind I instinctively make at the smell of liver and brussels sprouts. "I know it sounds awful, but it was so relaxing!"

She prattled on, but my mind had frozen on "Bergman something-or-other." It's not that I didn't think she looked fantastic. Hell. Mom looked beyond fantastic. She just didn't look like Mom. I'm not sure anyone back in Ten Commandments would recognize her. And maybe that wasn't such a bad thing, considering everyone in Ten Commandments could probably do with a makeover and a swift kick into the twenty-first century.

But this was too much of a jolt to my system at a point in my life when I had sustained my share of unexpected and unwelcome jolts. Right now I needed the comfort of familiarity. Like my ratty old chenille bathrobe. A cup of hot chocolate in my favorite Kermit the Frog mug. My old teddy bear. And yes, even my mommy. But this woman standing in front of me neither looked nor acted like my mommy.

Some things in life were supposed to remain as they always had been. Like mothers. And my mother clipped coupons to save ten cents on a bottle of ketchup. She didn't splurge on a day of pampering and a shopping spree at . . . at . . . "Bergdorf Goodman?" I asked, interrupting her one-woman sales pitch for Loretta-the-Personal-Shopper and the store's spa.

Mom snapped her French-manicured fingers. A French manicure! My mother, who always keeps her nails trimmed short so they won't get in the way of gardening, now possessed a full set of acrylics. I glanced back down at her feet. And a pedicure! "Yes, Bergdorf Goodman. That's it, dear. Such a beautiful store and a very friendly staff."

I'll bet, considering the bundle Mom must have dropped today. It was then that my peripheral vision picked up on the virtual wrecking ball swinging toward me. With mounting dread, I continued. "Mom, you don't have a Bergdorf's credit card. How did you pay for all this?"

"Well, that was a bit of a problem at first. They don't take Discover. Imagine that! I called to check before I left. Then I remembered seeing your American Express card when I rearranged your dresser drawers yesterday. So I borrowed it. I knew you wouldn't mind."

My American Express? My for-emergencies-only American Express card that has to be paid in full with each statement? The wrecking ball hit me broadside. I groaned.

"Honestly, Honora, there's no need for you to get so upset. I'll pay you back as soon as your father sends me some money."

Ah, a light at the end of the tunnel. "So you've talked to Dad?"

She grimaced. "No, not yet. I'm letting him stew for a while."

"Stew? I thought you said he doesn't even know you're gone. How can he stew? And what makes you think he'll send you money once he learns you walked out on him?"

"I only left because he ignores me."

"So when Dad sends you money, he won't be ignoring you, and you'll go home?"

"Of course not. He had his chance. I'm moving on. I told you that. By the way, you're on your own for dinner tonight. I'm dining with Hy."

"You have a date? With Oscar?"

"Who is this Oscar you keep talking about? I have a date with Hyman Perth. Your upstairs neighbor."

"Mother, you're married!"

She shot me a why-are-you-being-so-dense look and uttered an exasperated, overdramatic exhalation. "I'm separated. People are allowed to date when they're separated."

"Not if one of the two of them doesn't know they're separated!" My mother made no sense. I flailed my arms; my voice shot up several octaves. "When do you plan on telling Dad? Before or after he sends you the money to repay me?"

"I don't know why you're making such a fuss, Nori. You have a good job, and it's not like I'm some ne'er-do-well out to stiff you. You'll get reimbursed."

But when? In time to pay the Amex bill when it arrived in my mailbox at the end of next week? Doubtful. I knew I could no longer keep my unemployed status from her. Oscar the Grouch and Loretta-the-Personal-Shopper had forced me to spill the espresso beans.

But then again, maybe this newly metamorphosed Mom wouldn't react like the old one. Ten Commandments Mom would have let loose with an I-told-you-so lecture as she tried to forcibly drag me back to Iowa. Dr. Loretta Frankenstein's creation might have a completely different take on the situation. "Sit down, Mom. We need to talk."

She glanced at her watch. "It will have to wait, dear. I'll be late for my dinner engagement."

As if on cue, the doorbell rang. "I'll get it," Mom trilled in a singsong voice reminiscent of Mr. Rogers. Only it wasn't a beautiful day in my neighborhood today. Mom had seen to that with her extravagant shopping spree and newly acquired, self-induced single status.

I glanced toward the closed bedroom door and wondered what additional surprises were now hanging in my closet. Versace lounging pajamas? A Dior evening gown? A Judith Leiber rhinestone clutch? No, had Mom bought a Judith Leiber, she'd be carrying it with her on her "date."

I watched as she scooped up a napkin-decoupaged straw purse from the couch. I recognized it immediately as the twin to one she had given me. Red poppies. Being more a Kate Spade girl (even if I could only afford a faux version, purchased from a sidewalk vender in Times Square), I kept the poppy clutch on the top shelf of my closet. Along with the matching straw hat, belt, and shoes that screamed, "Iowa hick!" Ever since Mom discovered napkin decoupage about two years ago, few surfaces are safe from embellishment. And no birthday or Christmas has gone by without another addition to the growing stock in my closet.

I glanced back down at her feet. So why wasn't she wearing the matching poppy pumps? Had she forgotten to pack them? Too bad we're not the same shoe size. It might have kept her from purchasing those eight-hundred-dollar sandals she now wore.

Worse yet, from our conversation, I got the impression Mom had splurged on an entire new wardrobe at Bergdorf's, not just the one Donna Karan outfit and Manolos. My luck wasn't going well enough for her spree to have stopped with one pantsuit. And why should it? My Amex card has a really high credit limit.

Mom peered out the peephole and trilled, "One moment, Hy," as she started unlocking the deadbolts. Working her way from top to bottom, she muttered something under her breath about my closet of an apartment having more locks than the entire town of Ten Commandments. After some more grumbling, she slipped the chain and swung open the apartment door. Oscar the Grouch, minus the ratty green fur, stood on the other side of the transom.

For the first time in all our brief encounters, I took a good look at the man and nearly lost my breath. Always before, I had seen nothing more than a scruffy-looking senior citizen. Either I hadn't bothered to look too closely, or the Grouch cleaned up pretty good. Clint Eastwood good, in fact. Hyman Perth filled my doorway in all his shaggy-haired, goateed, chisel-faced, tall, lean, and lanky glory. The expression on his face told me my mother was about to make his day.

He didn't bother stepping into the living room. In typical Oscar the Grouch fashion, he grunted in my direction—albeit a somewhat friendlier grunt than normal—and offered his arm to my very married mother. And with that, Mom willingly left my apartment with the geriatric stud!

I locked the door behind them and headed for the bedroom, finding the credit card receipts stacked neatly on my dresser. With the help of my pocket calculator, I tallied up the damage. Two-thousand seven-hundred and eighty-four dollars later I reached for the phone and tried calling my father again. This time he finally answered.

"Mayor Stedworth here." Static accompanied my father's voice.

"Daddy? Thank God! Where have you been? I've been trying to reach you since yesterday."

He cleared his throat, the time-honored cue that I had uttered the unacceptable. Dad never raises his voice. He clears his throat and peers down his nose. I could feel that hypercritical stare now across a thousand miles, compliments of AT&T. And whether we were in the same room or connected only by fiber-optic cable, the result was the same.

"I mean, thank goodness," I corrected myself without further prodding.

Another throat clearing, this time signaling apology accepted from the man who doesn't even say *damn*. Nothing beyond a moderate *heck* or an infrequent *darn* ever makes it past his lips. A resounding *shit* would give my father apoplexy. *Fuck* would send him six feet under.

"And what other bad habits have you picked up in that city?"

"Daddy, I called to talk about Mom." Not my apparent fall from grace, but I didn't add that acerbic addendum. Dad hates sarcasm almost as much as he hates what he refers to as "gutter talk."

"Your mother?" The line crackled. In the background I heard what sounded like bits and pieces of every conversation in Iowa going on at once. "What about your mother?"

"Have you seen her lately?"

"Of course I've seen her. What kind of question is that?"

"When?"

Someone shouted my father's name. "Hold on, Nori." My normally calm father sounded harried and annoyed. I overheard a terse, muffled conversation in the background and what sounded like the revving of a dozen or so truck engines. A minute went by before Dad came back on the line. "What was that you were saying, Nori?"

"When did you last see Mom?"

More shouting. "Look, Nori. All hell's broken loose here. I don't have time for guessing games. What are you calling about?"

Hell? My father doesn't say *hell*! Any more than he says *damn*. Once, in a pique of teen smart-aleckness, I asked him if Satan lives in Heck. I got his trademark throat-clearing and a stare. But no matter what was happening in normally dull-as-dishwater Ten Commandments, it couldn't be worth the break-up of my parents' marriage. "Mom is in New York, Dad. Did you know she was coming?"

"Um, she may have mentioned something about it."

"May have?" I heard more racket in the background. More shouting. A siren. And lots of static. "Dad, what's going on there?"

"Look, Nori, I really have to go. You two have a nice visit."

"But, Dad—"

The line went dead. I had no idea what was happening in Ten Commandments. Dad had no idea that Mom had walked out on him. All in all, the phone call had been a resounding failure, leaving me with more questions than answers.

As much as I hated to admit it, I realized the only person who might be able to shed some light on this mystery was Eugene. Reluctantly, I scrounged around in my nightstand drawer until I found the phone book I had brought with me from Ten Commandments and flipped to the Ds.

I stared at the phone for several minutes. Was I about to make a huge mistake? The last thing I needed was for Eugene to misinterpret my call as encouragement to pursue a relationship that never existed except in the eyes of our parents. Not that Eugene had ever really pursued me. Being Eugene, he simply bowed to family pressure.

Both sets of parents, longtime friends, wanted nothing more than a passel of little Eugenes and Honoras rollicking around the town square. I'm convinced that Eugene asked me out only because he didn't want to disappoint his parents. And I only agreed to go out with him in order to get my parents off my back.

I shook off my trepidation and pounded out the numbers. I could handle Eugene. Thanks to a Stedworth-Draymore matchmaking scenario that had begun while I was still in utero, Eugene and I had grown up together. I knew him like a brother. But our relationship, despite years of parental prodding, had never developed beyond that of a platonic affection for one another—complete with the occasional sibling rivalry altercation. Like the time he decided to embalm my Barbie dolls and I got even by cutting his baseball cards up into paper dolls. The guy wasn't dense. Formaldehyde aside, he had to realize we had no chemistry.

"Oh?" asked Gertie as the phone rang on the other end. *"This bit of psychological insight is coming from the woman who thought she had chemistry with Dave the Deceitful Dermatologist?"*

Sigh! Point taken. Maybe Eugene was as dense about me as I had been about Dave.

"It's not too late to hang up," she suggested.

But it was. Eugene had answered the phone. "Draymore Funeral Home. Eugene Draymore speaking. How may I be of service?"

"Eugene, hi! It's Nori."

"Nori?" He hesitated long enough for me to wonder what sort of gears were spinning around in that closely cropped head of his. "How are you? Where are you?"

"I'm calling from New York."

"Oh. Um . . ."

Non-funereal small talk had never been one of Eugene's strong suits. Give him a room full of grieving relatives, and he always knew the right words. Catch him out of his element, and his tongue worked itself into a constrictor knot that would make any Boy Scout leader proud. I decided to cut to the chase.

"Eugene, I'm calling because I need to know what's

going on in Ten Commandments. I just had the strangest conversation with my father. He didn't even sound like himself."

"Understandable."

"Then something *is* going on there?"

"You could say that."

"Does it have anything to do with my mother coming to New York?"

Eugene's voice rose two octaves. "Your mother is in New York?" Eugene knew my mother. He knew how she felt about large cities, especially New York. "Are you serious?"

"Completely. I found her camped on my front stoop yesterday afternoon. And she's acting as odd as Dad. Claims she's leaving him because he ignores her."

"Well, under the circumstances I can see why the mayor might not have been spending much time at home lately, but still, she's got to understand the crisis we're in here."

Crisis? "What crisis? Mom didn't mention anything unusual going on at home."

Eugene laughed. Then his voice filled with a pseudo-serious inflection. He sounded like Uncle Zechariah ministering to the masses on a Sunday morning. "Let's just say Ten Commandments is in the throes of a complete breakdown of the tenets on which the town was founded."

I couldn't believe it. "The town is falling apart because my mother and father have split up?"

He laughed again, this time with irony lacing his chuckle. "No, Nori. I doubt anyone even knows your parents have split up."

"Including my father," I muttered.

"Well, like I said, he's had his hands full." With that, Eugene gave me a condensed version of Ten Commandments' fall from grace. Seems Uncle Ezra, Dad's bank president brother, had run off with the local tax collector, Mrs. Tibble, *and* the money for the new school gym. When Dad went in search of Uncle Jonah, his youngest brother and police chief, to report the disappearance of Uncle Ezra, Mrs. Tibble, and the money, he discovered Uncle Jonah in a compromising position with Uncle Zechariah's wife. "And it wasn't the missionary position the minister's wife was in," added Eugene.

I could almost see his eyebrows wiggling and couldn't believe the glee in his voice. Not that I didn't find the entire situation rather ironic and yes, more than slightly hilarious, but I didn't expect Eugene to feel that way. "You're enjoying this, aren't you?"

"Wait." He convulsed with laughter. "It gets worse. Your cousin LeRoy is back in town."

LeRoy Calhoun Stedworth was the last Stedworth to leave Ten Commandments before my recent departure. No one mentions Cousin LeRoy, the black sheep of the Stedworth family, in polite conversation. Few mention him behind closed doors. He fled Ten Commandments a decade earlier, one step ahead of the law. But Cousin LeRoy wasn't the sharpest pitchfork in the haystack. He was caught within hours, having stopped to make a withdrawal at a bank in a neighboring town—a bank where he didn't have an account. For the better part of the last ten years, he's lived as a guest of the federal government.

"He was paroled?"

"No. He completed his sentence. And you'll never guess what he's doing," teased Eugene. But he didn't wait for me to guess. He jumped right in with his big finish. Ta da: "He opened a triple X-rated drive-thru just over the town line."

"A drive-in movie theater?"

"Not drive-*in*. Drive-*thru*. And it's not a movie theater. He's got a combination porn shop and go-go bar, complete with topless dancers. You pull up and place your order, like going to McDonald's. Except you get a lot more than a Big Mac at the take-out window. He calls it the Ten Commandments Break. He's got billboards plastered all over the county: 'You Deserve a Break Today—from Ten Commandments.' "

No wonder Dad didn't sound like himself. How awful for him! His entire world was imploding around him. But how could Mom walk out on him during such a crisis? My mother didn't have a selfish neuron in her body, but you'd never know it by her recent behavior. "When did all this happen?"

"Yesterday."

"All of it?"

"All of it. Your dad found out about the missing money first thing yesterday morning. The billboards went up around the time he walked in on your Uncle Jonah."

"What a mess!" But at least Mom hadn't run out on Dad while he was trying to keep the town from self-destructing. She couldn't have known, and since she hadn't spoken with Dad since arriving, she still didn't know.

"You can say that. Think about it, Nori. Ten Commandments, a town established by God-fearing Christians, has turned into Sodom and Gomorrah on the Mississippi, and God isn't happy. Last night the mighty Miss' overflowed her banks and deposited a foot of mud and silt along Main Street."

"Oh, no!" That explained why I'd had trouble getting a hold of my father last night. And the Wicked Bitch hanging up on me this morning. And the sirens I heard when I did finally reach Dad a little while ago. But it didn't explain Eugene's overt enjoyment of the town's, and my father's, predicament.

I leave Ten Commandments, and Eugene Draymore, polite mama's boy, transforms into Bart Simpson. At least in spirit, if not deed. "Why are you enjoying this, Eugene? I thought you liked living in Ten Commandments."

"Things aren't always what they seem, Nori."

"What's that supposed to mean?"

"Just that maybe you don't really know me."

I guess he was right about that. But then again, he was the same Eugene Draymore who had drowned Cheerleader Barbie in a beaker of formaldehyde, so maybe I should have picked up on this wicked side of him years ago.

Had I ever seen him rip the wings off a butterfly? Kick a puppy? No. Eugene loved animals. As a kid, he always brought home injured strays and nursed them back to health. Throughout high school, he delivered meals to shut-ins and volunteered at the county hospital. As an adult, he continued to work for a variety of charities.

Eugene was neither cruel nor mean-spirited. His overt enjoyment over the downfall of Ten Commandments was an aberration in line with the Cheerleader Barbie incident. Which, in truth, he *had* apologized for afterwards. But then again, that was only after he had discovered his mutilated Pete Rose rookie card.

So now, more than ever, I needed to confront my mother. But when she returned from her "date," she didn't return alone. She invited Oscar cum Clint into my apartment and asked where I kept the sherry!

Sherry! Like it's the drink of choice for all twenty-somethings! Besides which, when did my mother start drinking? "I don't have any," I told her. "There's an open bottle of white Zinfandel in the fridge and maybe a few warm beers in the pantry."

She turned to Oscar/Clint. "Wine or warm beer?"

she asked with an I-really-did-try-to-raise-her-properly-but-there's-just-so-much-a-mother-can-do shrug of her shoulders and a roll of her eyes.

With a dismissive glance in my direction—one that indicated he understood my mother's travails—Oscar/Clint seated himself at my kitchen table like he was a regular patron of the establishment. "I suppose wine will have to do," he said, waiting to be served.

Well, excuse me for not having a bottle of—of whatever—handy! Feel free to insert the name of some expensive sherry if you know of one. I certainly don't.

"What would Martha Stewart think?" asked Gertie.

Oh, please!

Mom pulled two mismatched wine glasses from the cabinet and, with a frown, inspected them for chips before setting one in front of Hyman and the other across the table from him. Obviously, she wasn't planning on inviting me to join them in drinking my own wine.

I felt like an interloper in my own apartment. So what were my options? I could grab myself a glass *and* the remaining wine and head for the bedroom, leaving each with only one glass of Zinfandel, thus preventing a drunken orgy on my sofa.

"But they might wind up getting it on without any more alcohol," said Gertie. *"Who knows how much they drank at dinner?"*

True.

Option Two: I could grab my own glass and plop myself down at the table with them, forming a two's company, three's a crowd tableau.

"Which might give them reason to head upstairs," suggested Gertie.

Yikes! Mom and Oscar/Clint drinking at my kitchen table was bad enough. The Grouch entertaining Mom in his apartment? They had already shared tea up there this afternoon. Did that constitute a first date in his eyes? In hers? Exactly what was the normal modus operandi for the average middle-aged man and woman? Was the Grouch planning to bed my mother this evening? And worse yet, was my mother looking forward to a night of wanton sex with a virtual stranger?

Jeez! I had enough trouble visualizing my mother and father in bed together. As much as I enjoyed sex, like any normal kid, I clung to that misguided image from early adolescence that my parents only did it once. Standing up. For procreational purposes only.

My mother and the Grouch? I sure as hell wasn't going to break that hold-the-presses, this-just-in, earth-stopping, details-at-eleven news to Dad. Or to Mom, if she ever escaped from whatever alien had taken possession of her body. Hopefully, when E.T. was called home, he'd leave Mom with no memory of her escapades while under alien influence.

"You could wrestle her to the floor and sit on her until she comes to her senses," offered Gertie.

I studied Mom as she fluttered around the kitchen. With her rounded, matronly figure, she outweighed me by a good thirty pounds. *Yeah, that would work. How about a more realistic suggestion, Gertie?*

"Are you your mother's keeper? She's an adult. Let the cow chips fall where they may."

And shovel up the shit afterwards? No thank you.

I grabbed a sixteen-ounce tumbler out of the cabinet and plopped myself down at the table. Reaching for the wine bottle, I offered the Grouch my most beatific smile before turning to my mother. "I spoke with Dad this evening," I said, pouring the remainder of the Zinfandel into my glass. "He said he hopes you're enjoying your vacation and sends his love."

I then speared the Grouch with a meaningful glare.

"Did my mother mention she's been happily married for nearly thirty years?" They might still head upstairs, but if Mom wanted to make a fool of herself and ruin her marriage, I wasn't going to make it easy for her.

Chapter Eight

"So what did Grouchy Clint Clone say to that?" asked Reese. She and Gabe had joined me at Bean Around the Block the following morning. The coffee house was filling up early for a Saturday thanks to the buzz from the TV taping, but we arrived in time to claim a large table near the back. Although we had planned a nonstop-job-hunting-brainstorming session, the conversation quickly segued from the "hi's" and "how are you's" to "The Continuing Trials and Tribulations of the Girl from Ten Commandments."

"He told me I had nothing to worry about. That both my mother's virtue and her marriage were safe with him."

"Yeah, right," said Reese. "Believe that, and I've got a penthouse on the Upper East Side to sell you for only a thousand down and three hundred a month." She ripped apart her fat-free banana nut muffin and began picking out the walnuts and popping them into her mouth. "Did you notice the muffins in this dive are now as expensive as the ones in that designer bakery-to-the-stars in Tribeca? What's it called?"

"Muffy's?" supplied Gabe.

"Yeah, that's the one. Muffy's Muffins. How sickeningly Debutante-of-the-Year-Spence-Graduate cute." She glanced about Bean Around the Block and scowled. All the tables were now full; a long line snaked from the take-out counter to the door. "Three dollars for a lousy muffin. Thanks to Sarah Jessica Parker, I can't even afford breakfast anymore."

"Thanks to our pink slips, we can't afford anything anymore," I reminded her. "We shouldn't even be here."

"Eat, drink, and be merry," sang Gabe, waving his cup in the air, "for tomorrow we dine at the Dumpster." He winked at Reese before draining the remains of his mocha cappuccino.

Reese glared at him. "I was drunk, okay? I have *no* intention of posing with or eating out of Dumpsters. So give it a rest, will you?" Then she turned to me and offered an apologetic smile. "Sorry for the non sequitur interruption, Nori. So it turns out Oscar the Grouch looks like Clint Eastwood, and you're supposed to believe he has honorable intentions?"

"That's right."

"And why is that? You may be from Iowa, girl, but you're not that naïve."

"Maybe he's gay," said Gabe.

I shook my head. "I doubt it. A gay guy wouldn't look at my mother the way he did."

"Which was?"

"With a glint and a leer."

"He did invite your mother for tea," said Reese. "How many straight guys would do that?"

Gabe turned on her. "What? Only gay guys drink tea?" He waved his empty coffee cup under her nose. "In case you hadn't noticed, I'm gay, and I do *not* drink tea. As a matter of fact, I *hate* tea. Maybe he's English." He looked to me for confirmation.

"Right down to his fake Oxford accent." I shrugged. "I don't know. Aside from the accent, he seems as American as you or I. I think it's an affectation."

Gabe polished off the remainder of his chocolate-raspberry croissant and smirked around the mouthful at Reese.

She wasn't backing down. Reese was out to prove there was no way the Grouch could be a threat to my mother. "So how do you explain his intimate knowledge of Bergdorf's? No straight male I know could name Bergdorf's on a bet, let alone know where it's located."

Classic Reese. Totally illogical in her thought processes, but a true-blue friend. I hated to burst her bubble of irrationality. "Bergdorf's is one of his accounts. The guy's an importer."

All Reese could say to that was, "Oh, shit."

"Now what?" asked Gabe.

I shrugged. "Now nothing. Short of locking her into a chastity belt or hiring some thugs to drop a sack over her head and whisk her back to Ten Commandments, I guess I have to take Oscar the Grouch at his word."

"And after that you continued to sit at the table with them?" asked Reese.

"Hell, no! I tucked tail and excused myself to the bedroom. I spent the rest of the evening hiding under my quilt, watching *Comedy Central*. Mom finally came to bed after midnight."

"So she still doesn't know that you lost your job?" asked Gabe.

"Or about Dave?" added Reese.

"No, and as far as I know, she still doesn't know what's going on in Ten Commandments. I tried talking to her, but she yawned and said she was all talked out for the night. She was still sleeping this morning when I left the house to meet the two of you."

"Why don't you—"

I cut Reese off before she could offer her suggestion. "Why don't we get to why we're here? I'll dump the good news on Mom when I get home. If she's not out gallivanting with the Grouch."

"Gallivanting with the Grouch? With alliteration like that, you should try for a job in advertising or publishing," said Gabe. "You could be the next Ogden Nash or Shel Silverstein."

"Very funny."

"No, really," said Reese. "I think maybe Gabe's right. We'd all make great editors. I'd love to work for some glossy fashion or style magazine. Think of all the celebrities we'd meet."

"Uh-huh." Wouldn't we all like to work for some posh magazine. I dug in my briefcase for the *Times* classified section I had taken from the café yesterday and tossed it in front of Reese. "Be my guest. I read through this last night during commercial breaks. Not a slick fashion or style magazine position in the bunch. Not even an opening for a lowly editorial assistant at some third-rate tabloid."

"Is that the entire classifieds or just the editorial jobs?" asked Gabe, eyeing the thin section.

"Everything from accountants to zoologists," I told him. "Slim pickings."

Reese read the first ad in the editor listings: " 'International credit rating agency seeks qualified individual to edit research reports while working closely with analysts in corporate finance.' " She scrunched up her nose. "Forget it. I'm numbers challenged. Always have been. Always will be."

"Ditto," said Gabe.

Reese continued to read down the column: " 'Scientific copy editor. Senior medical editor. Managing editor for pharmaceutical trade magazine. Editor, Spanish language newspaper. Editorial director, multilingual for new publication on automotive engineering.' " She slammed the paper down and shook her head. "You've got to be kidding! What about *Vogue? Cosmo?*"

"Apparently not hiring. And neither are any of the

news magazines or decorating magazines. None of the book publishers, either. Not even that big category romance house."

Reese stared at me in disbelief. "I don't believe it! They *always* have openings. I interviewed with them a few years ago. They offered me a position, but I could have made more money slinging patties and asking, 'Do you want fries with that?'"

"We could always apply at McDonald's," suggested Gabe. "Look at what we'd save on food bills."

I screwed up my face. "Yeah, all the fat and calories you can scarf. No thanks."

"Beats Dumpster delights," said Gabe.

Reese smacked him over the head with the want ads.

"Is this a private fight, or can any hostile individual join in?" Mac Randolph, extra-large coffee cup in one hand, laptop in the other, and sexy smile playing across his face, had sauntered up behind Gabe. But he directed both his gaze and his question to me.

I stared up into his deep espresso eyes, and my stomach reacted with a wild flip-flop. Certainly not the reaction I expected.

"Maybe your belly's trying to tell you something," said Gertie.

Was it? I shoved her comment aside and addressed Mac. "This table is reserved for the unemployed. Do you qualify yet?"

He glanced at his watch, a Dick Tracy all-the-bells-and-whistles type, probably capable of relaying e-mail pink slips. "Not yet, but it's Saturday. Come Monday you might find me standing behind you at Unemployment."

"Have a seat," said Gabe, motioning to the empty place between us. "Misery loves company. By the way, who the hell are you?"

Mac laughed as he deposited his laptop on the floor and straddled the remaining chair at the table. I quickly made introductions. "Reese Blackwell. Gabe Hoffman. Mackenzie Randolph. Reese and Gabe are fellow ex-DataScroungers. Mac's the station manager at Big Apple Talk Radio."

"Radio?" Reese's face lit up.

"Down, girl. He's not hiring."

"Unless you've got some fabulous idea that will shoot our ratings off the charts and save my ass," said Mac.

"Hmm." Reese narrowed her eyes and took a quick peek at Mac's rear end. "I bet I could come up with something."

"Yeah, but would it be legal?" asked Gabe.

She swatted him again with the newspaper.

Mac ignored Reese and Gabe. "Finish your résumé?" he asked me.

I nodded in the direction of my laptop, which lay unopened on the floor alongside my chair. "For what it's worth. It certainly won't win a Pulitzer."

"Why is that? Not that they give out Pulitzers for résumés, by the way."

Like I didn't know that? My eyebrows arched into a classic *oh, really?* expression. Mac chuckled, then added sheepishly. "I guess you knew that, huh?"

"I'm from Iowa, not the Kalahari. We do get an occasional communiqué from civilization."

"Is that so?"

"Certainly. Why, only last week the Pony Express brought news about a man walking on the moon. Imagine that!"

Mac leaned back in his chair and raised his hands, palms outward. "Truce! I can't compete against your rapier wit." Then he leaned forward, elbows propped on the table, and grew serious. "So what's next? Any job leads?"

I shrugged. "Nothing in the paper. We were supposed to be formulating a game plan this morning."

I glanced over at my companions. Gabe fought off the newspaper attack with a bombardment of balled-up napkins that Reese managed to bat away in rapid succession. Suddenly, one landed with a plop in the dregs of my latté. I frowned into the cup. I had really wanted that last sip. At four bucks a shot, I couldn't afford to order another.

After yesterday, I had vowed to limit myself to one latté a day. Or more correctly, my shrinking bank account and my Bergdorf's-bingeing mother had forced me into the untenable position of having to cut way down on my high-priced caffeine addiction. Designer coffee had become a luxury I could no longer afford. Hell, living had become a luxury I could no longer afford.

"There's always CAA," said Gertie.

Caffeine Addicts Anonymous? Let me guess. They serve beer at their meetings? That silenced Gertie.

I grimaced once more at the soggy napkin that had sucked up the remainder of my coffee, then shifted my attention back to Mac. "But as you can see, some among us have decided to skip adulthood and head straight into their second childhoods."

So much for our nonstop-job-hunting-brainstorming session. I was on my own. "I'm heading for the library," I announced, grabbing my laptop and purse off the floor.

"What for?" asked Reese, swatting away another napkin fastball. This one grazed the head of a guy sitting at the table next to us, bounced off his bagel, and rolled onto the floor. He swung around and glared at Reese. She quickly dropped the newspaper bat onto her lap and gave him a *who, me?* look of feigned innocence before directing her full attention to me.

"My fingers have a date with the Manhattan Yellow Pages," I said.

The man turned back to his bagel and coffee. Reese stuck her tongue out at him. "Party pooper." Then she wrinkled her brow and turned back to me. "And you intend to let your fingers do the walking because . . . ?"

I stood and slung my purse over my shoulder. "I'm looking for a listing of employment agencies to call first thing Monday morning."

"Good idea," said Gabe, rising to join me. "Let's go, Reese." He nodded toward Mac. "See you around."

I held out my hand to stop them. "Sit. Continue your game. You two have nothing to worry about. I'm sure the Mets and Yankees scouts will be here any minute, fighting to sign you both up." Reese and Gabe looked at each other, shrugged, and sat back down.

"I'll walk out with you," said Mac. He nodded to Reese and Gabe. "Nice meeting you."

As we left Bean Around the Block, I couldn't help thinking of the Three Little Pigs.

"At least you're the pig building with bricks," said Gertie. *Oink.*

Chapter Nine

When I phoned Marjorie the next morning, she still hadn't spoken with Earnest. Given the difficulty of my task and the relative ease of hers, I was growing more than a little annoyed with her. And with Earnest. Didn't he even wonder where I was when he arrived home Thursday night? After all, it's not like we've ever spent any length of time apart, and on those few occasions when we have, each of us has always known where the other was.

By last night Earnest had spoken with Nori and knew I was in New York, but he sure as heck didn't know anything the night before. I began to wonder if he even realized I wasn't in bed beside him. Or if he cared. Talk about an ego crusher. But that was one of the reasons I up and left, wasn't it?

"And why in heaven's name haven't you spoken with Earnest?" I demanded when Marjorie began hemming and hawing.

"I don't think the timing is right, Connie."

I couldn't understand why Marjorie was having such difficulty getting a hold of Earnest. "What in the world is going on back home?"

Marjorie answered with a nervous giggle. "Well, not what you'd expect from Ten Commandments, that's for sure. More like a chapter out of *Peyton Place*. But then again, it isn't anything we haven't suspected for years."

"Marjorie!" My head pounded. I wasn't in the mood for riddles and games. Two glasses of wine with dinner, and another after arriving back at Nori's apartment afterwards, had given me a massive hangover this morning. Too late, I remembered why I didn't drink. Anyway, between the hangover, another night of little sleep, and a whopping case of ever-increasing guilt over leaving home without so much as a note of explanation to Earnest—even though I now wondered if under the circumstances, that guilt wasn't misplaced—I had no patience left.

Marjorie exhaled a heavy sigh through the phone lines. "All right, Connie, but you have to promise not to come running back because of what's happening."

"No fair! How can I make a promise like that when I don't know what's going on?"

"Promise or I won't tell you."

I thought for a moment, my mind conjuring up all sorts of morbid scenarios, but I brushed them aside as ridiculous. Earnest wasn't lying in a coma. He hadn't been struck by a semi on the interstate or chewed up by a thresher in the cornfield. If something awful had happened, Marjorie would've told me immediately.

Besides, Nori had spoken with Earnest last night, and according to Marjorie, whatever was happening began shortly after we left for the airport Thursday morning. I inhaled a deep breath, fortifying myself for whatever I was about to hear. "Okay. I promise."

Marjorie and I often speculated there was some hanky-panky going on between certain people in Ten Commandments. But when we connected the dots of circumstantial evidence, we always countered our whispered suspicions with logical explanations. We blamed our prurient musings on the tedium of living in a town where people sit around talking about nothing more exciting than the current prices of corn and soy beans. But it became clear, as Marjorie explained what had happened, that our cockamamie imaginary scenarios had come to life. "Is this some sort of joke, Marjorie?"

"If it is, the joke's on the town, Connie."

"And on us, to some extent. I can't believe it. We were right all along."

"Maybe we should learn to trust our own intuition more."

But I wasn't thinking of our uncanny second sight at the moment. My thoughts were drawn to my husband, caught up in the middle of his family's criminal acts and sexual shenanigans. "Poor Earnest. This must be tearing him apart. I should be by his side at a time like this."

"You promised, Connie!"

"I know, but. . . ."

"No buts. You have a job to do, and Earnest will thank you for it." She paused before adding, "Eventually. Besides, he's managing. Of course, none of us needed Main Street flooding right now, but the water's receding, and there hasn't been much damage. Just the usual mud and silt to shovel out. He doesn't even know you're gone, Connie. He hasn't made it home in two nights."

Well, that at least made me feel a little better. Earnest had probably initially assumed I was cooking meals for the emergency workers while he organized sandbag details. Same as any normal flood. But now he knew otherwise. I told Marjorie Nori had spoken with her father last night.

"So why jump all over me? Earnest knows where you are. As soon as things calm down, I'll handle the rest."

"We have a timetable we need to follow," I reminded her. "Besides, this changes everything. A wife's place is by her husband's side during times of trouble. Especially family trouble."

"Earnest isn't responsible for his brothers, Connie. He knows that. Ezra and Merline are Jonah's and Frank Tibble's problem, and Jonah can answer to his own wife and Zechariah for fooling around with Florrie. It's not your problem, and it's not Earnest's. You concentrate on what you're supposed to be doing."

Maybe she was right. I had to think of myself for once. Wasn't that my reason for coming to New York in the first place? Doing something for me? Only, after decades of putting me last, I was out of practice. Not to mention that I wasn't even sure what I wanted to accomplish. Make my husband pay more attention to me? Get my daughter to come back home and settle down with Eugene? "Sometimes I wonder if maybe I'm treating symptoms instead of the illness."

"What in the world is that supposed to mean? I swear, Connie, you're making less and less sense lately. Concentrate on the future. This time next year you and I could be planning a baby shower. You'll be so busy you won't have time to can pickled beets or paint cows on curtains."

But was that enough? Marjorie didn't get it, so I dropped the subject. This was something I'd have to figure out for myself. I turned the conversation back to the scandals in Ten Commandments. If truth be told, I never cared much for most of Earnest's relatives. Sanctimonious hypocrites, the lot of them. "Ezra and Merline, huh?"

Marjorie chortled. "What about Jonah and that holier-than-thou sister-in-law of yours?"

"The pious minister's wife?" I shook my head and snorted. Florrie walked around town with her nose up in the air—when she wasn't looking down it in scorn at everyone else.

"Unbelievable. I wonder how long all of this has been going on."

"At least as long as we've suspected, I'm sure. Probably much longer."

Marjorie promised to keep me filled in as events developed. She also promised she'd get going on her end of the plan.

"Remember, Marjorie, if you don't arrange things just right, it's going to screw up everything."

"I know. I know. You don't have to keep reminding me, Connie."

Somehow that didn't reassure me. I wanted everything over and done with already. Now more than ever, I wanted to be back with my husband. New hairdo and wardrobe aside, I wasn't cut out to be a modern free spirit. No matter how much I once dreamed of it. That was a long time ago. Another lifetime. Another Connie. Changing the outer package didn't change the inner woman—and my inner woman was just as confused and unhappy as ever. If not more so.

Both my headache and my guilt worsened.

And then Nori returned, bringing more bad news. She had lost her job.

I'm afraid, under the circumstances and given the state of both my head and nerves, I was less than sympathetic. "So what did you expect from a company with such a cockamamie name? If you had listened to your father and me and gone into teaching, you'd have security."

She threw her arms up in the air and stormed into the bedroom. "Thanks for the support, Mom." Then she slammed the door.

I winced. And sighed. Today was growing worse by

the nanosecond. I followed her down the hall and opened the door. The sight of my baby lying curled up on her bed, her ratty old teddy bear clutched to her chest, nearly broke my heart. As much as I didn't like the choices Nori had made over the past few years, I couldn't help hurting for her. It came with the mother-hood territory.

I sat down beside her and stroked her head. "I'm sorry, sweetheart. I guess I'm not myself today. I have a terrible headache."

She raised her head and glared at me. "And whose fault is that?"

I withdrew my hand. "Ouch." My daughter had driven a pitchfork into my heart. If she only realized I was doing much of this for her. But children never under-stand such things until they have children of their own.

"Yeah, right. Ouch. That'll teach you to stay up half the night drinking with a man who isn't your husband."

"We were discussing your job loss, not my social life," I reminded her.

"I'm not cut out to teach."

"How do you know? You never gave it a try."

"Of course I did."

"That was practice teaching. Having your own class-room is different."

She sat up and stared at me. "You're so right, Mom. Instead of a six-week stint, I'd have a one hundred and eighty-three day sentence each year until I was old enough to retire. No thanks. I hated those six weeks."

"You could learn to love teaching. It's a noble profes-sion. One you could be proud of instead of that scrounging-whatever-it-was."

"DataScroungers."

"Whatever." I dismissed the word and her former employer with a wave of my hand. "You could learn to love many things if you gave them a chance, Nori. But you don't. You have a stubborn streak as wide as the broadside of a barn, and Lord knows where you get it from. Certainly not my side of the family."

She put her hands on her hips and drew her mouth into a tight frown. "Are we segueing into a Eugene discussion here, Mom?"

"Eugene is a wonderful young man."

"Yes, he is, and I'm very fond of him, but I'm not in love with him. Never have been. Never will be. You can sing his praises until you've got laryngitis, but that isn't going to change."

I slapped my hands on the mattress and jumped up, turning my back on her. "Fine! I give up. Marry your fancy-schmancy Parker Avenue doctor who you've never bothered to bring home to meet your parents, and then you won't have to worry about getting a job. Which reminds me . . ." I spun around, crossed my arms over my chest, and confronted my daughter. "Now that I'm in New York, do I finally get to meet this mystery man of yours?"

"Park Avenue," she whispered.

"What?"

"It's Park Avenue, not Parker, and you won't be meeting him." Her voice shook. She turned her head away, but not before I saw the tears welling up in her eyes and how she fought to get a grip on her emotions.

So, I had been right. There was far more than a drenching by a mud puddle eating at my daughter when I arrived on Thursday. And still eating at her. And it had something to do with that rotten roadkill boyfriend of hers. I was certain of it. From the moment she had started talking about him during her weekly phone calls home, I knew he would wind up hurting my baby. A mother can sense these things.

Silence hung in the air. The second hand on the bed-side clock swept half a minute away before Nori finally spoke. "We broke up." Her voice quivered. "Thursday. Right before I came home."

"Oh, baby!" I sat back down on the bed and drew her into my arms. "I'm so sorry." And I was. Even though I knew the man wasn't any good for my daughter, I still ached to see her hurt by him. I patted her head and rubbed her back as she choked out one strangled sob after another. "Go ahead. Cry as much as you want." And she did, clutching me for dear life and showering my shoulder with her tears until Earnest wasn't the only one dealing with a flood.

"I'm glad you're here, Mom," she finally said after a few shuddering deep breaths once the crying stopped. She kissed my cheek. "I don't think I told you that before."

"That's all right. I understand."

"No, it's not all right. I've had a rough few days, but that's no excuse for the way I've treated you. I'm sorry."

"I thought maybe you were embarrassed by my coming. That you were ashamed of your country bumpkin mother because I'm not sophisticated and worldly enough to introduce to your Park Avenue doctor boyfriend."

"Oh, Mom, no! Of course not." Then she pulled away and stared wide-eyed at me. Her mouth dropped open. "Is that why you went to Bergdorf's? Because you were afraid you'd embarrass me in front of Dave?"

I shrugged. "Not really, but I suppose if I thought about it, maybe a small part of me felt that way."

"Mom, I'd never have anything to do with a man who couldn't love you for who you are. I've never been embarrassed by you or Dad."

"But you turned your back on us and your home for a more sophisticated life."

"And boy, did I find it."

I noted the irony in her voice. "Do you want to talk about it?"

She shook her head.

"Maybe you should anyway, honey. Don't keep all that hurt bottled up inside you. It's not healthy."

She lowered her head and shook it slowly from side to side. "I can't believe how naïve I was. It's like something out of a bad soap opera."

"He cheated on you?"

"Bingo." She raised her head and stared at me. A chuckle fought with a snuffle. "Is telepathy something women gain with childbirth? A side effect of expelling the placenta? Out with the afterbirth, in with the sixth sense?"

I smiled at her. "That and the fact that your emotions are about as transparent as a sheet of Saran Wrap right now." I placed my hands on her damp cheeks. "I'm sorry, sweetie. But better to find out sooner rather than later. I never had a good feeling about that one."

"But you never even met him!"

"I didn't need to. Every time you mentioned him on the phone, my earlobes starting itching like mad." I bent and kissed her forehead. "Go wash your face. I'll make us a pot of tea."

"Better make it double-strong. I have more bad news."

I studied my daughter's hurt-filled, remorseful expression. My heart jumped into my throat and then plummeted like a lead cannonball into my stomach. "Oh, Nori! You're not pregnant, are you?"

Her eyes bugged out, and she began to laugh. So hard that she clutched her sides and doubled over. I drew her back into my arms and stroked her head. "Oh, Nori! It's all right, sweetheart. I still love you. I'll always love you, no matter what, and I'll love your baby, too."

"No, Mom." She shook her head between fits of laughter. "I'm not pregnant, but thank you." She hugged me. "I love you, too, Mom. I don't tell you that nearly enough, do I?"

I stared at her as though she were speaking in tongues. "You're not pregnant?"

She shook her head again.

I exhaled a deep sigh of relief. "I just thought . . . the way you were so upset . . . then what else is wrong?"

She wiped the moisture from her face. "Everything in Ten Commandments. I called Eugene, and. . . ."

"You called Eugene?"

"Yes, Mom, but listen. I called Eugene to find out what was going on with Dad and you."

"There's nothing going on with Dad and me. How's Eugene? What did the two of you talk about? I'm so happy you're keeping in touch with him."

"Mom! Daddy's up to his eyeballs in shit, and all you care about is small talk?"

"Honora! Such language! You know how your father feels about those words."

She grabbed my shoulders and leaned in so close that our noses nearly touched. "Mom, listen to me. There's all sorts of trouble at home. Uncle Ezra ran off with Mrs. Tibble *and* the tax till, Uncle Jonah is screwing Aunt Florrie, Cousin LeRoy opened a drive-thru topless bar out on the highway, and the Mississippi overflowed and flooded Main Street again!"

"Oh, I know all about that."

"You know? Since when?"

"Since I spoke to Marjorie this morning."

"Mom, how can you sit here while Dad is knee-deep in shit? I don't understand. I've never known you to turn your back on Ten Commandments during a disaster—natural or personal. You're the mayor's wife, the first lady of the town. The first person to come running with a casserole, no matter what the emergency. Instead you're off getting drunk with my grouchy neighbor. What the hell's going on with you?"

How do you explain a midlife crisis to a twenty-five-year-old? How do you tell your daughter that after too many decades of accepting your life, suddenly you yearn for more? Only you're not sure what. And yet, at the same time you still want things to remain the same. I can't fathom my own mood swings. How can I expect her to understand the turmoil roiling inside me?

And I certainly wasn't going to spill the beans about the other reason for my trip. So I told her a little white lie of sorts instead. "I left your father because of times like this. The town and its reputation are all he cares about. He acts as if he's personally responsible for his brothers' and everyone else's sins. Like he's somehow failed Ten Commandments and everyone in it, and that's why your Uncle Ezra and Merline Tibble ran off with the tax money and your Aunt Florrie spread her legs for your Uncle Jonah."

Nori's eyes bugged out again. "'*Spread her legs*?' Mom, since when do you talk like that?"

"Well, that's what she did, isn't it?"

"Yes, but I'm used to you speaking in euphemisms—if you mention such things at all. Like 'Aunt Florrie's indiscreet behavior' or 'Uncle Jonah's unfortunate fall from grace.' Jeez, Mom, you didn't just change your hair and clothes yesterday. You changed your entire attitude. No one back home will recognize you. *I* barely recognize you!"

I smiled at her. "Good. I needed a change. As for Ten Commandments, I've suspected for years that everything wasn't as sweet and bucolic as certain people would have you believe. Nothing ever is, you know. Look at your own situation with what's-his-name."

"Dave."

"Yes, Dave. Anyway, anyone who would have you believe otherwise is only fooling himself."

"Are you referring to Dad?"

"Among others. Anyway, maybe it's time the truth came out and ruffled a few pretentious feathers."

"What truth?"

I thought for a moment before answering, then decided if Nori was old enough to live on her own in New York, she was certainly old enough to learn the truth about Ten Commandments—or at least what Marjorie and I suspected was the truth. "As far as I can tell, Jonah Stedworth's been cheating on Pauline for years. Before Florrie, it was Bonita Sue Gibbsborough, and before Bonita Sue it was Dorothea Adamson.

"And Florrie's no angel, either. She's a two-faced hypocrite who sticks her highfalutin' nose in the air while she wiggles her rear end in the faces of half the men in Ten Commandments. I wouldn't be surprised if Jonah was only the latest in a long line of affairs for her."

"Mom, are you sure about this?"

I frowned and shrugged my shoulders. "Well, if you mean, did I actually witness any of this hanky-panky, no. I can't say that I did. But there was certainly plenty of evidence that anyone who cared to open his eyes would have noticed."

"What about Dad? Did he suspect anything?"

"Your father has spent his life seeing only what he wants to see, Nori. I'm sure he knew what was going on. He probably knew more than anyone else, but he never discussed it with me, and I never brought up the subject with him."

"Why not?"

"Because we don't discuss things like that."

"You discussed them with Marjorie."

"That's different."

"Why?"

"Because your father's got this foolhardy notion that it's his ancestral obligation to make sure Ten Commandments lives up to its name."

"But when Uncle Ezra and Mrs. Tibble ran off, and he caught Uncle Jonah with Aunt Florrie. . . ."

"He can't pretend anymore, can he?"

"But, Mom, he must be devastated. How could you not be with him at a time like this? He needs you."

I sighed. She was right. Earnest did need me, and I needed him, but I couldn't go back. Not yet. Besides, I had another reason for being in New York, one I couldn't divulge to my daughter. Not if I wanted to succeed. In my heart I still believed I knew what was best for Nori, even if I didn't know what was best for myself. "He doesn't need me, Nori. He needs his Main Street Disney World image. None of it's real. It never has been. Ten Commandments is a sham."

"Then why do you want me to move back there and marry Eugene?"

"Just because Ten Commandments isn't utopia doesn't mean it's not a nice place to live and raise a family, Nori. And Eugene's—"

"Such a nice young man?"

Now she was getting it. "Exactly."

"But what about you and Dad?"

"Don't worry, dear. Everything will work out."

"So you still love him?"

"Of course I love him! What kind of question is that? He's my husband, isn't he?"

She rolled her eyes. "So if you still love Dad, then explain all that shit about 'we're separated.' And 'I've given that man thirty years of my life.' And 'I'm moving on.' What the hell's going on here, Mom?"

She had me there. If only I had thought things through more before I opened my big mouth, I might not have lied myself into a quagmire. I never was a good fibber. Opting for parental indignation and a quick exit cop-out, I marched into the living room. "Honora, I refuse to talk to you when your mouth is in the gutter." I then grabbed my purse and headed for the front door.

"Where are you going?"

"It's nearly four o'clock. I'm having tea with Hy."

Chapter Ten

Dumbfounded, I followed my mother into the living room and watched her reach for her purse and sashay—that's right, I said *sashay* because stroll, saunter, strut, prance or just plain walk won't cut it—out the door. *Is it me*, I asked Gertie, *or is my mother certifiable?*

"*Definitely certifiable.*"

Well, I'm glad we agree on that. So how the hell do I get her to go back home?

"*Promise to marry Eugene?*"

Oh, you're some help!

"*Admit it. A part of you is happy she's here.*"

And a part of me was. For all my complaints about her, my mother always knows when I need her. Maybe there is something to her itchy earlobe theory. Maybe some great cosmic force had told her I'd need her comforting embrace. So putting aside her own fears of the world outside Ten Commandments, she had winged her way east without a second thought.

"*Sometimes a girl just needs her mommy?*"

I suppose so. But Mommy had morphed into someone I didn't recognize. A mutated amalgam of June Cleaver and Candace Bushnell. I shook my head and laughed. *And here I've been worrying about how to tell her I caught Suz and Dave al fresco in the Jacuzzi without her learning I'm no longer a virgin.*

The scene, branded in my brain, mocked me whenever I closed my eyes. The tub of bubbles. The champagne. The platter of chocolate-dipped strawberries. I could barely contemplate their betrayal, let alone voice it.

"You had no problem telling Gabe and Reese and that good-looking Mac."

True. But when I told Gabe and Reese, I was still insulated by my anger and the newer shock of having lost my job. Telling Mac wasn't difficult, either. He's a stranger. He doesn't know Dave or Suz. Doesn't know how much I loved them both, how deeply violated I felt. *Besides, Gabe and Reese know I'm not a virgin and Mac probably assumes it. But my mother? At least not the mother I left behind in Ten Commandments. Yet here she is mega-vaulting past presumed chastity to the conclusion that I'm pregnant.*

"And correct me if I'm wrong, but she didn't seem all that upset by the prospect."

Don't think I didn't notice that. Yet a moment later, she's admonishing me for saying shit.

"But in the next breath she's talking about your Aunt Florrie spreading her legs."

Not to mention wiggling her rear end in the faces of half the men in Ten Commandments. Aunt Florrie. Uncle Ezra. Uncle Jonah. God-fearing, church-going pillars of a God-fearing, church-going community. All unbelievable hypocrites. And then there was my mother, who was beginning to sound like the poster child for CTA—Contradiction of Terms Anonymous. My head spun faster than Sarah Hughes at the Olympics. *It's like something out of a Jackie Collins novel!*

"More like Jackie Collins meets Stephen King."

How true. I was still having trouble adjusting to this empyrean shift in my universe. For years Aunt Florrie and I had baked gingerbread men together at Christmas. Uncle Ezra taught me how to milk a cow, and Uncle Jonah helped me learn how to drive. How could these same loving relatives be thieves and adulterers? *And my mother's known about it since forever?*

I thought I knew all there was to know about everyone and everything in Ten Commandments. Isn't that why I left? What rock of innocence had I been hiding under all these years? What else didn't I know? Maybe I was the delusional one in the family, living under the notion of a conservative, repressive town that was anything but conservative and repressive. *Not that I want to go back,* I told Gertie. *At least not permanently. Jeez! I'm not sure I can ever look certain family members in the eye again.*

"Yeah, the holidays are going to be a real bitch this year."

I groaned. Leave it to Gertie, mistress of the understatement. But she was right. Thanksgiving and Christmas in Ten Commandments, *après* scandal, would never be the same. Safe, boring Ten Commandments had betrayed me as much as Dave and Suz had. My childhood memories were now forever tainted. *Obviously, Uncle Ezra won't be playing Santa in the Thanksgiving Day parade down Main Street.*

"Think he took the red suit and beard with him when he skipped town?"

My mind conjured up an image of Mrs. Tibble sitting on Uncle Ezra's lap. Only he wasn't wearing the red pants. He wasn't wearing any pants at all. For that matter, neither was Mrs. Tibble.

"Ewww! Don't go there."

Too late. I had already grossed out both myself and Gertie. And it takes a lot to gross out Gertie. I shook the image of Uncle Ezra and Mrs. Tibble from my head and grabbed my laptop. Time to forget Ten

Commandments and do something constructive. Like find a job.

Only the moment I booted up the computer, I realized I had an even bigger problem. This wasn't my computer.

Chapter Eleven

"How many of those do you own?"

"What?" I followed Hy's gaze to the lavender and pink hydrangea-decorated straw shoulder bag I had set on the black granite counter of his ultra-modern, stainless steel kitchen—a kitchen easily twice the size of my daughter's entire apartment nine floors below. In such a setting my decoupaged purse looked about as out of place as a pork roast among Orthodox Jews. (And yes, I do know of such things. I may hail from Ten Commandments, Iowa, but that doesn't mean I'm ignorant of other people's beliefs and traditions.)

Hy turned his attention to a cabinet with frosted glass doors above the sink, retrieving a burnished stainless steel sugar bowl and cream pitcher. I settled onto one of the zebra print stools surrounding the island that served as a kitchen table. "Your bag," he said. "That's the third one I've seen you carry."

I shrugged as he placed a smoky gray glass mug on the placemat in front of me, somewhat surprised that he had even noticed my pocketbook. Earnest certainly wouldn't have. "So? Lots of women have more than one purse. Even women who come from Iowa."

He glanced down at my matching straw pumps as

he brought the teapot to the table and poured for both of us. "Did you make them?"

Okay, so maybe they didn't exactly go with my new sophisticated wardrobe, but I liked my purses. And my matching shoes. And hats. And belts. Even if they did embarrass certain people. Like my daughter, who kept the ones I had given her buried in the deepest recesses of her closet.

Besides, those high-heeled sandals Loretta had talked me into buying were not exactly comfortable for someone used to wearing penny loafers and low-heeled pumps. Talk about an impulse purchase. And having worn them, I now can't return them. I don't care how sexy Loretta said they make me look. They hurt my feet.

I scowled at Hy. He was dressed to match his apartment—all in black. Didn't anyone in New York ever wear any colors besides black and gray? I glanced at my purse and decided it didn't look out of place at all. It added some much needed color to this depressingly monochromatic room. As a matter of fact, both Hy and his entire apartment could stand a good splash of color, and I intended to tell him so. Right after I reproached him for his condescending attitude. "Well, that's not very gentlemanly, even if my accessories are too Midwest for you."

Hy laughed. "My dear Constance, you don't give yourself enough credit."

I eyed him suspiciously but couldn't help noticing that his voice didn't sound teasing. Or condescending. On the contrary, he seemed to be thoughtfully appraising my purse and shoes rather than condemning their lack of elegance and sophistication. "Credit for what?"

He sat down on the stool next to mine and took both

of my hands in his. Gazing into my eyes, he said, "Connie, I'm about to make you an offer you can't refuse."

And then he did. Except I didn't believe him. I pulled my hands out from between his and laughed. "You have got to be kidding!"

"I'm totally serious."

Still, I kept waiting for the punch line.

And waiting.

And waiting.

Eventually it occurred to me that maybe he *was* serious. As well as insane. "What makes you think anyone in New York—or anywhere else for that matter— would pay for my decoupaged handbags?" After all, as much as she loves me, my own daughter keeps hers hidden in a closet. For that matter, I often suspect that Marjorie and my other friends only carry theirs when they know they'll be bumping into me. And that's back in unsophisticated Ten Commandments, Iowa.

But Hy was persistent. "Trust me, Connie. I'm in the trends business. And I intend to make these purses of yours tomorrow's biggest must-have item."

Right. The man had gone delusional on me. "You told me you were an importer."

"I am. I import trends."

How can someone import a trend? Apparently, Hy had already figured that one out. Quite successfully, too, if his apartment was any indication of his bank account and stock portfolio. He drained his cup of tea. "I'll be right back." He stood up and strode from the kitchen. A minute later he returned with a newspaper and set it in front of me. "This is the Sunday Styles section of *The New York Times*." He flipped open the paper and pointed to some tacky-looking fuchsia and chartreuse vinyl purses embellished with five-and-dime plastic flowers and rhinestones.

I scrunched up my nose. Even in Ten Commandments the women had better taste than to be caught dead carrying something like that. "Those are hideous."

"Read the caption."

I bent over the paper and gasped. Those Salvation Army rejects were selling at a place called Henri Bendel for . . . I spun around and gaped at him. "Five hundred dollars?"

"Handmade by the fourteen-year-old daughter of a banker who lives on the Upper East Side. We've already sold six hundred, and the store only started carrying them last week. I've recently signed a contract to have them mass-produced in China, exclusively for Target Stores."

"Six hundred people have already shelled out five hundred dollars each for . . ."—I pointed at the monstrosities—". . . for those?"

Hy smiled. "It's all in the marketing."

By the time he explained his marketing strategy to me, he had me believing I was going to be the next Martha Stewart. Pre-stock scandal Martha, of course. Goddess of all things domestic. I'd be lying if I didn't admit the idea appealed to me. Suddenly I had visions of my face plastered all over Wal-Mart the way Martha was plastered over K-Mart. And then there was the Connie Stedworth magazine. The Connie Stedworth television show. The Connie Stedworth empire. I'd be a household name. I'd be a *somebody* finally, rather than an addendum to my husband and daughter.

I needed to lose twenty pounds. Fast.

"What else do you do?" Hy asked, pulling me from my reverie.

"Do? Well, I make a mean pickled beet that wins a blue ribbon every year at the county fair." Connie Stedworth gourmet foods?

Hy scrunched up his face. "I'm not sure the world is ready for pickled beets."

Okay, so we wouldn't be featuring a line of gourmet foods in the Connie Stedworth empire. Yet. I had brought some jars of pickled beets with me for Nori. Hy would change his mind after he ate some. "Come downstairs with me," I said, taking a last sip of tea. I'd show him my painted jumpers and the various other craft items I had made for Nori.

Then I'd feed him some pickled beets.

"Meet Iowa *haute couture*," I said a few minutes later as I pulled half a dozen painted denim jumpers from the closet and spread them across the bed. "Hardly what you'd find at that store you sent me to yesterday."

With one hand cupping his elbow, the other stroking his nearly white goatee, Hy stared at the array of painted cows, chickens, teddy bears, geese, strawberries, and sunflowers that wound their way around the hems and covered the bibs of each garment. "Retro sells."

He picked up a jumper and fingered the row of black and white speckled hens parading around a burgundy and taupe checkerboard border. "We've already revisited the tie-dyed sixties and the disco seventies. Everyone is regressing. Family is paramount, especially after what this country has been through over the past few years. Perhaps the time is right for a reemergence of the American country look of the eighties."

He dropped the jumper back onto the bed. Deep in thought and continuing to stroke his goatee, he paced back and forth over what little available floor space there was in Nori's bedroom. His eyes darted around the room, stopping occasionally on the few pieces of my handiwork that Nori hadn't hidden away in her closet. "Yours?" he asked, lifting up a dresser box I had decoupaged with Iowa tourist brochures.

I nodded.

He continued to pace. "And this?" He pointed to an ivy-painted flowerpot on the windowsill. Within it rested the remains of a geranium that had long since passed on to wherever neglected plants go when they die.

I offered him a sheepish grin and a shrug. Nori had never met a plant she couldn't kill in record time. "The pot only. I take no responsibility for my daughter's murderous tendencies toward all things green."

He bent down and squinted at the dead plant. "What in the world is this?"

I stepped around the bed to take a closer look, expecting to find a mealy bug or two attempting to eke out a bare-bones existence on the remains of a dead leaf. But Hy wasn't referring to anything creepy or crawly. He pried something off the surface of the caked dirt and held it up for closer inspection.

My belly flip-flopped. Red-hot heat surged up my neck and into my cheeks. I felt as embarrassed as the time my mother caught me reading *The Joy of Sex*. And I was already married then. "That's nothing," I squeaked out through a suddenly restricted windpipe. I grabbed for the item in his hand but he refused to part with it.

He held it up to the light of the window, turning it to inspect the one-inch object from all directions. He cocked his head; his forehead furrowed, his bushy white brows knitting together. Then he laughed. "I'll be damned. It looks like a younger version of your daughter."

I was filled with pride that he could so easily identify the caricature of Nori I had painted on the object, but I really didn't want to have to explain the origin of the item he held in his hand. "Um . . . yes . . . well, it's nothing. Really. Just a stupid idea I once had."

I don't know what I was thinking when I came up with that lunatic notion. Maybe I had suffered from PMS that day. The entire incident was too embarrassing to dredge up and explain. I distinctly remember tossing the piece out years ago. How strange that Nori had picked it out of the trash and saved it.

"Is it stone?" Hy weighed the irregularly shaped object, slightly larger than a marble, in the palm of his hand.

"Not exactly."

"No, I didn't think so." He bounced it in his hand. "Too light." He studied it once more. "And too oddly shaped for stone." He peered down at me. "Connie, this is fascinating. What exactly is it?"

I shook my head. "I'd rather not say."

Hy raised his head and stared at me, an expression of disbelief and astonishment settling over his face. "Why the bloody hell not?"

"You'll think I'm nuts."

"Why would I think that?"

"Because it was a crazy idea. And weird. Everyone said so."

He raised an eyebrow. "I'm not everyone."

No, he wasn't. And he hadn't patronized me and my countrified craft projects once. Hadn't referred to them as tacky or unsophisticated. Not that what he held in his hand was anything close to a typical "country" craft—either in technique or style or subject matter. Not by a long shot. This was no painted sweatshirt with little piggies or a floral decoupaged iced tea tray. Hy hadn't once laughed or rolled his eyes or made a face the way my highfalutin sister-in-law Florrie did behind my back. He actually expressed admiration for my creations. Wanted to market them.

I chewed on my lower lip, trying to decide whether or not to divulge my secret. But what was the worst that could happen? He'd roar with laughter the way Marjorie had? Still . . . "Promise you won't laugh?"

He nodded.

I took a deep breath. "It's a belly button casting."

Chapter Twelve

A quick call to directory assistance gave me the information I didn't want to hear. Like me, Mac had an unlisted phone number. Having no idea where he lived, I figured my only other option was to head for the building that housed WBAT.

Maybe he decided to go back to the office, rather than his apartment, after we parted at the library, I told Gertie as I hurried around the weekend crowds strolling along the streets of Greenwich Village.

"*Oh yeah, what every soon-to-be-fired management type does on a day off—put in unpaid overtime.*"

Okay, probably not, I conceded, *but maybe I can get an address or phone number from someone.*

"*Right. I bet they give those out to total strangers on a regular basis.*"

Of course not, but when I explain what happened. . . .

Gertie yawned. "*Sure, Nori. Whatever you say.*"

I decided not to speak another word to her. She was being her normal less-than-helpful self, even if she was probably right. As usual. Damn, she was getting to be a royal mega-boil on my derriere.

"*I heard that!*"

Truth hurts. Deal with it. I pushed open the heavy glass door and made my way across the lobby to the building directory. Eighteenth floor. I headed for the bank of elevators.

"Is Mackenzie Randolph in?" I asked the receptionist after stepping from the elevator a minute later.

Emitting a sigh of annoyance, the gum-snapping woman tore her attention away from the dog-eared romance on her desk. Without a glance in my direction, she pushed her glasses up the bridge of her nose and checked a sign-in board to her left. Next to Mac's name a button was slid to the "out" position. "Nope." She returned to her book.

"I need to get in touch with him."

She scowled at her novel. "Try Monday."

I glanced down at her nameplate. Maybe a more personal touch would work. I forced my lips into a smile and spoke in a voice that suggested we were the best of friends. "Look, Monica, I really need your help. This can't wait until Monday. Can you give me his number or address?"

She snorted. "Not likely."

"Please," I placed both my palms over the pages of her paperback. "You don't understand. This is an emergency."

Her growl told me I finally had her attention but definitely *not* her sympathy. She raised her head and glared at me through heavily made-up eyes that had narrowed into slits of hostility behind her bejeweled faux designer glasses. She pointed a razor-sharp, two-inch-long ruby nail at me. "No, sweetie. *You* don't understand. I don't care if Mr. Mac knocked you up and took off with your life savings. Your problems ain't my problems, and nothing you say is gonna make me risk losing my job. We don't give out personal info here, so take your 'emergency' and come back Monday."

Why did everyone suddenly assume I was pregnant? "But he has my computer and—"

She sucked in a deep breath. "Look, girl, do I have to call security, or are you gonna get outta my face?"

"Fine. Thanks for nothing." I tucked tail and headed for the elevator. Monica the Reception-Bitch meant business, and I had no intention of risking a run-in with Dick the Supercop or any of his overly zealous private security cronies. The way my luck was going, I'd wind up spending the night in a lice-infested cell with half a dozen transvestite streetwalkers. Sharing a bed with my mother was bad enough.

"Told you so," said Gertie.

I stabbed at the down button. *Oh, stick it!*

She ignored the insult. As I exited the building she spoke up. *"Where to now, Sherlock?"*

The only other place I might find him was Bean Around the Block. Since Mac had no way of getting in touch with me, maybe he'd head there once he realized he had the wrong computer. *If* he realized he had the wrong computer. For all I knew, he wouldn't notice the mix-up until Monday morning. Which wouldn't be the worst thing in the world, I supposed.

"Unless he reads some of your files."

I came to such a quick halt that a woman walking behind me slammed her suitcase of a purse into my thigh and stabbed her stiletto into my foot as she swerved to avoid me. She turned and glared—all six feet and easily two hundred and fifty pounds of her.

I opened my mouth to apologize. After all, the collision was my fault, and I wasn't about to tangle with an Amazon. Even on a good day the odds would be against my survival. But in one swift breath, before I could utter a word, she cursed me out with a four-letter-word barrage that stood a good chance of making even George Carlin blush. Then she gave me a shove for good measure and continued on her way.

I groaned. From both the physical pain spreading

through my foot and leg and the horror settling like a lead meteorite in the pit of my stomach. Most of my files ranged from sleep-inducing boring to dull-beyond-belief benign. Except for one. I squeezed my eyes shut and whispered a swift prayer that Mackenzie Randolph was a gentleman and wouldn't snoop around in a lady's private software. Especially my Gertie folder. But what were the chances of that, considering the gods had recently pulled the Carpet of Fate out from under me, and I had plummeted headfirst into the Land of Crappy Karma?

"Slim to none?"

For future reference, Gertie, rhetorical questions don't require answers.

"I'll remember that."

Sure you will.

"You know, I liked you a lot better when you were a lonely little kid."

And I liked you a lot more before you developed an attitude.

"You mean, like you?"

Touché. I suppose we'd both changed drastically over the years. And in the case of one of us, not necessarily for the better.

"That would be you, right?"

See what I mean? Who needs an imaginary friend with a 'tude? *Don't answer that,* I warned before she could toss in her fifty cents worth of opinion.

"Fine with me. Besides, seems you have bigger problems at the moment."

We had arrived at Bean Around the Block. I stepped inside the crowded coffee shop and scanned the room. Gertie was right. At the back of the café, camped out in one of the overstuffed chairs tucked into a corner, sat Mackenzie Randolph, his attention riveted to the screen of the open laptop perched on his knees. *My* laptop.

So much for hoping he'd act like a gentleman. I twisted

the shoulder strap of his computer case in a death grip as I limped off to confront the cyber-voyeur. Fury seethed through every pore of my body.

"Watch out, Mackenzie Randolph. The wrath of Honora Stedworth is about to come crashing down on your head."

Damn right, Gertie! Hellfire and brimstone the likes of which even Ten Commandments has never seen. The man was about to die an agonizing public death. Figuratively if not literally. I didn't care who heard me castigate him into a glutinous mass of mushy hominy. He deserved it. I was tired of being used and abused by men. First Dave. Now Mac.

The closer I got to the subject of my indignation, the more vehement my fury. Every injustice ever visited upon me, going all the way back to my childhood run-ins with Kurt Zwickel, surfaced in a pulsing, throbbing head of outrage about to explode on the unsuspecting cyber Peeping Tom seated across the room.

I came to an abrupt halt in front of his chair; I glared down at him. My mouth opened, ready to spew forth the total accumulation of twenty-some-odd years worth of pent-up frustrations.

My unsuspecting prey glanced over the rim of his reading glasses and smiled. "Hi, Nori. I was hoping you'd stop in." He spied the case cushioned against my hip. "I see you discovered our little mix-up."

Little mix-up? Maybe I'd call it that if the man weren't presently snooping in my most personal thoughts.

"You don't know that yet," cautioned Gertie.

True. I held both my breath and my temper as I cocked my head to view the file Mac had accessed.

And then I saw them.

Snuggled together on the loveseat several feet from Mac's chair.

Head to head.

Tongues and limbs entwined.

Dave and Suz.

All the fight drained out of me before I could hurl a single blistering syllable at Mac. I stood riveted to the floor, unable to move, unable to speak. I could only stare at them, once again sucked into the vortex of Thursday's humiliating betrayal.

Dave hated Bean Around the Block. "You've got to be kidding," he said when I once brought him. He wrinkled his nose as if he'd stepped in an enormous pile of steaming horse crap, grabbed my hand, and yanked me out the door. Now that Bean had made it to the A-list by way of HBO, I guess he no longer considered it *slumming* to patronize the Greenwich Village coffee house.

"Nori?" Mac reached up and gave a quick tug to my jacket sleeve.

I had to get out of there before Dave and Suz came up for air and spied me. Confronting them alone in Dave's Jacuzzi was bad enough. Watching them suck face in public was more than I could bear. I'd already suffered emotional rape at the hands of those two. I didn't need a heaping of public humiliation for good measure.

"Nori, what's wrong?" He followed my line of vision. "Uh-oh. That's not . . . ?"

I didn't answer him. A three-pronged assault of rage, panic, and pain choked off my windpipe. I frantically blinked back the tears threatening to drown both my eyeballs and my soul. Spinning on my heel, I ran for the exit, hoping I'd make it before Dave and Suz broke their lip-lock and noticed me.

Crappy karma and Mackenzie Randolph followed me as I half-ran, half-hobbled down the street.

"Hey, Nori! Wait up!"

I kept running. With each limping stride his computer whacked against my hip bone, causing even more pain to my already assaulted body. Mac caught up to me within half a block.

He grabbed my elbow; I stopped short. The last thing I wanted was to fall apart in front of him. In front of anyone.

Turning away, I inhaled what I hoped would be a deep calming breath but instead sucked up a gulp of noxious diesel exhaust from an idling delivery truck that obviously hadn't passed the emissions control test. The vile fumes triggered a coughing spasm camouflaging the shaky sobs that had threatened to erupt from my throat. Tears caused by the stinging emissions mingled with the emotional ones already swimming around my eyeballs. Saved by a polluter. I nearly choked on the combination of fumes, tears, and irony. God certainly works in mysterious ways.

Mac patted me gently on my back as he guided me away from the spewing truck. "Are you okay?"

I nodded between hacking wheezes until I finally caught my breath. "Fine."

"Good. Now would you mind telling me what got into you back at Bean? Was that your ex?"

I nodded once more and sighed. "Guess I overreacted a bit, huh?"

"Understandable."

"He hates Bean. And he knows it's a favorite place of mine." I forced myself to ask the question I wasn't sure I wanted answered. "Did they see me?"

Mac shook his head. "They never came up for air." He rubbed the stubble on his jaw. "So you think he wanted you to discover them there?"

"Brilliant deduction, Mr. Holmes. Ever consider becoming a detective? You've already proven you can snoop into people's private lives."

"Huh?"

I motioned to my computer dangling at his side. "You were reading my files."

To his credit he flushed with guilt. At least he was man enough not to lie his way around the flagrant violation of my privacy. "Yes, well, actually, I want to talk to you about that."

I stiffened. "Talk about the height of hubris! You read my diary and then expect me to discuss it with you? I don't think so."

Mac blanched. "Your *diary?*"

"What did you think you were reading, a download of *Crime and Punishment*?"

"I thought it was e-mail correspondence you had saved to a Word file. Are you telling me that *you're* Gertie? Damn! This is too good to be true."

"What?" I grabbed for my computer, shoving his at him. "You, Mackenzie Randolph, are a pervert."

He grinned at me. "And you, Nori Stedworth, are the answer to both of our prayers." Then, instead of taking his computer and handing me mine, he placed his palms on either side of my face and kissed me.

I should have yanked myself out of his grasp. Kicked him in the shin. Slapped his face. Spit in his eye.

One of the above.

Some of the above.

All of the above.

Instead, I did none of the above. Instead, I kissed him back.

In the background I heard Gertie chuckle.

Her laughter brought me to my senses. I broke the kiss. "Why did you do that?"

He grinned. "Because I've been wanting to ever since I met you?"

Not the answer I expected. "You did it to throw me off balance. To change the subject."

He shrugged his shoulders. His grin grew wider, hi

expression taking on a Dennis the Menace appearance that announced mischief was second nature to him. "You seemed to enjoy it."

I felt the heat surge through every pore of my body. No point in denying his assertion. Either to myself or him. My skin still tingled from his touch; my flushed cheeks confirmed his statement. Dave was a good kisser, but compared to Mac, he was a rank amateur. If they gave out an Oscar for Best Kisser, Mackenzie Randolph would strut off the stage with the phallic gold dude every time.

Still, I wasn't about to let him know that. At least not verbally. I crossed my arms over my chest, narrowed my eyes, and raised my chin. "That's totally beside the point."

"Sure. If you say so. Now can we talk about you and Gertie?"

The man had no shame. "No. Not now. Not ever. Just forget what you read."

"And why would I want to do that?"

"Because I'm asking you to, and if you have any shred of decency about you, you'll honor my request."

He screwed up his face and scrubbed at his jaw as if deep in thought. Tension twisted both my nerves and my intestines into a rat's nest as the seconds ticked by. Finally, with a twinkle in his eyes and another devilish smile playing across his too-handsome-for-his-own-good face, he shook his head. "Sorry. No can do."

If looks could kill, Mackenzie Randolph would now be vulture fodder.

Apparently, along with reading my computer files, he also read minds. He held up his hands. "Hold off with the execution until you hear me out, Nori."

I hitched my chin higher. "Why should I?"

His lips twisted into a bad-boy smirk. "Because I'm about to make you an offer you can't refuse."

153

I've heard some trite lines in my time. This one ranked up there with "Haven't we met before?" and "What's your sign?" Did he really think I'd fall for a Tony Soprano wannabe imitation? I smirked back. "Wanna bet?"

"Why don't you reserve judgment until after I plead my case?" He grabbed my elbow and steered me toward the entrance of Lemongrass, a small bistro two doors down from where we stood. "Let me buy you dinner."

I dug in my heels and mulled over his offer. Part furious, part embarrassed by his intrusiveness, I wasn't sure I wanted to spend a moment more with him. After all, I had no idea how much he had read. I'd only noticed the file header on the computer screen before the shock of seeing Dave and Suz rammed me in the solar plexus. Had Mac just begun to scan my files or had he spent hours indulging on my most seriously private musings? Another wave of scorching humiliation surged from my toes up to the tips of my ears.

But he had also piqued my curiosity. What exactly was this offer he was so certain I couldn't refuse? If I didn't give him the opportunity to explain, I'd never know. Then again, did I *want* to know? After all, there was that old adage about curiosity killing the kitty.

"Yeah, but satisfaction brought her back. What do you have to lose by listening to him?"

Gertie was turning into a card-carrying member of MRCLU, the Mackenzie Randolph Civil Liberties Union. A regular Mac-Advocate. Still, she presented a valid point. And there was that kiss.

"Hmmm. Don't forget about the kiss."

How could I? Mac's kiss toppled off the Richter scale. A man who kissed like that definitely deserved the benefit of any doubt.

"And maybe a second chance?"

Maybe. After all, how else would I get the opportunity to experience another one of those kisses?

"Now you're talking."

Inhaling a deep breath and hoping I didn't regret my decision, I nodded to him. "All right. I'll have dinner with you, but you'd better have a damn good excuse for snooping around in my files."

"In or out?" He motioned to a row of small wrought iron tables and chairs, half unoccupied, lining the entrance to the restaurant.

"In." In case Dave and Suz happened to stroll down the street after they finished slurping each other's various and sundry body parts.

"Two for dinner?" the host asked as we entered. When Mac nodded, he led us to a white linen-covered table off to one side of the cozy dining room. I took the seat that placed my back to the window. Again, just in case.

Mac seemed in no hurry to launch into his explanation or make his *offer.* He picked up the beverage menu and began studying it. "Wine, beer, or cocktail?"

"A Bellini, please."

The waitress appeared. Mac ordered my drink and added a Sam Adams for himself. Then he turned his attention to the dinner menu.

I reached across the table and placed my palm over the selections. "Let's talk first."

"What's your rush?"

"I may not have an appetite for dinner after I hear what you have to say."

Mac laughed. "But I may need to mellow you out quite a bit first. I've got a lot on the line here. I figure a few drinks. A nice dinner. A sinful dessert. Then I'll spring my plan on you."

I sighed. "That's what I'm afraid of. So whatever you have in mind, it's something I won't agree to until I'm tanked and stuffed. Then you'll go in for the kill?"

Mac switched from Dennis the Menace to a Sylvester-with-Tweety-Bird-in-his-mouth expression. "Well, I'd prefer to think of it as mellowed out and sated."

"Semantics."

"All the same, if you don't mind, I'd rather not take any chances."

"And why is that?"

"Because right now I feel like I need to declaw and defang you."

I started to growl at him, but my heart wasn't in it. I had made the mistake of focusing on his lips, ostensibly searching for telltale yellow feathers. Or so I had convinced myself. All too unfortunate a choice of focal point on my part. The slightest hint of a five o'clock shadow set his lips off like a spotlight trained on a performer. And oh, could those lips perform.

I felt the growl segueing into a needy groan. I tried to mask my unbalanced state with a flippant retort. "And whose fault is that? I didn't go snooping in your computer. I respected your privacy. The moment I realized I had your laptop, I turned it off and went looking for you."

Mac placed both his palms on the table, leaned forward, and inhaled sharply. "Okay, maybe we need to get this out in the open. Look, Nori, I didn't mean to snoop, and I didn't. Not at first, anyway. And even then, not intentionally. I figured if I went back to Bean, you'd eventually show up. I'd been waiting over two-and-a-half hours, and I was bored. I turned on the computer hoping to find a few games to play. Gertie sounded like a game."

"A game?"

"You know, like Lara Croft? Or Ms. Pacman?"

I granted him the point with a tight nod. "Fine, but you had to have realized your mistake the moment you clicked on the icon."

He grew sheepish. "I did. And I really did start to

exit. I swear. But then I caught a few lines of type, and . . ." He raised his hands, shrugged his shoulders, and sighed. "I'm sorry. I was hooked after the first sentence. I couldn't stop reading."

"How far did you get?" In other words, how embarrassed should I be? But I didn't add that aside.

He extended me another sheepish grin. "Not as far as I would have liked. Maybe three, four pages. You showed up a minute or two later."

Now it was my turn to sigh—a huge sigh of relief. Mac's snooping had netted him no more information than I had already verbally given him: The Dave and Suz Debacle. The Burrito Blunder. The Mom Melee. The Career Calamity. He had gotten no further than the *Why Me?* bitch-and-moan prologue to what had quickly become a rather lengthy tome in the few days since I'd resurrected Gertie. My secrets safe, I could now afford to be magnanimous. "Okay, I rescind the price on your head, but what does my diary have to do with making me an offer I can't refuse?"

The waitress appeared with our drinks. Mac held up his hand. "Can we order first?"

"You still feel the need to tank and stuff me?"

He cocked his head and morphed from Sylvester Cat into Pierce Brosnan. In full ultra-suave James Bond mode. "I reserve the right to answer that question *after* you're sufficiently mellowed and sated."

I acquiesced. After all, who could refuse Pierce Brosnan? Without glancing at the menu, I turned to the waitress. I'd eaten here often and knew the house specialty. "I'll have the trout amandine."

"Make that two," said Mac, handing her the menus. "And a bottle of Chardonnay."

I glanced first at my untouched Bellini and then at his equally filled-to-the-brim pilsner glass before raising a questioning eyebrow at him.

He stared me right in the eye, his expression unreadable. "Like I said, I'm not taking any chances."

One hour and far too many calories and alcohol units later, Mac finally dropped his bomb. An entire wine cellar of Chardonnay couldn't have prepared me. "You want *me* on Big Jock Rant Radio? To do what? Explain the infield fly rule from a female perspective?"

Mac leaned back in his chair and crossed his arms over his chest. "Hey, if you can explain the infield fly rule from *any* perspective, I'm all ears. I still have trouble understanding that one myself, and I played second base in both high school and college."

"Great! And you're a guy. You're supposed to be born knowing things like that. It's in your genes." I leaned back in my chair and mirrored his arms-crossed position. "You've had your little joke, Mac. Now can we get serious?"

"I am serious." He took a deep breath and placed his hands on the table. "I've been going about this all wrong. Wracking my brains to come up with a new angle on yet another sports talk show when we have too many already. You were right."

"About what?"

"When you complained about the station and mentioned why you didn't listen to it. Do you remember what you said to me the day we met?"

I shook my head. I met Mac within hours of my life imploding around me, and he expected me to remember a casual conversation about a radio station I never listen to?

"You asked me if I ever think about the other half of the population? Those with double-X chromosomes. You said the shows are all the same, hour after hour. The only things that change throughout the day are the names of the guys doing the ranting and raving and the sports figures or teams they're ranting and raving about."

"But if I remember correctly, you said the owners were committed to that format."

"The talk format, yes. But not necessarily the all-sports format. What WBAT needs is a jock counterbalance. Someone to draw in the other half of the populace. You can do that, Nori. I see it in your writing. At first I thought some sort of point-counterpoint type show with you and your friend Gertie. But now that I know it's all you, that's even better. You could go up against different guests each segment."

"Like a female Howard Stern?" I shook my head. "I don't think so."

He wasn't deterred. "Or maybe it could be an essay sort of spot. Like a female Andy Rooney. Or a call-in show. Like a young, hip Dr. Laura."

Mac was on a roll. I held up my hand to stop his mile-a-minute, wasn't-coming-up-for-air discourse and douse him with a bucket of reality. "You're forgetting I have no broadcast experience."

He brushed away my objection with a wave of his hand. "No problem. Neither did any of our jocks before we sat them in front of a mic."

"And what would I talk about?"

"The same things you and Gertie talk about."

"Who's going to be interested in that?" And besides, who says I want to share my private thoughts with the entire New York metro area? Or at least the segment of it that listens to WBAT.

He speared me with one of his megawatt, bad-boy grins. "I would."

I'll bet he would.

"Especially the parts about him."

159

Those get deleted as soon as I get home, I told Gertie. *I'm not taking any more chances on computer mix-ups with Mackenzie Randolph.*

I turned my attention back to Mac. "One more listener isn't going to save your job. Besides, you don't count. As the station manager, you already have to listen."

"Trust me, Nori. This is going to work. You need a job. I need to save mine. What do either of us have to lose by giving it a try?"

Gertie the Mac-Advocate piped in again with another nickel's worth of unwanted advice. *"He's got a point. What do you have to lose, Nori?"*

My sanity?

"I think that fell by the wayside several days ago."

Cute. Editorial comment from the cheap seats. How about if you let me handle this, huh, Gertie? I'm a big girl. I can make up my own mind.

"Then explain to me exactly why I'm here."

Is it considered homicide if you strangle your imaginary friend?

"It's a death penalty offense."

I was afraid of that. I settled my elbows on the table and cradled my head in my hands. A whopper of a headache lurked right behind my eyeballs. I closed my eyes and massaged my temples with my fingertips. "I need time to think about this," I told Mac.

"Take all the time you want. As long as you agree by tomorrow."

My eyelids popped open; my jaw dropped. "Tomorrow? But tomorrow's Sunday."

He nodded. "And Monday is the end of the month. My last day of employment unless I can pull off a programming miracle between now and then."

I groaned. He was dumping his fate in my hands. Unfair. I wasn't in control of my own life—how could I be held responsible for someone else's? Although, if I did succeed in this hare-brained idea of his, we'd both win. "How much money are we talking? Enough to keep me from moving into a cardboard box?"

"What were you making?"

I told him.

"Not a problem." But his voice didn't sound all that convincing to me.

"What do I have to do?"

"Go home and write something. A few paragraphs."

"On what topic?"

"Anything that's been bothering you."

Hell, I could write an epic on that subject. I just doubted anyone would want to hear it. "Okay." I inhaled a deep breath and extended my right hand across the table. "We'll both probably regret this, but you've got yourself a deal, Mackenzie Randolph."

He took my hand and shook it. Although I would have much preferred his sealing our agreement with another one of his kisses.

Mac insisted on walking me back to my apartment, even though it was only around the corner. I debated the entire short distance as to whether or not to invite him in for a cup of coffee. Not because I didn't want to appear presumptuous. Any other time, I wouldn't have thought twice about it. Especially after having already savored one of his kisses. This wasn't any other time, though. There was a very good chance that come Monday Mac would be my boss. And then there was Mom. A simple introduction wouldn't suffice. She'd bombard Mac with all sorts of intrusive questions and would continue her probing long after he'd left. I didn't want to deal with that tonight.

Mac left me no choice, though. At my door he said, "How about a cup of coffee for the road?"

I couldn't exactly be rude now, could I? "Sure.

You've got your choice of hazelnut, mocha java, or Kenyan," I said, as one by one I unlocked the deadbolts and then swung the door open.

Mac didn't answer me. I glanced up at him, saw the shocked expression that covered his face, then followed his line of vision across the room. To a half-naked Hyman Perth lying supine on my couch. And my mother bending over him just below his waist.

Chapter Thirteen

"Mother!"

Nori's shriek drowned out Pavarotti's mournful, plaintive rendition of "Rudolfo" and startled the bejabbers out of me. I jumped, stumbled backwards, and tripped over one of Hy's discarded shoes. Hy bolted upright. I reached for his arm to steady myself. His pants slid farther down his legs. As he grabbed for them, his elbow knocked the bowl of casting medium from my hand. I lurched for the bowl, missed, and kicked over the bag of plaster lying at my feet.

Plaster of paris spattered seven ways to Sunday. A cloud of plaster dust rose into the air like a burping volcano, then began to settle. All over Hy. All over me. All over the living room.

I always mix way too much. This batch had been no exception. I can never get the water-to-powder ratio right. First I add too much water, then I compensate with too much powder, then too much water. And so on. I hadn't realized how much I'd mixed until I saw the fallout settle over the room. I needed a tablespoon at most and wound up with over a quart before I managed to get the consistency right.

A large dollop had landed smack-dab in the middle of the forehead of some strange man who stood beside Nori. He scooped the white glop off his brow and stared at it. Deep furrowed lines of puzzlement replaced the spot where the plaster had nailed him.

Who was he? She hadn't gotten back together with that fancy-schmancy epidermis doctor, had she? That would certainly complicate things. As much as I hated seeing my daughter in tears, their break-up made my job a lot easier.

Nori batted at the plaster dust still hovering in the air and continued to gawk, her head bobbing back and forth from me to Hy and back to me. "Mom, what in heaven's name are you doing?"

I searched around for the roll of paper towels I had brought in from the kitchen. Where were they? If I didn't begin mopping up the mess soon, it would start hardening. "We were listening to Puccini before you starting wailing like a banshee."

"Puccini? Screw Puccini!" She pointed to Hy. "Why is he naked?"

It took Herculean effort, but I forced myself to ignore my daughter's foul mouth. A mother's influence only extends so far, and it was obvious mine hadn't made it past the Ten Commandments town limits. I gave up on the paper towels and walked over to the stereo. Taking care not to drip plaster on the CD player, I lowered the volume on *La Bohème*, although I considered it a shame to replace such a masterful tenor with the shrill discord resonating from my only offspring. Why did she have to be so judgmental and close-minded when it came to me?

"What does it look like we're doing?"

The man standing next to her stifled a chortle with a fake cough, swatting at the air in some useless attempt to blame the dust for his spasms, but he didn't fool me. Or Nori. She glared him into silence, then turned her scowl on me. "Trust me. You don't want me to answer that."

"Honora!" I stooped to pick up the Tupperware container that held the remains of the plaster and discovered the paper towels sticking out from under the sofa. With a grunt, I lowered myself to my knees and pulled out the roll. "Someone has a very dirty mind, young lady. I'm making a belly button casting, as you can plainly see, not giving a blow job!"

"Mom!"

"A belly button casting?" The man standing next to her raised his eyebrows. "Now that has potential."

"What!" I didn't know who this person was, but he'd better not be thinking of stealing my idea.

Nori's scowl deepened. I wished she wouldn't do that. I've told her before it will give her early wrinkles. "Over my dead body," she told him.

"And mine." I added. "Whoever you are, you can just forget it. Belly button casting is my creation, and I've given Hy marketing rights. We're drawing up contracts with the lawyers on Monday."

"Marketing rights? Mom, you can't go around pouring plaster into strangers' navels. What on earth has gotten into you?"

"Strangers? Who said anything about strangers? I'm going to make castings of celebrities. Hy plans to mass market the reproductions. He thinks they'll be the next big craze. Bigger than Beanie Babies."

"Celebrities?" She glared at Hy. "He's no more a celebrity than I am!"

"I was demonstrating my technique on him."

This time the man with Nori didn't bother to mask his laughter. "This is priceless!"

Nori elbowed him in the ribs then turned her wrath on Hy. He had slipped his pants back up and was in the process of pulling his turtleneck over his head. "What kind of con game are you running here?"

To his credit Hy fought to keep his temper in check,

even though anger over the affront to his integrity had turned his face as red as one of my jars of pickled beets. "I am a businessman, not a con artist," he said in a tightly clipped voice. "And you may not want to admit it, my dear, but your mother happens to have immense talent."

"Talent you intend to exploit?" Nori's voice rose several octaves. Sarcasm dripped from each syllable.

Hy's voice grew tighter and deeper. A purple vein popped out on his temple and began to throb. "Talent, young lady, I intend to *nurture*."

Before those two came to blows, I stepped between them; not an easy task, since at this point they stood nearly nose-to-nose. And growl-to-growl. "We really do need to take care of this mess before it hardens. Nori, you get the vacuum. Young man"—I turned to Nori's friend or whoever he was—"there's a bucket under the sink. Fill it with water and bring it in here. Hy, you take the paper towels and start wiping up as much of the wet plaster as you can."

All three of them stared at me as if I were speaking in tongues. "What are you waiting for?" I clapped my hands together, sending up a cloud of plaster dust. "Move!" Without another peep, they broke ranks and set off on their designated assignments. Now all I had to do was figure out a way to smooth their ruffled feathers. And convince my daughter I hadn't lost my mind.

Some tasks are easier than others. Cleanup took two hours of hard labor. Plaster is a stubborn foe, whether in dry or wet form. Overcoming misconception and distrust takes far longer. Nori had classified Hy as the enemy. Convincing her otherwise proved daunting.

"I want to see everything before you sign it," she told me after I explained Hy's plans for my crafts to her, "and I want Dad here, too. You owe him that much."

"Not a problem. I'm sure your father will be very happy for me," I told her, trying hard to suppress the grin bubbling inside me. Nori was making things all too easy.

I couldn't wait to call Marjorie. I felt like a new woman. Suddenly my life had purpose. Thanks to Hy, I was about to embark on a new career and a new life—a life where I was appreciated for being more than just an appendage to my husband and daughter. For the first time I would be a *me*. And if all continued going my way, a year from now I might also be a grandmother.

There was but one giant horsefly in my happy balm, and he presently sat across from me at Nori's kitchen table. Turns out he wasn't the fancy-schmancy doctor. He was someone new, but the moment he'd walked into the apartment with Nori, my earlobes had begun itching as if I were wearing poison ivy earrings.

As far as I was concerned, he had no business being part of the discussion. This was between Hy, Nori, and me, but he had convinced my daughter that it might prove beneficial to her to have an impartial witness to our impromptu meeting. So there he was, a stranger I knew nothing about, other than the little he had offered about himself—his name and that he managed a radio station—learning way too much for my liking. However, Hy didn't seem concerned, so I tried hard to ignore the red-flag-warning-signals my earlobes kept waving at me.

Chapter Fourteen

"Write about what happened tonight," said Mac as I walked him to the door several hours later. "Belly button castings, plaster of paris fallout, crazy neighbors, and crazier mothers. The whole nine yards. That should cover at least a month's worth of spots."

After our lengthy kitchen table summit, Mom and Hy had excused themselves and headed up to Hy's apartment—to do God knows what, and I don't want to know anyway. Although I had my suspicions. Especially since she departed with what was left of the bag of plaster of paris. I chewed on the inside of my cheek as I contemplated, then quickly rejected, Mac's suggestion.

"Forget it. I don't need Oscar the Grouch slapping me with a lawsuit."

"Oscar the Grouch?" Mac frowned. "You've lost me. What does a monster who lives in a trash can on *Sesame Street* have to do with any of this?"

I explained my nickname for Hy, then added, "That man's up to something. I don't trust him."

"Maybe you're overreacting. He seems to know what he's doing."

"That's exactly what scares me."

Mac leaned against the doorjamb and scrubbed at the day's worth of stubble that covered his jaw. He looked too damn sexy for his own good. Or mine. I shook the thought from my head.

"I don't think you have to worry," he said. "He's drawing up legal documents."

"Through *his* lawyer."

"So get your mom to hire someone to represent her interests." He paused, shifting his weight from foot to foot, and cocked his head as if weighing whether or not to say more. Which he finally decided to do. "You know, Nori, I've got to tell you, I don't see anything suspicious here. Not that I can imagine anyone wanting a casting of Arnold Schwarzenegger's belly button, but stranger things have happened. Maybe your neighbor is on to something.

"And I think your mom's a riot. You have *got* to write about her for the radio piece. Trust me. You'll bowl the head honchos over. It was all I could do to keep from laughing my head off this evening."

I had noticed, but I shook my head, again dismissing the idea of using my mother's midlife crisis as source material.

"I already have an idea for the segment."

"Oh? What?"

I offered Mac one of his Sylvester-Tweety Bird smiles as I opened the apartment door for him. "You can read it tomorrow. Good night, Mac."

The next morning I met Mac at Bean Around the Block and presented him with what might turn out to be my first broadcast piece.

Sigmund Freud once posed the question, "What do women want?" The answer continued to elude him throughout his lifetime. No great surprise there. Freud was a guy. And a chauvinistic one to boot. He never bothered to go to the source. If guys want to under-

stand women, they need to learn to ask questions and listen to the answers, two things guys aren't very adept at doing because they believe that real guys don't need directions. News flash: You need directions. Big time. Your entire species is clueless.

Let me introduce myself. I'm Gertie. After you listen to me, you'll probably dub me your worst nightmare. But you will listen because the geniuses at this station are convinced you need to hear what I have to say, and in a brilliant programming move, they've sandwiched me in between their two highest-rated jock ranters.

For those of you tempted to tune me out and switch over to Howard Stern, I guarantee if you keep an open mind and stick with me, you might learn a thing or two about women and decrease your strikeout ratio.

So without further ado, welcome to:

THE TAO OF GERTIE
LESSON NUMBER ONE: FLUSH THIS!

Now listen up, all you macho, testosterone-laden jocks: It's time for a little English lesson. So tear yourselves away from the fridge, the TV, or that favorite Internet porn site of yours; put down the beer can; sit up straight in your torn Barcalounger; and pay attention.

Webster's defines "seat," and I quote, as: "a place or space to sit; a thing to sit on; the part of a chair, bench, etc. that supports the buttocks; a part or surface on which another part rests or fits snuggly." End quote.

The human derriere—that's ass, for those of you who didn't take French or who have minimal IQ points—was not designed to defy gravity. (Don't take my word for it, though. Ask your wives or mothers or any woman over the age of twenty-five.) Therefore— and here's where you guys have to pay close attention, so try to keep those brain cells focused a few seconds longer—a seat, by definition, must be a horizontal surface.

Got it? Good! Now kindly lower the toilet seat into its proper parallel to the horizon position each and every time you're through taking a whiz. And don't bother with the excuses. We've heard them all, and none of them hold water—or in this case, a completely different type of liquid. Thank you, gentlemen, and have a nice day.

Mac placed the printout on the table in front of him, leaned back in his chair, cupped his hands behind his head, and whistled through his teeth—loud enough that several other Bean patrons turned to stare at us. "Now, that's what I call a rant."

I shrugged as I sipped my latté. "No more so than all those rabid jocks who spout off over your airwaves for hours each day about the reasons for the Mets' latest losing streak or the price of Knicks tickets."

"But why toilet seats?"

I shrugged again. "Because nothing illustrates the great divide that separates the sexes better than the toilet seat issue. It's a classic."

He scrubbed his jaw. "Still, Gertie sure doesn't mince words."

I placed my cup on the table and crossed my arms over my chest. "Correct me if I'm wrong, but you did tell me to write about something that bothers me, didn't you?"

I could almost see the five hundred watt light bulb switch on in that little bubble over his head. "I left the toilet seat up last night, didn't I?"

"Bingo! Hand that man a chocolate cigar."

He offered me one of those sheepish grins of his. "Hey, it's a guy thing. And besides, I live alone."

"Then pee in your own apartment."

Surprise settled across his features. "This really bothers you, doesn't it?"

"It bothers all women, Mac. Especially when we stumble into the bathroom in the middle of the night and wind up doggie-paddling in the commode."

"You could always switch on the light to see where you're going."

I shook my head. "Great. And have the sudden brilliance of a hundred and fifty watts startle me fully awake at three in the morning? No thank you."

"Beats a wet bottom."

Men are so clueless. And not only about toilet seats. I leveled my most condescending smile at him. "How considerate of you."

He leaned back in his chair and ran his fingers through his hair. "I don't know, Nori. Maybe I expected you to write something more relevant."

"More relevant? Your audience is going to switch stations if I talk about glass ceilings or equal pay for equal work. Those are rants to level on CEOs, not sportsaholics." I reached across the table and tapped the paper. "Maybe I misunderstood you, but I thought you wanted me to push some buttons, get these guys annoyed enough to call in and spout off about something other than football stats for a change. And hopefully draw in women listeners as well."

He stared down at the sheet of paper. "And you think a treatise on toilet seat position will do that?"

"I think speaking out about all those little daily irritants that drive women up a wall will. Toilet seat position is simply one of them. None of this is earth-shattering, but it does speak to the issues of communication and respect between the sexes."

"Our listeners are going to demand we can you the minute this first essay airs. They'll chalk your rants up to being on the rag."

I laughed. "Now that's an expression I haven't heard since my great-grandmother passed away.

"Look, Mac, you want to spur ratings. I'm giving you controversy. What better way to achieve your goal? These guys are going to hate me. Think of all the liberals who tune in to Rush Limbaugh to hear which one of them he's bashing today. This isn't National Public Radio. I don't expect to change the world, but I might educate a few Neanderthals. And if not, well, hopefully I'll generate a terrific on-air slugfest."

Mac's face lit up to match the megawatt brightness of the imaginary light bulb that continued to blaze over his head. His eyes twinkled with devilment. "You're right. I hadn't thought about it in those terms. This is a hundred times better than I imagined. We'll need to hire more switchboard operators to handle the calls. Our very own WBAT *War of the Roses*."

He spread his arms wide as if to indicate a theater marquee. "I can see it now. Gertie versus the Jocks. Radio's answer to pro wrestling."

Not an analogy I cared to hear. Anything that smacked of wrestling brought back too many memories I'd rather keep buried at least six feet under. "So you think the station owners will go for this idea?" And did I really want them to? As much as I needed a job, and as much as I didn't want Mac to lose his job, I wasn't all that confident about diving headfirst into jock-infested waters. No matter how much I had fought to sell the idea.

"Trust me. They're going to love it."

And they did. By the end of the day I had cut a demo tape, the head honchos had heard it, and I had a contract sitting in front of me. Mac's unemployment clock was ticking down, and Sunday or not, he wasn't taking any chances. He wanted me signed, sealed, wrapped, and delivered before the clock struck midnight.

Lois Winston

Back at Bean Around the Block, I studied the hastily drawn-up contract. When I had finished reading, I pushed the sheets back across the table to Mac. "I can't sign this."

His jaw dropped. He looked as though I had told him he had one hour to live. Or one hour of employment left, which was pretty damn close to what he'd have if I didn't sign on the dotted line. "Why not?"

"I don't want my name associated with the segments. There's nothing in here about using a pseudonym. As far as WBAT and your listeners are concerned, I'm Gertie, not Honora Stedworth. Everything I say over the airwaves will be Gertie's words, Gertie's musings, Gertie's uncensored fantasies. Not mine. I want neither my name nor my image in any way connected with the station."

"What difference does it make?"

"It makes a gargantuan difference when you come from Ten Commandments, your father is the mayor, and your uncle is the local minister. Can you imagine the repercussions if these spots somehow find their way back to Iowa? I don't want to be responsible for giving my parents apoplexy. Or worse." I had already given them enough grief by turning my back on the life they had planned for me and leaving the bucolic land of *Father Knows Best* for the hedonistic home of *Sex and the City*. I didn't need the added guilt of possible coronaries on my conscience.

"You have nothing to worry about, Nori. Our signal strength isn't that powerful."

I passed him the pen. "Still, I'm not taking any chances. Especially with some of the topics I have in mind. I want an addendum."

Mac shrugged. "Okay. No problem." He picked up the pen, wrote one in, then initialed it.

I read what he had added and nodded. "Fine. Now I'll sign." He let out a long sigh of relief as I added my initials next to his, then signed and dated the document. I was now officially embarked on a new career, but I still wasn't sure what I had gotten myself into.

I soon learned.

My toilet seat diatribe aired during drive time the next morning. As Mac predicted, the switchboard immediately lit up like the Radio City Christmas tree. Men called in to rant; women called in to rave.

"What's the big deal? If the friggin' seat's up, flip it down."

"Why can't men ever put things back the way they found them?"

"You don't hear us complaining when you leave the seat *down*, do you?"

"That's the trouble with you men. You never listen. Didn't you hear a word she said? It's a *seat*. It's supposed to be *down*."

"S'matter? You ain't got no hands, princess? You can't lower the freakin' seat?"

"If men had to sit to pee, they'd make sure all toilet seats were permanently nailed down."

"Maybe this Gertie ain't got the brains to figure out how to work a toilet seat."

"Maybe that last caller needs to fall into the bowl the next time he sits to take a crap."

The war of the sexes had begun.

THE TAO OF GERTIE
LESSON NUMBER SIX: BIRTHDAYS DO
MATTER!

Why is it that the average guy can remember the most obscure sports statistics from a decade ago yet can't remember the birth date of the woman he's been going steady with for two years?

Joe Jock has no problem recalling the date Cal Ripkin

*ended his consecutive games streak or Barry Bonds
broke Mark McGwire's home run record. Harry Hotrod
knows to the exact hour when he last changed the oil
and spark plugs on his classic 'sixty-four Mustang.*

*But both are numerically challenged when it comes
to remembering their girlfriends' birthdays, let alone
Valentine's Day. And forget about the anniversary of
the day they met. That's like expecting Bart Simpson
to ace advanced calculus. Never going to happen.*

*Is it a chromosome deficiency or just plain insensi-
tivity? My money's on the latter. Guys remember
what they want to remember, and when compared to
NASCAR or Michael Jordan or the Super Bowl, we
women don't make the cut. Unless, of course, their
Johnsons need stroking. Then we're temporarily
moved to the head of the line—at least for the next
three to five minutes. And the television is usually
playing in the background so they can keep one eye on
the really important action.*

"You sure have dated some creeps," said Mac the following Monday after my first week of segments had aired.
"Do I take it from this that none of your boyfriends ever
remembered your birthday or Valentine's Day?"

With my latest tirade in his hand, he stood in the doorway of the closet-sized office WBAT had assigned me. It
wasn't much—only a battered desk with an unmatching
chair, a phone, a computer, and a filing cabinet—but it
was all mine. An honest-to-goodness office, not a cubicle.
And it came complete with a window, even if the glass
did contain a thick outer coating of grime that nearly ob-
scured my view of the industrial-sized air-conditioning
unit perched on the roof of the office building next door.

"One did," I said. "After I complained about him using my bath towels to polish the chrome on his Harley,
he bought me another set for my birthday."

His eyes grew wide. "You dated a guy who rode a motorcycle?"

"Worse. I dated a guy who shopped at the dollar store. Not only did he give me towels, but he managed to find the cheesiest set in Manhattan."

"Still, I can't picture you on the back of a hog."

"Ever try parking a car in Manhattan?"

"Park? Hell, I don't even drive in the city." He eyed me from head to toe, shook his head, and laughed. "Sorry, Nori, but you don't strike me as a biker babe."

"I wasn't for long. And certainly not after that birthday present."

"We're not all alike, you know."

"True. There are a multitude of subgenres to the creep species." And I should know. Look at Dave. Here I thought I had finally found Mr. Right, and he turned out to be Mr. Wrong-As-You-Can-Get. "At least my rotten track record has provided me with a new source of income." My first week's paycheck, several days late due to an accounting snafu, had arrived an hour earlier. I picked it up and waved it at him. "Solvent again."

"And soon to be more so," he said.

"What do you mean?"

Mac perched his rear on the edge of my desk. "The big boys like what they're hearing. Gertie's a hit. Ratings are up. Higher than I'd dared to dream. They want to give you live airtime."

"Live?" I wasn't sure I liked the sound of that. "And do what?"

"I'm picturing an hour call-in show. 'Gertie Gets Even.' You begin each segment with one of your short *Tao of Gertie* essays. Then we open the lines to callers. Sort of an on-air *Dear Abby*. People tell Gertie their problems, and she offers solutions."

Now I knew I didn't like the sound of it. I wasn't Dr. Laura. "There's nothing new about that idea. Radio is crammed with on-air shrinks. At least they have credentials. I'm not a therapist."

"Neither is Dear Abby, yet people write to her for help. We don't want a shrink. We want Gertie's slant on our listeners' problems. And we're betting our listeners want it, too."

"And what if Gertie can't come up with a solution? It's not like I'm going to have time to mull these questions over in my head. You're talking immediate repartee. No cue cards. No research. No time to think." I shook my head. "I can't do that."

"Sure you can. You've got the sharpest, quickest wit of anyone I've ever met. You've always got a snappy rejoinder on the tip of your tongue."

"Maybe, but I never have a live mic in front of that tongue. What happens when the tongue gets tied up in a double-square knot?"

This time Mac had the quick comeback. Obviously, he had taken the time to plan a counterargument for any objections I might raise. "We open the lines to our listeners. You harvest solutions from them. Act as a moderator or facilitator. Trust me, Nori, once you get started, you'll have no trouble. You were born to do live radio."

I contorted my face into a scowl. "I was born to Bible-belt conservatives."

Mac chuckled. "See what I mean?" Then he did a quick conversational one-eighty. "By the way, what's new on the navel-casting front?"

I groaned. My mother and her Svengali had spent the better part of last week tearing through Manhattan on a kamikaze marketing blitz that rivaled George Lucas's for the *Star Wars* franchise. "Turns out Hyman Perth has more celebrity connections than Regis Philbin. He's had Mom bending over so many belly buttons from Tribeca to the Upper West Side that I think she's developed a permanent stoop. She now has concise navel intelligence on soap opera stars, Broadway stars, the Mets, the Yankees. Even former mayor Rudy Giuliani."

Then I offered the *pièce de résistance*. "She called a few minutes ago. Tonight she's casting David Letterman's belly button in front of sixty million viewers."

Mac pursed his lips together and produced a long, low whistle of amazement. "How many of those viewers live in Ten Commandments?"

"You wouldn't think many, considering Letterman's particular brand of humor, but he's an Indiana boy, and that's close enough to Iowa for them to consider him one of their own. Even if half the time they don't get the jokes."

"And the other half?"

"Those turn them as red as my mother's prize-winning pickled beets. So to answer your original question, too many—including my father, who never goes to bed until after Dave's Top Ten List."

Mac motioned to the phone on the opposite side of the desk. "Think you should warn him?"

Chapter Fifteen

Maybe it was being in the Ed Sullivan Theater that triggered the sound of Paul Lind's voice singing a song from *Bye Bye, Birdie* over and over in my head. Only, as I paced back and forth in the Green Room, awaiting my fifteen minutes of fame on *The Late Show*, Paul's broken-record rendition of the lyrics had been altered to: *Dave Letterman! Dave Letterman! I'm going to be on Dave Letterman!*

"Nervous?"

I eyed the assistant-to-the-assistant-to-the-assistant producer assigned to babysit me. Her skintight black jeans with strategically placed holes and slits fell several inches short of her pierced navel. Her cropped, elasticized neon pink T-shirt barely covered her wannabe boobs. A gold hoop hung from her left eyebrow; a matching stud adorned her right nostril. She looked about twelve years old.

A nervous titter escaped through my lips before I could rein it back. "What gave me away? The path I've worn from one end of the room to the other?"

She glanced down at the nubby tweed carpet and chuckled. "You're not the first. I'll clue you in on something. Even the mega-stars pace the green room. It's tradition."

I forced the corners of my mouth into a smile, then

helped myself to a second petit four from the buffet table. What could she know about tradition? I have a jar of mayonnaise older than her.

As I nibbled at a corner of the cake, I bemoaned my solitary state. All that self-confidence Hy had imbued me with had fled to Bora Bora the moment he'd announced I was on my own this evening. And right about now I'd give anything to be in Bora Bora along with that AWOL self-confidence. Appearing on television was nerve-wracking enough. Having to do it solo was tantamount to asking me to scale Mount Everest in flip-flops and a bikini. I whined and pleaded to no avail.

"Sorry," he said. "I have a previous commitment that can't be rescheduled."

"So rebook me on Letterman. I'll go on some other night. I don't mind."

His jaw dropped. He stared at me as if I had suggested he slop Leona and Ralph Shakelmeyer's hogs. When he recovered enough to speak, I got a crash course in the finer points of pecking orders, public relations, and show business. "*The Late Show* books months in advance. You have no idea how many strings I had to pull. I only succeeded in getting you on so soon because they had a last-minute cancellation."

Meet Connie Stedworth, ferret replacement. Fernando, the gargling ferret, booked for Stupid Pet Tricks, had managed to escape his cage upon arrival at La Guardia last night. An extensive search proved fruitless. Or ferretless. Nearly twenty-four hours later, Fernando continued to elude capture. I hope he hasn't gone into the sewers. I hear they have alligators down there.

Anyway, Fernando's loss—literally—was my gain.

I helped myself to another petit four. What difference did it make? I hadn't been allotted enough time to lose

Off.

those twenty pounds, anyway. Besides, I needed something to calm my nerves—especially after the door opened and Mel Gibson walked into the green room.

Did I ever mention I've had a secret crush on Mel ever since *Braveheart*? There's just something about a man in a kilt. Sigh. Anyway, Mel scoped out the room, offered Miss Multi-Piercings a nod of recognition, then zeroed in on me with that huge ear-to-ear grin of his. "Mel Gibson," he said, extending his hand. "And you are?"

Before I could grasp his hand, the multi-pierced one stepped between us and completed the introductions. "Mel Gibson, meet Constance Stedworth. She paints belly button portraits."

"So you're the one!" Mel's grin widened even further—something I hadn't thought physically possible until I saw it with my own eyes.

Thanks to the Hyman Perth publicity juggernaut, my fame had spread as fast as the aroma of manure on a breezy spring day in Ten Commandments. Apparently, once you cast one celebrity belly button, *all* celebrities want theirs cast. My quirky creations were fast becoming status symbols among the rich and famous.

Before I realized what was happening, Mel yanked his shirt up to his pecs and tugged his jeans down to his hips. "Do mine."

Half an hour later I was fondling Mel Gibson's belly button on national television. I couldn't wait to tell Marjorie!

I called her the moment I returned to Nori's apartment. Her reaction wasn't exactly what I had expected. Not by a longshot.

"Constance Stedworth! What in the world have you gotten yourself into?" I held the phone away from my head to keep Marjorie from bursting my eardrum with her shrill condemnation. "For heaven's sake, you're supposed to be working on getting Nori and Eugene together so we can have grandchildren, not entering your second childhood. Good Lord, belly button castings! I thought you gave up on that crazy idea years ago."

All of a sudden she sounded too much like some of Earnest's relatives. "I expected that sort of censure from everyone else back in Ten Commandments, but not you," I told her. Not Marjorie, my former childhood partner in crime. She was supposed to be happy for me. Encourage me. But here I was forced once more into the position of having to defend myself. First with my daughter. Now with my best friend.

She exhaled a loud sigh through the phone line. "I know you were unhappy. I know you wanted a bit of adventure, but you've certainly taken dealing with menopause to new heights with this lamebrain idea. Or maybe new lows is more like it." She uttered that last sentence under her breath. "You'd best get a grip and come to your senses before Earnest has you committed. And at this point, I'm not sure I'd blame him. What *were* you thinking?"

I sniffed back my hurt feelings and defended my decision to go into business with Hy. "It's not a lamebrain idea. Hy thinks belly button castings have great marketing potential. Besides, I'm having fun. I'm meeting all sorts of interesting people, and you know what?"

"What?"

"They think *I'm* interesting. I'm not just Earnest's wife here. I'm someone in my own right. Someone people want to know. Celebrities are standing in line, waiting for me to cast their belly buttons and paint their portraits on the castings. And it sure as hell beats canning pickled beets back in Ten Commandments!"

Marjorie clucked her tongue as if trying to reason

with some addle-brained octogenarian. "I think this Hy fellow has you bamboozled. Why would anyone want to buy a belly button casting? It's a good thing Earnest is making arrangements to fly East. You certainly need rescuing."

So Marjorie had finally fulfilled her end of our scheme. "What did you tell him?"

"That you're on the verge of a nervous breakdown. Which, now that I hear what you've been up to the last week, isn't far from the truth."

"Marjorie! That wasn't what we agreed to." She was supposed to make Earnest jealous by leading him to believe he had a rival for my attentions in New York. Which, in a way, he had. No need to fake a fictitious suitor. That part of the plan had worked out better than I could have imagined. Only in reality my "suitor" had courted me as a business partner, not a paramour.

She brushed off my objection with a *tsk*ing noise. "Does it matter? I needed something drastic, something that would tear him away from the chaos going on here. We didn't expect the town to go to hell in a handbasket as soon as you left."

"And thinking that after thirty years he had competition wasn't drastic enough?"

Marjorie heaved a sigh through the phone line. "He confessed he's been puzzled by your behavior for quite some time. He chalked it up to 'the change' and figured he could wait it out. Under the circumstances, I don't think he would have taken our original ploy seriously. At least a nervous breakdown is a legitimate reason for this lunatic belly button idea of yours. I only hope seeing you on television tonight doesn't give *him* a nervous breakdown."

I hadn't thought about that. In the week and a half since I arrived in New York, Earnest and I had spoken only once. He called from his office last Sunday after church. He sounded tired and flustered, but before we had said much more than hello to each other, the conversation was cut short. Louisa Schrumm, his martinet of a secretary who I swear never leaves the office except to go to Bible study Wednesday evenings and church on Sundays, broke into the call with yet another Ten Commandments emergency. "Mr. Mayor, you have less than five minutes to get over to the Grange Hall."

"I'm on my way." As soon as we heard the click signaling she had hung up the extension, he said, "I'm sorry, dear. I have to get to a meeting." In typical Earnest fashion, the town came first, last, and always.

"But we need to talk . . ."

"It'll have to wait. Enjoy your visit with Nori. Give her my love."

"Earnest, please . . ." He had no time for what was on my mind. All that mattered was the town. Ten Commandments. First. Last. Always.

"I'll call you later tonight. We'll talk then."

He never did call back. I hadn't heard from him since, and my injured pride prevented me from phoning him. I reminded myself that his devotion to his town duties was one of the reasons I had left in the first place. Nothing had changed, and nothing ever would if I caved in now.

But maybe it was time I shelved my pride if I wanted a marriage to come home to. Being a workaholic was one thing. Seeing your wife cast belly buttons on national television was something else entirely. As hurt and frustrated as I was, I couldn't spring that on Earnest without any warning. "I'd better call to prepare him."

Marjorie snorted. "Somehow I doubt anything you say will prepare him for seeing his wife drooling over Mel Gibson's naked body."

"He wasn't naked. Only a few inches of his belly were exposed. And I wasn't drooling. I was casting. It's art, Marjorie."

"Maybe in New York, but by tomorrow morning tongues in Ten Commandments are going to be wagging about the apple not falling far from the tree."

"What's that supposed to mean?"

"Think Cousin LeRoy and his topless drive-thru bar."

"Oh."

"Yeah, oh."

"Wait a minute. Technically, LeRoy isn't my cousin, though. He's Earnest's."

"Frankly, I don't think anyone in town is going to split that particular hair."

No, they wouldn't. While busy creating the new Connie, I was inadvertently destroying the old Earnest. With all his other problems, how could my ultraconservative husband view my appearance on Letterman as anything other than another nail in his political coffin? Especially considering the reaction I'd received from my normally supportive and liberal-minded friend.

Painting chicks and ducks on denim was one thing. Painting celebrity portraits on castings of their belly buttons was something else entirely. Especially when done in front of millions of people across the country.

And Hy envisioned signed limited-edition collector's items as well as mass-produced replicas fashioned into earrings, pins, magnets, plant pokes, buttons. All sorts of knickknacks and bric-a-brac adorned with my belly button castings. The possibilities, he assured me, were endless. And from the reception we had received so far among New York's retailing elite, I had to believe him.

"Tiffany's has already come aboard to sell high-end jewelry pieces fashioned from my castings," I told

Marjorie. "Tiffany's. On Fifth Avenue. You know? Where Audrey Hepburn had breakfast?"

Maybe that would sway her. If belly button castings were good enough for Tiffany's, how could Marjorie—or anyone else in Ten Commandments, for that matter—object?

She heaved a deep sigh into the phone. "Look, Connie, I'm sorry for sounding so critical. I think it's wonderful that you met Mel Gibson and David Letterman. Frankly, I'm envious. Hell, I'm green with envy! *I've* never met a celebrity, not even when Walter and I took that vacation to California a few years ago. But you've strayed from your task. We had a plan. You're in New York to get Nori and Eugene together, and well . . . for heaven's sake, why belly button castings?"

"Because they're unique."

"I'll say." I could almost see her rolling her eyes a thousand miles away. "Not that Tiffany's or anything else will matter after everyone in Ten Commandments sees you on television tonight."

Again, I had to agree with her. The self-righteous, holier-than-thou citizens of Ten Commandments would never get past the sight of their mayor's wife diddling with Mel Gibson's navel. I saw but one solution. "I don't suppose you could arrange a power outage for the entire town, could you?"

When the phone rang at half-past midnight, I knew Marjorie had failed me in her assignment as a saboteur. Not that she had any experience with electrical equipment, but how hard could it be to knock out a transformer? The woman had definitely let me down.

I had tried to reach Earnest for several hours after concluding my call with Marjorie, but no matter which phone I called—home, office, or cell—I connected with recorded messages instructing me to ring one of the other numbers. I had little choice but to leave a message on each. "Earnest, it's Connie. Please call me at Nori's as soon as you receive this. It's important."

An hour later my messages became a bit more desperate. "Earnest, I really need to speak with you before you tune into Letterman this evening. Please call me."

Half an hour before the show's scheduled air time, I really began to panic. "Earnest, don't you dare turn on that television until you call me!"

During the commercial preceding my appearance, I made one final, desperate plea. "Earnest, I love you. Please keep an open mind!"

"I couldn't get through to him, either," said Nori. "I tried earlier today." She reached over and patted my clenched hands.

I continued to grip the receiver of her cordless phone. We were sitting together on her lime-green and orange tweed Salvation Army sofa, awaiting my television debut. All the excitement of the taping—which *The Late Show* staff assured me went exceedingly well—had long since deserted me. I suppose it had flown off to Bora Bora to join my self-confidence.

After my sobering conversation with Marjorie and my inability to reach Earnest, I now worried that my selfish desire to be a "somebody" would irreparably damage both my husband and my marriage. On the other hand, I resented that certain people believed my life should be a win/lose scenario, with me always stuck on the losing end. Why, in order to secure my husband's standing in the community, did I have to stifle my own creative growth and sacrifice my happiness? I wasn't doing anything sinful or wrong. So why was I suddenly riddled with guilt? I had only wanted to expand my own limited horizons, but in doing so, I might have made the life of the man I love a heck of a lot more difficult. And just at a time when he could least deal with it.

I knew Earnest was up to his eyeballs in assorted town and family problems, but I also wondered why he hadn't called me after Marjorie dropped that bomb about my being on the verge of a nervous breakdown. She'd inferred that my recent behavior made no sense to him, but his current behavior made even less sense to me. So he booked a flight to New York. He still could have called.

And now he neither answered his phone nor returned my calls. Marjorie must have spilled the beans about my appearance on *The Late Show*, and he was too furious to speak with me. I loved Earnest dearly, but he could be one incredibly obstinate, close-minded man when it came to his image and standing in Ten Commandments. I turned to Nori. "Do you think your father will forgive me?"

She sighed. Then she wrapped her arm around my shoulders and squeezed. "Mom, I still don't understand this new you, but one thing I do know is that Dad loves you. And always will. No matter how foolish all this will probably appear to him or how embarrassed he may get over it."

I shrugged out of her embrace. "And that's supposed to comfort me? You certainly have a way with words."

Nori grabbed the remote and raised the volume on the set as the commercial ended. Alan Kalter announced Dave's next guest—me. As I watched myself walk onstage, a shudder raced from my toes to my scalp; my knuckles turned white from my stranglehold on the phone. I groaned. "I look so fat!"

"They say the camera adds ten pounds."

"Ten pounds, my great-granny Mathilda! Whoever *they* are, *they* lie." I jabbed my index finger in the direction of the television screen. "That camera's making me look thirty pounds overweight."

Nori chuckled. "Then you have nothing to worry about. No one back in Ten Commandments will recognize you. We can tell them it was *another* Connie Stedworth."

Heat surged up my neck and into my cheeks, but it wasn't a hot flash. "Actually, Dave and I had a bit of a discussion about Ten Commandments."

Nori merely rolled her eyes and shook her head. She said nothing more. Her attention was fixed on the television screen where, as I bent over Mel Gibson's exposed torso and molded plaster of paris into his navel, I babbled on to Dave about my hometown, my family, Hy, and our new business venture.

Earlier that afternoon I had cast and painted Dave's belly button since there wouldn't be time to produce a finished product during my appearance. However, Dave wanted a live casting demonstration. Originally, he'd tapped Paul Shaffer as my on-camera guinea pig. Then Mel offered, and there was no way the producers were going to pass on Mel.

As usual, I mixed far too much plaster.

Mel, who lay supine on Dave's desk, glanced at the plastic bucket in my hands. His mouth fell open. He reached down and inched his jeans a bit higher on his hips. "Um, exactly *which* body part did you say you were casting?"

Dave wiggled his eyebrows. "Relax, Mel. The FCC won't allow Connie to cast the family jewels on network television. That's why she did mine before the show." A suggestive slide of the trombone in the band accompanied a roar from the audience. I had laughed nervously as beet-red embarrassment wormed its way into every pore of my body. The heat of humiliation now returned as I relived the events via the television screen.

Beside me, my daughter lowered her head into her hands. "Oh, Mom!"

At least this time the excess plaster didn't wind up spattered over everyone. Considering my shaky nerves and even shakier hands, that in itself was a small miracle.

The show finally ended, and Nori clicked off the television. She turned to me, and we sat there staring at each other for a minute, neither saying anything.

"Well?" I finally asked.

She shrugged. "I'll admit, if you weren't my mother, it would have been funny."

That's when the phone rang. I stared at the receiver still clenched in my hands. I knew it was Earnest. Somehow I could tell by the angry tone of the ring.

Chapter Sixteen

Mom answered the phone midway through the first ring. "Earnest?" The dread that clouded her features and echoed in her voice segued first to puzzlement and then a frown of annoyance as she handed me the phone. "It's for you. That Mac person."

That Mac person? "He's my new boss, Mom."

"A boss who calls after midnight?"

"Excuse me." I rose from the couch and headed into the kitchen for some privacy. Mom did have a point, though. "Isn't it a bit late for a business call?" I asked, dispensing with any form of greeting once I closed the kitchen door.

"Your mother's a riot. She had Mel Gibson and Dave Letterman eating out of her hand."

I yawned. All I really wanted right now was a decent night's sleep, something I knew I wouldn't receive until the blanket-stealing Queen of Toss and Turn headed back to Ten Commandments. "And this declaration couldn't wait until tomorrow?"

"I really like her."

"Yeah, I like her, too. When I'm not contemplating matricide."

"Admit it. You thought the show was cool."

I shrugged, not that Mac could see the gesture. "Okay, I admit it, but you're not the one who's going to have to deal with the hellfire and brimstone fallout headed this way from Ten Commandments." I slumped against the pots and pans cabinet and leaned my elbows on the cracked Formica countertop. "By the way, the feeling isn't mutual."

"You don't like me?" He sounded stunned.

"*She* doesn't like you."

"Why not?" Hurt outmuscled stunned. "I'm a nice guy."

"Granted."

"Everyone likes me." Petulance steamrolled hurt out of the picture.

"Everyone but my mother. She views you as a threat to her plans."

Mac laughed. Good-bye, petulance; hello, relief. "That's absurd. She can't still think I'm going to steal her belly button idea."

"It's not that."

"Then what?"

"You're not Eugene."

"Who the hell is Eugene?"

"The man she's chosen to father her grandchildren."

"Oh, that makes so much more sense. Not to mention sounding a bit feudal."

"She doesn't see it that way."

"And how do you feel about this Eugene guy fathering your children?"

I snorted into the receiver. "Never going to happen. I'll join a convent first."

"That's a relief."

"Why?"

"Because I intend to father your mother's grandchildren."

I dropped the phone onto the counter. The dishes in the drainer rattled. But not as much as my nerves. One kiss and a dinner and he's making the leap to happily-ever-after? Hardly. Mac just had a warped sense of humor.

"Are you certain?" Gertie sighed. *"You have to admit, it was one dynamite kiss, and he enjoyed it as much as you did."*

Stay out of this. I hardly know the man.

I picked up the phone and took a deep breath before I addressed his audacious pronouncement. "A little presumptuous on your part, don't you think?"

But Mac was no longer on the line.

I disconnected the phone on my end. *He was joking,* I told Gertie.

"Whatever you say."

Of course he was. But why, after getting flattened by an unexpected tsunami, was I now drowning in a sea of disappointment?

"Because you've fallen for him."

Don't be ridiculous.

"Who, me? I'm not the one who went weak in the knees over one kiss."

Before I could answer her, the phone rang again. As before, I refrained from any pleasantries and jumped right into the conversation. "If that was an April Fool's joke, you're several weeks late."

"Excuse me?"

"Dad?"

My father's voice boomed through the phone. "Nori, what in the world is going on there? This morning Marjorie Draymore tried to convince me my wife is on the verge of a nervous breakdown. Your mother, the Rock of Gibraltar. Can you imagine such insanity? I couldn't get her to shut up until I promised to fly to New York. Between you and me, I think Marjorie's inhaled too much formaldehyde."

"Mom's not having a nervous breakdown," I assured him.

"I didn't think so, but then your mother leaves a

dozen of the strangest messages for me tonight. Some nonsense about calling her before watching television." He harrumphed. "As if I have time for television these days!"

"Then you didn't see Letterman?"

"I'm hardly in the mood for comedy right now."

"More flooding?"

"That's the least of my problems." His words came across more like a growl than a statement. "Ingrates. Each and every one of them. I'm glad your mother isn't here to see what's going on."

"What *is* going on, Dad? Where were you all day? Why don't you ever answer your phone anymore?"

He exhaled a sigh of part annoyance, part exhaustion. "Not now, Nori. I'm assuming your mother is asleep already. Tell her we'll be there late tomorrow."

"What!"

The phone went dead. For the second time that night I felt like a hit-and-run victim.

"He didn't want to speak to me?" I had returned to the living room and plopped down on the sofa next to Mom to tell her about Dad's brief call. Her face sagged. She looked as forlorn as the withering remains of her vegetable garden after the first major frost.

My guess was that she flew from Ten Commandments to Manhattan without so much as a second thought and was now consumed with remorse over her rebellious flight. Even if she did claim to be having the time of her life establishing herself as the Belly Button Queen. I knew my mother. Deep down inside all she really wanted was a bit more attention from Dad, but this was a hell of a way to achieve it.

"And one other thing," said Gertie.

What's that?

"For you and Eugene to give her grandbabies."

195

My stomach soured at the thought. *She's going to have to settle for batting five-hundred because there's no way in hell or Ten Commandments or anywhere in between that her second wish will ever come true.*

I placed my hand over the ones Mom was wringing in her lap. "Dad assumed you were asleep and hung up before I could tell him otherwise."

"Oh." She turned her watery eyes to me.

I had never seen my mother cry, but at any moment I expected the floodgates to open. The thought unsettled me. Mothers were supposed to comfort their children. There was something unnatural about the process working in reverse.

"How did he sound?"

"Tired. Harried. Somewhat annoyed."

She sighed, then sniffed. "Annoyed with me." A tear broke loose from its mooring and trickled down her cheek. "It's all my fault. I should have returned home as soon as I heard about the trouble. I'm such a selfish person. He'll never forgive me, and I don't blame him."

Poor Mom. I wasn't sure what else to do, so I wrapped my arm around her shoulders again and squeezed as I kissed her cheek. "Actually, he said he was glad you weren't there to see what was going on. Whatever that means. I suppose we'll hear all about it tomorrow."

Mom seemed in better spirits the next morning, or maybe she just masked her anxiety well. She hummed as she stood over the stove, frying bacon. I shuffled into the kitchen, desperate for a jolt of caffeine. Once again, her nocturnal triathlon of tossing, kicking and snoring had prevented me from getting more than a bare minimum of Zs. Each time I drifted off, she startled me awake with a fairly accurate imitation of a bull moose in heat, followed by a swift kick and a blanket-stealing shift of position. How long can a person go without sleep before losing her mind?

Or maybe I had already lost my mind, since yesterday I had allowed Mac to talk me into a live format. My intestines twisted into a rat's nest. The smell of the sizzling bacon didn't help.

Live radio. No cuts and retakes for bloopers. Just me. Alone in a radio booth. Live. What if I froze? What if I couldn't think of something to say? Or worse yet, what if I said something totally stupid?

"Like all the other hosts they have on talk radio? You'll fit right in."

If that's supposed to make me feel better, it doesn't.

"Hey, I try."

Try harder.

I reached for the coffee pot. "Good morning," I mumbled to my mother. I poured myself a cup of coffee and sank into one of the mismatched kitchen chairs, which were now not as mismatched as they were before Mom's arrival. Each had received a fresh coat of pale blue milk paint. Purple and yellow pansies now adorned the chair backs and seats. The table had gone through a similar transformation, with a garland of pansies trailing up each spindle leg and circling the perimeter of the tabletop. I had to admit, her handiwork did liven up my dreary little kitchen with its crazed linoleum, peeling paint, and cracked countertop.

When she first arrived, Mom had suggested we scrape and paint the walls as a weekend mother-daughter project, then she'd stencil a border around the perimeter, but that was before she hooked up with the King of Kitsch. Now she devoted most of her time to belly buttons. Her whirling dervish transformation of my kitchen table and chairs had taken place on a day when Hy was otherwise occupied.

"Good morning, dear." She placed a glass of orange

juice in front of me and kissed the top of my head. "Did you sleep well?"

"Hmm."

"*Liar.*"

Shut up, Gertie.

"Did your father say what time his flight was due in?" She simultaneously cracked two eggs into the frying pan, then placed two slices of bread in the toaster.

Ignoring the orange juice, I bent over my mug and inhaled the head-clearing, eye-opening aroma before taking a sip. "He said he'd be arriving late." But as I sipped my coffee and the drowsy cobwebs began to clear from my brain, I remembered that wasn't what he had said. He had said *we'll* be arriving late tomorrow. Had Marjorie insisted on coming with him?

"*Marjorie, the cohort who drove your mom to the airport? You really think your father would want her tagging along?*"

Maybe she's switched sides. After all, Mom admitted last night that Marjorie was appalled by the whole belly button casting shindig on Letterman. Knowing Marjorie, this had surprised both of us. I wondered if she had stayed up to watch the show and if so, why she hadn't called afterwards, considering she's Mom's oldest and closest friend.

"*Maybe she had a stroke when she saw your mother bent over Mel Gibson's naked body.*"

He wasn't naked. Besides, I could see half the town keeling over from the shock of seeing Mom getting intimate with Mel's belly button, but not Marjorie. She isn't your typical Ten Commandments-ite. Frankly, I wouldn't be surprised to learn that Marjorie had put Mom up to flying to New York in the first place.

If Marjorie saw the show last night, she had probably turned green with envy. Which was also probably why she jumped all over Mom when she found out what Mom was up to. She wasn't so appalled by the idea of belly button castings as she was of Mom having so much fun without her. Which was also probably why she was jetting east with my father. Marjorie wanted in on the action.

Mom placed the platter of eggs, bacon, and buttered toast in front of me. "Jam?"

I shook my head. "No thanks. You're not eating?"

"I already ate, sleepyhead. I'm going to shower while you have your breakfast.

As soon as I heard the water running in the shower, I scraped the bacon, eggs, and toast into the trash and covered the evidence with the empty juice container and some crumpled newspaper. Mom's version of a hearty breakfast—more fat than I normally ate in a month—was difficult to stomach on a good day. And considering the day looming in front of me—live radio in the morning, my dad and Marjorie this evening— today stood little chance of being labeled "good."

Ninety minutes later I stood outside the radio control booth, my knees shaking. "I'm going to make a complete fool of myself," I told Mac.

"No, you're not. I have total faith in you."

"You and how many other fools?"

He laughed. "See what I mean? Even when you're falling apart, you've got a snappy retort on your lips."

"Reflex action. Abject fear triggers my sarcastic side." Not to mention what it was doing to my stomach. I felt like my innards had been sliced and diced by a set of Ginsu knives. And that was without the benefit of Mom's grease-bathed bacon and eggs.

I glanced at the clock and took a deep breath, releasing it in a rush. "I guess it's now or never." Given my druthers, I'd choose never, but I had already committed myself to this lunacy, thanks to my inability to say no to Mac.

There ought to be a law against charming, sexy bosses. Too late I realized I was a pushover for Mac's hooded bedroom eyes and killer smile. With one look he unleashed a massive dose of latent sex appeal, and my common sense headed south. As far south as Antarctica. And the worst part about it? The man seemed totally unaware of his power.

A moment later I found myself seated in front of a microphone. Across from me, one of the ranting jocks—an ex-football player with a shaved head, tattooed biceps, and a neck as thick as one of my thighs—was finishing his segment. He glanced over at me, his mouth contorting into a sneer, and immediately segued into what sounded like a rehearsed speech. "You've heard her tirades; now hear her live. Stick around, guys—if you dare. Next up: The Queen of Mean herself, the Lorena Bobbitt of the airwaves. Mess with her at your own risk, and don't you dare leave the toilet seat up 'cause that ballbusting Gertie's about to get even. But first, these messages from our sponsors."

He flashed a less-than-friendly smile at me as a commercial for the Stanley Cup playoffs played in the background. "They're all yours, babe."

I responded with a glare. *Lorena Bobbitt? Ballbusting?* "Looks like I hit a nerve. You guys can dish it out, but you can't take it, can you?"

"I don't go around slamming women. I talk sports on my show. We all do. Mac should have his head examined for bringing you in. You're going to drive our listeners away in droves."

I hoped his sentiments weren't shared by the other program hosts. The various people I had met at the station had welcomed me warmly, but I had only come into contact with management and ancillary staff up until now, not the jocks.

"Don't let him rattle you," said Gertie.

No way. Evidently, this man wanted to see me die a quick but torturous on-air death. I wasn't about to give him the pleasure. My pride and competitive nature—not to mention my Iowan stubbornness and growing anger over his chauvinistic attitude—stomped all traces of previous nervousness into oblivion. I returned his sneer with a condescending smile. "I see. That explains why both market share and revenues are up since I signed on."

"A fluke that won't last. You're a two-bit trick that'll grow old and tiresome before the end of next week." With those parting words, he stormed out of the booth, slamming the door behind him.

"Asshole."

You said it, Gertie. His patronizing manner reminded me of Dave. The Dave I remembered after I had shed those rose-colored glasses. That in itself was enough to fortify my resolve. No way would I give that jock jerk the satisfaction of seeing me fail. Gertie was going to get even, all right. And by the time we were through, every jock at this station would owe his paycheck to us.

I glanced into the control room. On the other side of the glass booth the engineer and Mac both gave me a double thumbs-up. The last of the commercials ended. A fanfare of trumpets and drums heralded the pre-recorded intro to my new show, *Gertie Gets Even.* The ON THE AIR sign lit up. I was live and alone and chomping for chauvinistic bear.

THE TAO OF GERTIE
LESSON NUMBER EIGHT: CLEAN IS NOT A
FOUR-LETTER WORD!

Few things divide the sexes more than the concept of clean. Far too many men can't seem to grasp the importance of a filth-free living space. Most women

aren't "neat freaks" as men like to label us. We don't
want to eat off your floors. We just prefer not to stick
to them after we've passed out from the reek of
mildewed towels, outdated milk, and the dog you for-
got to walk. Therefore, in the interest of my fellow
double-X chromosomers and our acute olfactory
glands, all male listeners please repeat after me: People
live in houses; animals live in barns.

Got it?

Barn floors, for those of you who have never ventured west of the Hudson River, are covered with straw
to absorb the waste products of their inhabitants—
cows, goats, horses, pigs, jackasses, and various other
assorted livestock. Living room, kitchen, bathroom, and
bedroom floors are covered with hardwood, linoleum,
tile, or carpet, products that are not meant to absorb potato chips, empty beer cans, decomposing pizza boxes,
ratty underwear, or any other waste products spilled,
dropped, or discarded by the resident male biped.

In other words, gentlemen, if you want your girlfriend to step over your threshold for a night of pas-
sion instead of turning up her nose and running for
the nearest subway stop, you need to follow a few simple rules. There are only six, but if memorization is
not your strong suit, consider having them tattooed
on your arm for easy reference. It sure would beat that
snarling rattlesnake curling around your bicep.

Rule One: If you use it, put it away. Trust me. No
woman wants to enter your bathroom and discover
that container of jock-itch powder sitting on the sink.

Rule Two: If you wear it, hang it up or toss it into the
hamper. You don't want an obstacle course between the
entrance to your apartment and your bed, do you? Besides, if your date trips over those exercise togs that
have been lying in a heap on the floor for three weeks,
forget about any mattress gymnastics that night. In-

stead of kissing her good night, you may find yourself kissing your bank account good-bye when she takes you to court over her injuries.

Rule Three: If you drop it, pick it up. See Rule Two.

Rule Four: If you open it, close it. Stale food is for pigeons, squirrels, and assorted vermin no woman wants to discover lurking in your cabinets and crawling across your counters. Lids were invented for a reason. If a chimp can be trained to use them properly, so can you.

Rule Five: If you dirty it, clean it. With soap, detergent, bleach or disinfectant. This rule applies equally to dishes, glasses, utensils, cooking implements, sinks, bathtubs, stoves, countertops, floors, clothing, and every square inch of your body—not only the areas that show. Women want to be turned on by you, not turned off by that disgusting ring around your bathtub or the equally disgusting one around your neck.

Rule Six: If you wear it out, toss it out. Bikini briefs may be sexy, but not if they're dingy and ripped. And for God's sake, lose that ten-year-old stretched-out, faded, and stained Nirvana T-shirt. Even the Salvation Army would refuse it as a donation.

Still want to live like a slob? No one's stopping you, but when your first date with the cute chick in the accounting department is also your last date with her, make a quick inspection of both your apartment and yourself. Chances are you struck out because you're still living like a child, except now you don't have Mommy to pick up after you.

When I finished Gertie's Rant-of-the-Day, I announced that the remainder of the program, after the commercial break, would be devoted to our new "Ask Gertie" segment. Callers could query Gertie on personal situations related to today's "Tao" segment. "And if I don't have an answer for you, we'll open the lines to other callers for their suggestions."

The first commercial kicked in. I leaned back in my chair and heaved a deep sigh. The hard part was yet to come, dealing with the listener call-ins. What if they were all jerks with attitude like the guy who hosted the show before me? I needed a megadose of Gertie Gumption. Now.

"Glad to know I'm finally getting the respect I deserve."

Just don't disappear, I begged her.

"So I suppose I'd better hire a cleaning service before I invite you over, huh?"

I swung around to find Mac slouching in the doorway. "Please don't tell me I just described your apartment."

He cocked his head and thought for a moment. "The gym clothes have only been on the floor since the day before yesterday, and I don't have a dog."

"How sticky are the floors?"

He offered me one of his Sylvester grins. "I refuse to answer under the grounds that it may incriminate me."

I countered with a smile of understanding. "Don't call me; I'll call you."

The only guy I ever dated who kept a spotless apartment was Dave. And that was only because he employed a Russian immigrant who came in three times a week. She even kept his refrigerator and pantry stocked so he didn't have to bother making a weekly trip to the Food Emporium.

Dave didn't believe in wasting time doing anything he could hire others to do for him. At first I saw nothing wrong with this perspective. Who wouldn't want someone else to deal with life's daily drudgeries? In hindsight, I now found Dave's attitudes arrogant and condescending, especially the derogatory way he spoke of his housekeeper.

"Another side effect of the rose-colored glasses," suggested Gertie.

True. When it came to Dave, I'd seen what I wanted to see.

"Until you had seen too much."

Thanks, Gertie. Not a reminder I needed at the moment. I shook the Jacuzzi image from my brain.

"Ready?" asked Mac.

Hardly, but I no longer had time to dwell on my past blindness. The phone lines were lit up like Rockefeller Center at Christmas. And every one of those strangers on the other end sought Gertie's advice. Fools. I couldn't solve my own problems. How was I supposed to deal with theirs?

I inhaled a deep breath and nodded, albeit feebly and not very honestly. "I guess."

Mac gave me a thumbs-up and stepped back into the control booth.

The final commercial ended. The engineer pointed his finger at me, and it was sink-or-swim time. Too bad I'd never advanced much beyond a frantic doggie paddle, living in landlocked Iowa.

I gulped back my panic, took a final deep breath, and plowed ahead. "Welcome back. You're listening to WBAT-Big Apple Talk Radio. I'm Gertie, and this is "Gertie Gets Even." Go ahead, caller. You're on the air."

"Hiya, Gertie."

Something about the woman's Brooklyn accent sounded frighteningly familiar, but I forced myself to continue. "How can I help you?"

"Well, y'see, I've got this boyfriend. He's real to-die-for. Hollywood looks *and* he's a doctor. But not the kind that's gonna be out at all hours on emergencies. Office hours only."

"Why is that?" As if I had to ask.

"He's a skin doc. Y'know? A dermatologist. Deals mostly with acne."

I wondered if Suz could recognize my voice as easily as I recognized hers. And if so, would she out me on the show? I grabbed a tissue from a nearby box and draped it over the mic to muffle my voice. "The topic today is men who live like pigs." Which certainly didn't include Dave. He might fit the swine category for other reasons, but a lack of cleanliness wasn't one of them.

She puffed out a sigh of annoyance. "Yeah, I know. I'm getting to that."

"So?"

"Y'see, he's got this Russian chick, Svetlana, who comes in and cleans for him. She sure doesn't look like any housekeeper I've ever seen."

"In what way?"

"She's every woman's worst nightmare. A five-foot-six size two with double-D boobs and blonde hair that doesn't quit till it reaches her ass."

I'd never met Svetlana, but Dave had told me she was a sixty-two-year-old, roly-poly grandmother. "Just because she looks like a movie star doesn't mean she's not a cleaning lady." Even I didn't believe that lame excuse, so how could I expect Suz or my listeners to swallow it?

"I found a leopard thong between the sheets the other day, and it's definitely not mine. He's banging her, all right. No doubt about it."

"Did you confront him?"

"I waved the thong in front of them without saying a word. They both turned scarlet."

"Sounds pretty damning to me."

"Right. So I'm thinking maybe I should offer to clean his apartment."

"And?"

"And then he'd have to fire her. End of problem."

Was she really that naïve? Worldly Suz? It was hard to believe. And a bit gratifying. "Let me get this straight. You believe if you remove the temptation, he'll remain faithful to you?"

"Of course he will."

"Not likely. That thong might belong to Svetlana, but your boyfriend's the leopard. As the saying goes, leopards don't change their spots. Not to mention that other saying: Once a cheat, always a cheat." And what goes around, comes around. Suz got what she deserved. I smiled to myself as I stabbed at the button, ending the call. "Next caller. Go ahead. You're on the air."

Chapter Seventeen

"Great job," said Mac as I stepped from the booth. "I knew you'd be terrific at this once you got into it."

I half expected him to wrap me in his arms and bestow another one of those mind-numbing, toe-tingling, turn-my-life-inside-out-and-upside-down kisses. Disappointment overwhelmed me when all I received was one of his classic killer smiles and a pat on the shoulder, even though we weren't alone and even though I knew getting involved with the boss was a really bad idea.

Still . . .

No one had ever shown such faith in my untested abilities before. My parents assumed I'd flounder and fail in New York. Not only did they expect me to tuck tail and come running home, they looked forward to it, eager for that time when I'd see the foolhardiness of my rebellion and decide to get on with the life they wanted me to lead: Ten Commandments schoolteacher and wife of Eugene Draymore.

Although with Mom's new entrepreneurial spirit, I had to wonder if she still felt that way. At least about the teaching. Nothing could change her mind about Eugene. However, having broadened her own horizons and wowed them on Letterman, she might actually now understand why I wanted to choose my own career path.

Not that she knew the direction that path had recently taken. By committing a few deliberate sins of omission, I had led her to believe I was essentially doing the same type of work at WBAT as I had performed at DataScroungers—research. Best she continued to believe that, too. Even in her newly liberated persona as Belly Button Artist to the Stars, Mom wasn't ready for Gertie.

To my surprise—and delight—I discovered Reese and Gabe waiting for me in my office. Gabe slouched against the filing cabinet. One hand shoved into the pocket of his khaki cargo pants, his nose hidden behind an open file folder, he read aloud one of my recent "Tao" segments. Reese, simultaneously giggling and rolling her eyes over his Shakespearean theatrics, lounged in my chair with her Manolos propped on what had been, when I left, a fairly neat stack of papers. I didn't care. It was good to see them. "How'd you two make it past the one-woman combination FBI-CIA-ATF at the front desk?"

Gabe stopped reciting and raised his head. "You mean Monica? She's my cousin."

Too bad I hadn't dragged Gabe with me the day I came in search of Mac and my computer.

"So, this is mere coincidence?"

"Nah." Gabe waved his hand, crossed the miniscule floor space separating the filing cabinet from the entryway, and planted a kiss on my cheek. "I had no idea Monica worked here until we walked in."

"Why didn't you tell us?" asked Reese, swinging her feet to the ground and jumping up to embrace me. "This is wild! Who'd have guessed that Honora Stedworth of Ten Commandments, Iowa, is Getting-Even Gertie?"

But she and Gabe had. "How'd you find out?"

"Elementary, dear Stedworth," said Gabe, tapping his forehead with the file folder. "We recognized your voice, of course."

Of course. "Did you hear the show that just aired?"

They both nodded.

"Recognize my first caller?"

Another double nod from the dynamic detective duo.

"Think she recognized my voice?"

Reese snorted. "Bimbo Bambi? She's too wrapped up in herself to recognize her own mother."

I hated to admit Reese could be right about Suz. I had once considered Suz my best friend. Shows you what an excellent judge of character I am. However, even I had recognized Suz's obsession with herself. Most women make a trip to the ladies' room to touch up their makeup. A little powder on a shiny nose or forehead. A fresh swipe of lipstick. Suz scrubbed her face clean and applied a new coat with each visit.

I often wondered if her obsession with perfection was her way of trying to camouflage her Brooklyn roots. Unfortunately, even a gallon of Georgette Klinger's premium foundation couldn't mask her nasal Brooklynese. Suz might look East Hamptons but her voice and mannerisms shrieked Prospect Park.

"No more talk of backstabbing bitches," said Gabe. "Sounds like she's getting hers in spades, and it couldn't happen to a more deserving tramp. Grab your bag, Nori. We're taking you to lunch."

Lunch? I glanced at my watch. It was barely past breakfast. "A little early, isn't it?"

"Never too early to start partying," said Gabe. "Besides, we have lots to celebrate. We need to get a head start."

Since my official duties at the station ended with my completion of that day's show, I was free to come and go as I pleased—as long as I had tomorrow's rant prepared before going on the air. I shrugged. Why not take off for a few hours? Gabe, Reese, and I had lots of catching up to do. Wait until they heard the latest about Mom. Or had they, too, seen last night's edition of *The Late Show*?

"There's one thing I've been dying to know," said Gabe as he waved to Monica, then stabbed the down arrow for the elevator.

I indicated the station with a wide sweep of my arm. "How I wound up here?"

Reese rolled her eyes and smirked. "Like we couldn't figure that one out ourselves."

"What do you mean?"

"Don't start playing Miss Innocence, girl. I want all the details about you and Mac." She elbowed me in the ribs, triggering a surge of heat that beelined from my toes to my cheeks. "And I mean *all.*" She underlined her last word with a second rib jab.

"Okay, that, too," said Gabe. "But first, where in the world did your mother come up with that belly button idea of hers?"

No need to wonder about last night any longer, but Gabe's question barely registered. I was more focused on Reese's query. "There's nothing going on between me and Mac."

"What about that kiss?"

All right, besides a kiss. But that was between Mac and me. No one else. Except, apparently, Gertie, since I couldn't keep the die-hard buttinsky from sticking her nose in my business.

Reese stared at me with one of her sure-Nori-tell-me-another-one-I-won't-believe looks. I broke eye contact with her and turned to Gabe. "The history of belly button casting takes a bit of explanation."

His eyes grew wide with anticipation, and he rubbed his hands together as if a Renaissance banquet had been spread out before him. "I'm all ears." I loved this childlike quality of his. It took so little to amuse him.

I glanced over at Reese as the elevator pinged its arrival. She tendered another eye roll to the heavens before stepping in.

"So?" Gabe apparently had no patience to wait until we had arrived at the restaurant to hear my story. "Spill the beans."

I laughed. "Funny you should mention beans because that's how it all started."

He raised one eyebrow.

Reese folded her arms across her chest, crossed her ankles, and slouched against the elevator's back wall. Her body language proclaimed she couldn't care less about belly button portraits. She wanted me to get to the good stuff—the dirt on my budding romance with Mac.

The elevator ground to a halt at the lobby. As I stepped out, I began my tale. "Once upon a time there was a very obstinate, defiant little girl who absolutely refused to eat certain foods her mother insisted she eat."

"Why?" asked Gabe.

"Because she didn't like them."

"No, why did her mother insist she eat them?"

"Because they were good for her. Anyway, chief among these were liver, brussels sprouts, and lima beans, but this particular tale is about lima beans."

"Oh for the love of . . ." Reese threw her arms up in the air, then onto her hips. "What the hell do lima beans have to do with belly buttons? Get to the sex. Have you slept with Mac yet or not?"

"*Shh!*" I hazarded a quick survey of the lobby, hoping no one had heard her. No heads turned in our direction. No one had paused, ears perked, awaiting juicy gossip. I heaved a sigh of relief and glared at Reese before continuing to walk toward the door. "Not. And I'm not going to. He's my boss."

"So what? He's a hunk who has the hots for you."

I stopped short and spun around to confront her. "How do you know?"

Reese slapped her hand against her forehead. "Please tell me you're joking. Jeez, Nori, anyone with only half a functioning brain cell can figure that one out."

"And that the feeling is mutual," added Gabe with a smirk and a wink.

That surge of heat returned to my cheeks. "It's that obvious?"

Gabe and Reese sandwiched me in a sideways hug as we left the building and headed down the street. "But there is a cure for what ails this patient," said Gabe. He wiggled his eyebrows and flicked an imaginary cigar in homage to Groucho Marx.

"What's that?"

"You know what they say about falling off a horse?"

"I am not sleeping with my boss!" And to emphasize my pronouncement, I changed the subject back to the history of belly button portraiture, my words falling from my mouth in double-time. "Once upon a time there was a very obstinate, defiant little girl who absolutely refused to eat her lima beans."

Reese huffed a sigh of resignation. Gabe offered Reese a shrug, then cocked his head in my direction as we entered Curds 'n Whey, a small café two doors down from the station.

After settling into seats at a corner table, we placed our beverage orders, a Bloody Mary for Gabe and mimosas for Reese and me. Then I continued. "The little girl's mother insisted she eat those lima beans, but the little girl was extremely ingenious. She found countless ways to trick her mother into thinking she had eaten the lima beans when she had actually hidden them in her pockets, stuffed them into her socks, or stuck them down her shirt."

"And her mother never caught on?" asked Gabe.

"The little girl wasn't allowed to leave the table until she had finished the lima beans, so she was able to conceal them covertly while her mother washed the dishes."

"So what happened?" asked Gabe.

"Yes, please don't keep us on the edge of our seats here," said Reese as she proceeded to push back her cuticles.

"One day the little girl left the dinner table with her shorts pockets stuffed with lima beans. What she had forgotten was that one of the pockets contained a fairly good-sized hole. As she walked across the kitchen floor, she deposited a trail of lima beans in her wake. Her mother, discovering the evidence, called to her. When the little girl pivoted to return to the kitchen, she slipped on the lima beans and wound up breaking her leg."

"Ouch!" Gabe winced.

"And the correlation between broken legs and belly buttons?" asked Reese, accepting her drink from the waitress who had arrived at our table.

The waitress shot Reese an odd look as she set the remaining drinks on the table in front of Gabe and me. I suppose it isn't every day she hears *broken legs* and *belly buttons* mentioned in the same sentence, but she shrugged off her curiosity when none of us deigned to supply her with an explanation. Grabbing a pad from her apron pocket and a pencil stub from behind her left ear, she asked, "Ready to order?"

We decided on omelettes, Western for Gabe, Spanish for Reese, and mushroom for me. After the waitress jotted down our orders and headed for the kitchen, Gabe raised his glass. "To us," he toasted.

"Exactly what are we celebrating?" I asked.

They both grinned. "You're not the only one who

landed a job. Reese and I lucked out with a temp agency yesterday. I'm taking over next week for an office grunt at ABC who was called up for the Reserves."

"And as soon as I get back from St. Croix next month, I'm stepping in for an editorial assistant at Primedia who's going out on maternity leave," said Reese.

"So no Dumpster scrounging?"

She glanced over at Gabe before answering, but he seemed lost in thought as he munched on a stalk of celery and stared out the window. "I *was* kidding about that, you know."

"Sure you were," he said, returning his attention to us. He lifted his glass and clinked it against ours. "As the Bard of Avon so aptly put it, 'All's well that ends well.' Or so they tell me." He scowled into his drink before polishing off the Bloody Mary in one long swig, then held up his empty glass, signaling the waitress for another.

Reese reached over and patted his hand. They exchanged a knowing glance before he expelled a heavy sigh.

"What aren't you telling me?" I asked.

Gabe shook his head and stared into his drink. "Life will go on," he muttered.

"Damn right it will," said Reese, wrapping her arm around his shoulders and giving him a good hard squeeze. "Besides, you can do better than some affected SoHo gallery owner who doesn't know art from rat pickings." She turned to me. "Gabe and Abe broke up."

"Oh, Gabe!" I reached across the table, but he waved my hand off.

"The Big Guy giveth, and the Big Guy taketh away. Yin yang and all that crap." The waitress arrived with his second drink, and he took a gulp before continuing. "For every celebration there must be an anti-celebration to keep the universe in balance, right?"

"Is that the way life works?"

"Seems so. Anyway, Abe is history. Kaput. Nothing more than a month-long one night stand." He shrugged and forced a smile. "Now, back to that poor little girl with the broken leg, if you don't mind."

I glanced over at Reese. She nodded. If Gabe wanted to hear the history of belly button casting, then that's what he'd get. I continued my story. "The little girl wound up spending six weeks of a very hot summer in a full leg cast. No swimming. No bike riding. No roller skating. She whined and complained constantly.

"Her mother, being a creative sort and also feeling a bit guilty over forcing her daughter to eat the lima beans that caused the broken leg, began thinking up ideas to amuse the child. One day she mixed up a batch of plaster so the little girl could make a hand print. The little girl thought that was a stupid idea. Kindergartners made plaster handprints, and she was in second grade.

"The mother was losing what little patience she had left at that point. She had a bucket of fresh plaster, a pouting seven-year-old, and a garden full of ripening produce that needed canning. That's when she lost it. She told the little girl to lie down and pull up her T-shirt. Then she plopped a dollop of plaster into her belly button and told her not to move. The child was too stunned to disobey.

"After the plaster hardened, the mother took a look at it and realized it resembled a face. The next day she painted the child's portrait on the casting."

I fiddled with the stem of my mimosa glass, twirling it between my fingers. "My father was horrified when he discovered what she had done."

"Why?" asked Reese. She had finally taken a mild interest in my story.

I shrugged. "Dad always worries. It's that image thing he's so obsessed with."

"As in, what would the good people of Ten Commandments think?"

"Exactly. So Mom tossed the casting into the trash, and we both promised not to mention a word of it to anyone. But I retrieved the belly button portrait and kept it all these years. She was showing Hy some of her handiwork in my apartment when he noticed the casting sitting in a flower pot on my bedroom window sill."

I leaned back in my chair and took a long sip of my drink. "And that, my friends, is how the hottest must-have to hit New York in decades came about."

"Damn, I wish I'd thought of that," said Gabe, smacking his palm onto the table. "Belly button castings!" He nudged Reese. "Sure beats photos of Dumpsters, huh?"

She scowled at him. "I don't think either of us should ever mention Dumpsters again."

"Deal."

"Good. Now that your curiosity has been satisfied, can we please get to sex?"

"I hate to disappoint you, my dear, but you're just not my type."

Reese punched him in the shoulder. "Not you, dimwit. Nori."

Gabe studied me for a moment. "Sorry, she's not my type, either."

Reese growled.

Chapter Eighteen

Throughout the day, Hy made certain that I had little time to dwell on Earnest's impending arrival. He had scheduled back-to-back meetings with an advertising agency on Madison Avenue and what he referred to as a high-end *chatke* manufacturer, headquartered in Brooklyn.

"*Chatkes?*" I asked as our cab inched along in bumper-to-bumper traffic on the Manhattan Bridge. Nori had purchased several *chatkes* from the corner deli one evening to go along with the pot roast and carrots I cooked for dinner. She served them topped with applesauce. Tasty but . . . "What do potato pancakes have to do with belly button castings?"

"Not latkes," said Hy. "*Chatkes*. It's a Yiddish term for knickknacks and collectibles."

"Oh."

He chuckled. "Not a word used much back home?"

Not that I could remember. "The only time you hear Yiddish spoken in Ten Commandments," I told him, "is when someone is watching an old Barbra Streisand movie or *Seinfeld* reruns."

Barbra I like. When she sings. Her movies I can take or leave, so mostly I leave them. As for *Seinfeld*, I never could see the humor in a show where a group of obnoxious, self-absorbed, boring people sit around talking about piddling nonsense. So, no, I suppose I'd never heard *chatke* used in Ten Commandments.

Rain pelted the cab in an angry staccato. We crept along as sluggishly as corn grows during a drought, but the taxi meter continued to spin as swiftly as a tornado. "I could drive to Sioux City and back in the time it's taking us to get across this bridge."

Hy raised an eyebrow.

"Okay, so I tend to exaggerate. Maybe just there, not there and back."

Hy glanced at his watch and grimaced. "I don't doubt it. We'd make better time if we walked."

I stared out the window. Fifteen minutes had passed since the cab pulled onto the access road to the bridge, and we were still less than halfway between Manhattan and Brooklyn. "You go ahead," I told him. "I'm not up for a hike. Not in these shoes." In an effort to impress the executives at the ad agency and not come across looking like a country rube, I had worn one of my new outfits and forced my feet into those killer shoes Loretta-the-Personal-Shopper had talked me into buying. Not a good choice on the best of days but a disastrous selection for a trek along a rain-drenched bridge.

He drummed his fingers on his thigh. "We have time. I don't want to be late for our next appointment, though."

"I didn't realize we had another after this."

He turned to me and grinned. "I was keeping that one a surprise."

Hy was like a kid with a fistful of dollars let loose in a candy shop. I loved his exuberance, the way he grabbed onto an idea and ran with it. The way he had seen the potential of my crafts and encouraged my endeavors. The optimist in me couldn't wait for Earnest to meet Hy and hoped some of his enthusiasm for my work would rub off on my stodgy husband. The realist in me knew otherwise. Earnest would hate Hyman Perth.

Just like Nori. I still couldn't understand why my daughter thought Hy was a grouch at best and a con man at worst. I shuddered when those narrow-minded Stedworth genes she inherited from Earnest's side of the family kicked in and reared their ugly heads. Nori might think she had left Ten Commandments behind, but she brought much of its baggage along with her to New York. Her suspicions concerning Hy were but one manifestation of those latent genes. Then there was her lack of enthusiasm over my budding career. She had no idea how much that hurt me.

No matter what she professed to the contrary, my daughter was firmly entrenched in the Ten Command-ments mentality that a mother's duties consisted of the Three C's—cooking, cleaning, and carpooling—not gallivanting around Manhattan in an attempt to satisfy her muse. I'm certain she blamed that on Hy, as well. Although she never came right out and said it, in her mind mothers weren't supposed to have muses. Or needs. Or desires.

Did she expect me to spend the next thirty years cro-cheting afghans and canning pickled beets? I had sac-rificed myself on the alter of June Cleaver long enough. The twenty-first century had arrived, and I was tired of living entrenched in the nineteen-fifties.

I bit my tongue as much as possible and chalked her narrow-minded attitudes up to her youth. Once she and Eugene had a few babies, she'd understand my need to be more than only a wife and mother. She may have inherited those censuring Stedworth genes from Earnest, but she had also inherited my Abernathy genes and was more like her mother than she realized. My daughter had a great deal to learn about life, but I had no doubt she'd wind up more like me than she could possibly realize at this point in time.

Especially once she married Eugene. As much as I liked the boy and wanted this union for my daughter, I saw too much of his father in him and not enough of Marjorie. What was it about Ten Commandments men? Were their only role models Ward Cleaver, Larry Flynt, and Robert Vesco? Were their choices limited to stalwart fifties family men like Earnest, sex entrepreneurs à la cousin LeRoy, or embezzlers like Uncle Ezra? Eugene needed his horizons broadened. Marjorie and I would have to work on him. After the wedding.

"Don't frown," said Hy. "I'll have you back in plenty of time before your husband arrives."

He startled me out of my introspection. "What? Oh, sorry. I was thinking of something else."

"Something that's worrying you?"

I offered him a smile and shook my head. "Ever hear the expression, 'Youth is wasted on the young'?"

"Your daughter?"

"Partly . . . she's so inflexible at times."

"She's very young, Connie. She needs time to grow up and mature."

"I know."

He reached across the seat and patted my hand. "I know she doesn't like me, but I admire her feistiness. And her protectiveness of you. She has your best interests at heart, even though her concerns are misplaced."

Quite a perceptive analysis coming from a man who had fathered no children and who had known my daughter and me for such a brief period of time. If only Earnest were capable of such understanding—of both his daughter *and* his wife. But Earnest was as flexible in his thinking as a drought-stricken stalk of corn. Not that corn stalks think, but like the brittle stalk, Earnest never bends or yields to the winds of change. He snaps. Only he does it silently. My husband never raises his voice.

Apprehension over my husband's reaction to my newfound career resurfaced and knit my intestines into a tangle of stomach-cramping knots. Would Earnest view my activities as selfish and damaging to his reputation? Undoubtedly. I loved the man with all my heart, but broad-minded he wasn't. Especially when it came to his family.

Earnest built his life and career around the status quo. He thrived on the comfort of familiarity and decried change. He still hadn't come to terms with Nori rebelling and moving to New York, and now he had to contend with familial troubles back home. Lord knew how he had dealt with all of that. Not well, I imagined. Now he'd have to contend with my new life. Would so much change be more than my stuck-in-his-ways husband could handle? Was I risking sacrificing my husband and marriage on the altar of self-fulfillment?

I closed my eyes and said a silent prayer, begging God to bestow on Earnest an extra helping of patience along with a large dollop of understanding. A dash of humor wouldn't hurt, either, I added as a last-minute plea. But my prayer did nothing to calm my own nerves.

By the time the cab pulled into a no parking-no stopping-no standing spot across the street from Goldfarb Novelties, I had worked myself up into a tizzy of guilt.

Mr. Goldfarb's company occupied the second floor of a warehouse in DUMBO. Why a city would name a section after a flying elephant was beyond my comprehension, but Hy said it was an acronym. Something about the area down under the Manhattan Bridge. New York, it turns out, is a city of acronyms: SoHo,

NoHo, NoLIta, Tribeca. I had no idea what they stood for, but I had a sneaking suspicion it was all some sort of secret code employed to confuse and rattle hapless tourists.

According to Hy, DUMBO was the next Tribeca, an area once rundown but growing trendier and more desirable by the minute. As we dodged puddles and traffic from where the cab dropped us off to the building's entrance, I glanced around. Structures that looked like bombed-out shells, victims of vandalism and neglect, stood side-by-side with their pristinely restored counterparts. Construction trucks filled every available parking space, the overflow double- and triple-parked along the street. Beefy-armed men in jeans and T-shirts darted back and forth, toting materials and tools.

We dodged workmen to enter one of the under-construction buildings, making our way up a set of stairs still in desperate need of renovation. Solomon Goldfarb, a rotund whirlwind of a man with an unlit cigar stub shoved between his lips, greeted us at the top of the staircase. "Mind the mess," he said, pointing to a chaotic pile of lumber and hardware as he ushered us into his showroom.

"*Oy vey!* Some way to run a company, eh? But whatcha gonna do? Shut down for six months while these garbanzo beans take their sweet time hammering and painting me out of business?" Mr. Goldfarb directed this comment to Hy.

Then, without taking a breath he switched gears and focused his attention on me. "Connie Stedworth!" He grabbed my hand with both of his and gave it a firm shake. "I finally get to meet the Belly Button Queen. My good friend Hyman here told me all about you. What a million-dollar idea you came up with, little lady. Your talent. My know-how. Hy's marketing genius. We're gonna make a fortune. We can't lose." He tugged on my hand, which was still held firmly between his. "C'mere. Let me show you what I got in mind."

He led us into his private office and closed the door. "Over here." He snatched the cigar from the side of his mouth and used it as a pointer to indicate a sheet-draped table in the corner on the room. Stepping to one side of the table, he grabbed a corner of the white fabric, and with a grand flourish, whisked the covering away. *"Voila!"*

I stared at the objects on the table, my jaw hanging open. "Oh, my."

"Pretty damn impressive, huh?" He stood with the sheet draped over his shoulder, his arms crossed over his puffed-out chest. His grin spanned the full width of his face.

I leaned over the table to better examine the samples, each standing on a pedestal of varying heights. Hy had provided Mr. Goldfarb with several original celebrity belly button castings. Each celebrity had agreed to allow the use of his image, with the royalties going to designated charities. From the original castings, Mr. Goldfarb had fashioned molds to create replicas looking so much like the originals that even I couldn't tell the difference. And he had accomplished this amazing feat in only a few days.

But it didn't end there. He had taken the reproduced castings and used them in the most ingenious ways. I especially liked what he had done with the casting I'd made of Steve Martin's belly button. The actor and comedian was currently starring in a play on Broadway and was one of the first celebrities Hy had contacted. Mr. Goldfarb had mounted his casting in the bottom of a martini glass.

"I call that the 'Steve Martini,'" he said, following my gaze.

The other items were equally . . . unusual. A miniature backgammon set with David Letterman belly buttons vying against their Jay Leno counterparts. Luckily, Jay was televising from New York last week and had agreed to a casting although I hadn't appeared on his show. Donald Trump adorned a gold-plated money clip. And then there was the Rosie Posy, a crystal bud vase with a hand-blown glass rose whose center was a Rosie O'Donnell belly button casting.

"Of course this is only the beginning," said Mr. Goldfarb. "I have lots more ideas up here." He tapped his index finger against his temple.

Hy nodded toward the samples. "Well, Connie? What do you think?"

My gaze shifted from one item to the next. All were well-crafted works of art in their own right. Whimsical. Funky. Not the least bit tacky. However, I doubted anyone in Ten Commandments would agree with that assessment, including my husband. The knots in my intestines hitched tighter at the thought, but I masked my distress with a bright smile. "I like them."

Mr. Goldfarb whooped with excitement, then pressed us into sharing a celebratory toast before we left. Although I only took a few sips of the cognac he provided, by the time we flagged down another cab and headed back into Manhattan, I felt like all twelve members of the Ten Commandments Drum and Bugle Corps were tromping around in my stomach, their blaring, discordant melodies reverberating in my skull. That infernal troop of tin-eared octogenarians never could carry a tune worth a darn, but it didn't keep them from subjecting the rest of the town to their annual butchering of Sousa every Memorial Day, Labor Day, and Fourth of July.

I wanted to curl up in bed and pull the covers over my head. Instead, we had yet another business appointment. Beside me, Hy tapped out a steady staccato of beep-beep-beeps on his hand-held computer. "Any chance we can postpone this one?" I asked. "I'm about to crash."

His finger poised mid-beep, he turned to me. "Too much excitement for one day?"

"Too much, period. I haven't come up for air since the moment I met you. Is this the way your life is all the time? Racing from one appointment to the next?"

"Sometimes. Launching a product is always a frenetic undertaking, requiring precise timing and coordination. But I'm not merely creating demand for a product or even a product line this time. You sat in on the meeting with the ad people. We intend to create a demand for all things Connie Stedworth. The belly button castings are but the first bricks in the foundation of the Connie Stedworth empire. We catch the public's attention with something wild, then build on our initial success."

I chewed on my lower lip. "The Connie Stedworth empire," I murmured. My fanciful daydream suddenly sounded like an intimidating nightmare. "I'm a housewife from Iowa, not a Harvard MBA." And certainly not cut out to be the next Martha Stewart. Look what happened to her. And she was no country bumpkin, even if she did claim to grow her own corn. Something I always had my doubts about. The woman probably employed a dozen full-time gardeners and landscapers, plus kept a horticulturist on retainer.

He laughed. "I'll remind you of your humble roots a year from now when we go public."

"Go public? Like in stock IPOs?"

"Of course."

My head whirled with far too much information to process in a month, let alone a day. "So where are we headed now?"

"For a meeting with your publisher."

"My publisher? I haven't written a book."

"Not yet, but you're about to."

He then proceeded to lay out his idea for the Connie Stedworth belly button casting cocktail table book, featuring me casting celebrity belly buttons. And the Connie Stedworth belly button wall calendar featuring photos of all the Connie Stedworth belly button products. "Why else do you think we brought along a photographer to each of those celebrity casting sessions?"

"For a scrapbook?"

Hy laughed at the joke. Only naïve me hadn't been joking. I pretended otherwise, though, sank further into the taxi's lumpy cushions, and forced a chuckle.

He saw right through my sorry attempt at deception. "You weren't kidding, were you?"

The heat of embarrassment flooded my cheeks. Either that or I was experiencing another one of those damn hot flashes at the most inappropriate of moments. I ducked my head and shrugged. "Worldly, I'm not, in case you hadn't noticed." But when I hazarded a sideways glance at him and our eyes met, I cracked up.

The hysterical release fed upon itself. As each laugh erupted, another started building inside me. The snowballing effect infused me with courage. The more I laughed, the better I felt. The knots in my stomach relaxed; the drum and bugle corps in my head called it quits.

The fog of guilt and indecision that had insinuated itself into my thoughts lifted. Suddenly, everything came into focus. Hy believed in me. He made me believe in myself. "Everything's going to work out," I told him between uncontrollable fits of belly laughter.

He tossed me an I-told-you-so smile. "I never doubted it."

We weren't talking about the same thing, but it

didn't matter. By the time we entered Nori's apartment, I was downright giddy with self-confidence and still bubbling with laughter.

"What's so funny?"

The question—and the questioner, his arms crossed over his chest, a scowl etched onto his haggard face—axed my newfound self-confidence mid-chortle.

Chapter Nineteen

Mom stared at Dad.

Dad stared at Mom.

"*Uh-oh*," said Gertie, always the master of the understatement.

A tension-filled silence blanketed the room.

Mom recovered first, her words sputtering, her face guilt-ridden. "Earnest! We . . . um, I mean . . . uh, I didn't expect you until later."

"Obviously." Dad's lips pressed into a tight line.

When Mom reached out to touch his arm, he flinched as though she had zapped him with a stun gun. He stepped aside and glared at Hy, quickly scanning the ultra-sexy, Clint Eastwood look-alike from his shimmering head of thick platinum hair down to his custom-made Italian boots.

Although nowhere near the *GQ* cover model that Hy was, Dad generally held his own in the looks department, as long as you ignored the excess pounds and the receding hairline. But even back when he was trimmer and not yet follicly challenged, Dad was no Clint clone. His frown told me he was well aware that he came up short in comparison.

Dad turned his attention back to Mom. She wore the Donna Karan black silk pantsuit. Her crimson pedicured toes peeked out from the strappy silver Manolo Blahnik sandals. Her newly colored and styled hair framed her Georgette Klinger made-up face.

"He's got to admit she looks ab-fab," said Gertie. *"Very elegant and very New York."*

All compliments of Loretta-the-Personal-Shopper and my Amex card, I reminded her. She definitely didn't look anything like Earnest Stedworth's wife Connie. At least not the wife he last saw in Ten Commandments, Iowa.

Dad's frown deepened. His eyes filled with a hurt I never expected to see in my always-in-control father. The world as he knew it and expected it to be had spun out of control and crashed at his feet. First at home with his run-amok relatives. Now here in New York.

I wish I had had a chance to prepare him for Mom's transformation from denim-clad Iowa nobody to designer-draped Manhattan somebody. He was aware of neither Hy nor her budding career as America's newest crafts doyenne, let alone her ascension to the ranks of Belly Button Artist to the Stars. He had missed her television debut last night and apparently hadn't spoken with anyone in Ten Commandments who might have caught it. Which in itself was odd. I would have thought the tongue-wagging citizens of Ten Commandments would be speaking of little else after last night.

Unfortunately, Dad had arrived only minutes before Mom and Hy returned. I had had no time to catch him up on current events. Besides, I was still recovering from the sight of his traveling companion. Last night, when Dad said, *we'll be there late tomorrow,* I mistakenly assumed *we* referred to him and Marjorie. Not Eugene.

With the appearance of my parents' handpicked future son-in-law, I began to suspect a conspiracy, possibly one involving Mom, Dad, *and* Marjorie. Too much of what had transpired since Mom's arrival continued to make little sense to me. I scrambled to mentally fit the various puzzle pieces together, searching for clues in comments she had made over the past few weeks. However, when she walked in moments later with Hy, and I saw Dad's wounded expression, I dismissed the theory.

Eugene, it turned out, was in New York for a morticians' symposium. He had booked his flight weeks earlier. The timing was purely coincidental.

No one else in the room seemed capable of much besides glares and sulks and averted glances, except Eugene. He sat in the corner of the room, in my well-worn, circa-nineteen-sixties avocado-green armchair, intently observing the circus playing out before him as if he were watching an episode of *Six Feet Under*. For the sake of my parents and their marriage, I decided it was up to me to take charge of the tension-filled fiasco unfolding in my living room.

I began with a simple introduction. "Dad, this is my upstairs neighbor, Hyman Perth." I waved my hand in Hy's direction, then back toward my father. "Mr. Perth, my father, Earnest Stedworth."

Hy offered his hand. "Mr. Stedworth. A pleasure to finally meet you."

Dad eyed him suspiciously, offering a begrudging grunt in place of a handshake.

"That went well," said Gertie.

I frowned at my father before nodding in Eugene's direction. "And this is Eugene Draymore, a neighbor from back in Ten Commandments."

"Neighbor?" Mom raised an eyebrow. "He's a good deal more than just a *neighbor*."

"Family friend," I amended, scowling at her.

She raised her other eyebrow.

I ignored her. With all the shit that had hit the fan, leave it to my mother to focus on something so totally unimportant. I opened my mouth to tell her so.

"I wouldn't," warned Gertie.

My mouth snapped shut, bowing to Gertie's superior insight. No point adding a bale of dry hay to the already incendiary situation.

I was at a total loss as to how to proceed. My introductions had done nothing to ease the tension.

"Your mother needs to have a heart-to-heart with your father," said Gertie.

And Dad needs to listen with an open mind. That much I had already figured out for myself. Dad, however, had never been much of a listener, open-minded or otherwise, when it came to his own kin. He was too entrenched in his Nick-at-Nite concept of the ideal family. Until now.

"Someone switched the channel on him."

I'll say. The Osbournes and the Bundys had replaced the Nelsons and the Cleavers, and my poor father was at a loss as to how to cope with the seismic shift in his universe.

The ringing of the doorbell broke the percolating tension that engulfed my crowded apartment. In my rush across the living room, I nearly tripped over my own feet. I didn't care who was at the door. At this point I'd welcome the diversion of an Avon lady or a politician.

Instead, I got Reese and Gabe, and since my basement apartment opens directly onto a small exterior landing, I couldn't get rid of them before they muscled their way inside. Under the circumstances, I would have preferred half a dozen proselytizing Jehovah's Witnesses. At least the Jehovah's Witnesses would have been clueless of Connie Stedworth and her burgeoning belly button empire.

"Hey! We've been thinking about it," said Gabe, "and we decided we need our belly buttons cast." He wrapped a damp leather arm around my shoulders and planted a wet smacker on my cheek.

"Right," said Reese. She shook the rain from her multicolored dreadlocks and added a peck to my other cheek. "And since we have an 'in' with the Belly Button Queen's daughter . . ." She stopped short when I closed the door, and she spied the roomful of people. I watched as her glance skipped from one person to the next and she drew the obvious conclusion. "Your father's here already?"

I nodded.

"Oops."

Gabe offered up a sheepish grin. "Guess this isn't a good time, is it?"

I shrugged. "Guess not."

But it was too late. My father had heard every word. His eyes bugged out; his jaw dropped as his attention shifted from Gabe to my mother. "Belly Button Queen?" I could tell the exact moment he made the connection to that afternoon so many years ago when my mother had lost her patience and slapped a glob of plaster onto my stomach. My father, the man who never raises his voice and has *never* to my knowledge taken the name of the Lord in vain, bellowed, "Jesus Christ, Connie! Have you lost your mind?"

My mother wobbled on her Manolos and turned white under her Georgette Klinger. "Earnest, I can explain." But she didn't. Her head snapped from Hy to me and back to Hy, her expression begging one of us to jump in and take command of the out-of-control situation.

Hy quickly put two and two together and arrived at the only possible conclusion. He turned to my mother. "You haven't told him about us?"

Not the best choice of words under the circumstances.

Dad's jaw dropped even farther and his voice boomed even louder. "*Us!* What exactly does he mean by *us?* What the hell's going on here?"

Mom stared at Dad for a split second, her face registering the shock of hearing profanity erupting from her normally soft-spoken and decidedly reverent husband, before she threw her hands up in the air and screamed at him. "Not what you're thinking!" She turned her attention back to Hy. "No, I haven't told him about us. I haven't had a chance to talk to him about anything. He rarely answers the phone, and when he does, he's always too busy with his precious town business to listen to me."

Then she pierced Dad with a stony glare, stomped her foot, and stormed out of the room. A moment later, the slam of the bedroom door reverberated throughout the apartment.

Dad stared after her, his face as red as a jar of Mom's pickled beets. His fists clenched into tight balls, he turned on Hy. "What have you done to my wife?"

Before Hy could answer, I stepped between them. "Dad, you need to calm down before you have a coronary."

"What I need is answers. From him." He jerked his chin toward Hy. "You stay out of this, Nori."

My father is not a violent man. Even with all his conservative views, he never subscribed to the spare-the-rod/spoil-the-child theory of child-rearing. When I was growing up, the punishment fit the crime, but it never included spanking. My father didn't believe in corporal punishment or solving disputes with physical force.

To my knowledge, I was the only kid in Ten Commandments who never got walloped on the rear at some point during childhood. As a teen, I once asked Mom about that. She said it had something to do with his time in Vietnam but refused to elaborate.

Even though, in my opinion, Dad's style leaned more toward benevolent dictator than Ghandi-like statesman, his pacifist nature had always dictated his actions. Until now. Before his fists made contact with Hy's face, I grabbed my neighbor and urged him toward the door. "I think you'd better let me handle this," I told him.

Hy dug his heels in. "No, I owe your father an explanation. He seems to be under the mistaken impression that your mother and I . . ."

"That you what?" yelled Dad, reaching over me to grab for Hy's arm. I blocked him with my body, sandwiching myself between the two men.

"This is no time for chivalrous platitudes," I told Hy, jerking open the door with one hand and shoving him outside with the other. "Let me do the explaining. You go upstairs before he makes mincemeat out of your face."

He eyed Dad once more and nodded. "Maybe that's a good idea."

"You bet your sweet Armani it is." I closed the door in his face and spun around to confront my father. "What has gotten into you?"

He sputtered for a moment, his face changing from pickled beet red to near purple, before he could force out any words. When he finally gained enough control of his emotions, instead of answering my question, he bombarded me with some of his own. "With me! What's gotten into your mother? Who is that man? What is she doing with him?"

I slumped against the door and heaved a sigh. My mother should be the one offering the explanations for her seemingly bizarre behavior, not me. I walked to the bedroom and knocked. "Mom, please come out and talk with Dad."

Silence. I opened the door and found Mom staring out the window. Tear tracks streaked her cheeks. As soon as she heard me enter, she swiped at her face in a vain attempt to hide the evidence, but her efforts only further striated her expensive makeup.

"Mom?" I crossed the room and placed my hand on her shoulder. "You have to talk to him. He'll understand."

She inhaled a shuddering sniffle. "Will he? You saw how he reacted. I've never seen him like that."

"He's scared. He thinks he's losing you. Go straighten things out."

She shook her head. "I can't. He's too close-minded. That's why you left. I realize that now."

"I left because I wanted to lead my own life, not live a life planned for me by someone else, no matter how well-meaning his intentions." I paused, trapping her gaze with mine. "Or yours."

She turned to face me. A fresh stream of tears trickled from her eyes. "So do I, Nori. I've been living a dictated life for too long. I didn't realize how long until I came to New York." She inhaled another sniffle, and a sob caught in her throat. "Until I met Hy."

A shiver skittered up my spine. "Mom, you're not falling for Hy, are you?"

Her eyes widened. "Of course not! How could you even think such a thing?"

"And you still love Dad?"

She stabbed her French-manicured finger in the direction of the living room. "That man out there is not your father. Or my husband. I don't know who he is, but he's not the man I married."

I couldn't disagree with her. Dad certainly wasn't acting like Dad had ever acted. "You didn't answer my question."

She collapsed onto the bed with a sigh. "Yes, I still love him."

"And he loves you."

She answered me with a raised eyebrow and an

acerbic snicker. The first snicker I had ever heard from my mother. But then again, it was an afternoon of firsts. After all, I had never before heard my father curse, either.

I countered the snicker with a bit of rationality. "If he didn't love you, would he have bothered to go ballistic out there?"

She turned away from me and shrugged. "Who's to say why men act the way they do?"

I wanted to grab her by the shoulders and shake some sense into her. Instead, I tamped down my own violent urges and tried for some diplomacy. "I'm going to take Eugene, Reese, and Gabe for coffee so you and Dad can have some time together to straighten everything out."

"I doubt that's possible."

"You won't know unless you give it a try."

I left the bedroom and headed back to the living room, feeling as though the mother-daughter dynamic had flip-flopped onto its head. *She's acting like a recalcitrant child,* I told Gertie.

"And he's acting like a bully."

Right. So now it was up to me to bully some sense into the bully. I had only stood up to my father once before.

"Oh?"

All right. I didn't stand up to him. I ran away.

"That's more like the truth."

And he's still holding a grudge over that one act of defiance.

"He'll get over it. Eventually."

Sure, when I give in and see things his way.

I stopped at the entrance to the living room. Reese and Gabe stood in the middle of the room trying to avoid eye contact with my father, who kept glaring at them. I imagine he must have been badgering them for information on their belly button comments. Eugene hadn't moved from his observation chair in the corner of the room. "You, you, and you," I said pointing my finger at each of them in turn. "Get your coats on, and come with me."

"Where to?" asked Reese.

"Bean. And you," I said, walking up to my father and staring him down, "go *listen* to your wife."

I had never spoken so forcefully or bluntly to my father, much less ordered him around. He stared at me, speechless, as if he didn't recognize me. I hardly recognized myself. After all, Earnest Stedworth's daughter would never speak to her father in such a disrespectful manner.

"No, she tucks tail and runs off to New York instead of standing up for herself."

So I'm a coward when it comes to my own life, I told Gertie, *but now I'm fighting for my parents' marriage. The stakes are much higher.*

"Or maybe you're finally developing a backbone."

Maybe. Possibly. I did feel more in control on my own turf. Back in Ten Commandments, I often felt as though it was me against the entire town. Everyone seemed to know what was best for me. And no one hesitated to tell me. Or cared what I wanted. It had never occurred to me that others might feel the same way. Like Mom.

Without waiting for Dad to recover from his shock and reply, I grabbed my coat and purse, yanked open the front door, and stepped onto the landing, where I waited for Reese, Gabe, and Eugene to join me.

"Wow! What a tyrant," said Gabe over his shoulder as he walked beside Reese and ahead of me and Eugene. "No wonder you left home."

"He's usually not like that," said Eugene. "I've never seen him lose his temper or raise his voice." He turned to me. "Have you?"

I shook my head. "Never."

Gabe stopped short and spun around to face Eugene. "Who are you, by the way?"

I realized I had neglected to introduce everyone, a lack of social graces I rushed to correct as we hurried along through the scurrying evening commuters and a light mist of rain. "Reese Blackwell. Gabe Hoffman. Eugene Draymore."

Gabe stared, eyes wide with surprise, his mouth hanging open. "*You're* Eugene?"

Reese landed a light jab to Gabe's upper arm. "Who else would he be, Bozo?"

Gabe shrugged. Then he extended Eugene both his hand and a huge grin. "Welcome to New York."

Chapter Twenty

A few minutes after Nori left the bedroom, I heard a light rap on the door. "Connie? May I come in?"

I inhaled a deep breath before crossing the room and swinging open the door. Earnest stood on the other side, his face still slightly red but his overall demeanor appearing more confused than confrontational. And haggard. His normally straight shoulders were slumped; his face sagged. My meticulously groomed, always-in-control husband looked disheveled and disconcerted. His hair needed a trim; his clothes needed a pressing.

His expression begged for reassurance that his world hadn't come apart at the seams. But it had. In ways he didn't yet comprehend and maybe wouldn't accept. And I couldn't offer him any reassurance. Not until he offered me some. For the first time in my life, I had experienced a sense of being *me,* and I was thoroughly enjoying this encounter with my new self. I had no desire to go back to living as a mere appendage of my husband. Not when I now knew the thrill of being a *somebody.* No wonder Earnest relished his position as mayor. Being a somebody was far more fulfilling than being a nobody.

He hesitated for a moment before saying, "Nori suggested I listen to what you have to say."

I walked over to the one below-level window and stared out at the narrow service alley. Half a dozen pigeons pecked at a rain-soaked, discarded fast-food sack. "Instead of jumping to conclusions?"

He huffed out a loud breath. "Without jumping to conclusions."

I glanced over my shoulder at him. "And without interruption?"

He stared at me.

I crossed my arms over my chest. For once in my life I demanded the stage. It was his turn to sit silently in the audience. "Earnest, you have to promise you'll hear me out. All of it, before you say a word."

He sighed. Then nodded. Reluctantly. "All right. No interruptions."

It was a beginning. I glanced down at the dead plant on the windowsill. Nori's old belly button casting still sat on top of the dried and caked dirt. I plucked it out of the clay pot and slipped it into my pocket. Then I walked over to my bewildered-looking husband, slipped my hand into his, and led him into the kitchen.

"Would you like a cup of tea?" I asked, grabbing the kettle off the stove.

He slumped into a chair and nodded before propping his elbows on the table and covering his face with his hands. "Connie?"

I set the kettle under the tap and waited for it to fill with water. "Hmm?"

He lifted his head but stared down at the table rather than looking over at me. "Would you answer a question first? Before you say whatever it is you want to tell me?"

I shut off the tap, placed the kettle on the stove and turned up the flame. I knew what Earnest was about to ask me. When he raised his eyes for a brief moment, I saw the worry swimming in them. Part of me was disappointed that he could even think such a thing of me, but another part felt joy because it told me my husband still loved me. Though I had never doubted that in the past, recent events had raised all sorts of questions.

I twisted the wedding band on the third finger of my left hand. Earnest had placed it there thirty years ago, and I had never removed it. "I know what you're going to ask, and the answer is no. I haven't betrayed my marriage vows, and I have no intention of betraying them. Or you. Ever."

He sat back in the chair, and expelled a deep sigh of relief. "Whatever's going on with you, Connie, I love you. I always have and always will."

I sat down opposite him and placed my hand over his. "I know. I feel the same way about you."

He emitted another enormous sigh. "Life back home got crazy right after you left. I haven't had more than a few hours of sleep each night in nearly two weeks. I'm sorry I turned into a raving maniac a little while ago. I don't know what came over me."

"I know. And I'm sorry I left at such an inopportune time. I could have been of help to you, had I been there."

He smiled at me. "Leona Shakelmeyer organized meals for the rescue squad during the flood. Everyone complained. Most unappetizing ham sandwiches I've ever tasted." He shook his head and chuckled. "And Ralph a pig farmer. Kind of ironic, isn't it?"

I smiled back at him. "Leona shouldn't be allowed within a mile of a kitchen. She thinks she's Fannie Farmer, but the woman doesn't know the difference between a muffin and a muffler. Which explains why her muffins always taste like car exhaust."

Earnest laughed again. His face relaxed. He squeezed my hand. "Come home, Connie. I know all about this menopause stuff. After Marjorie called me, I did some reading. There are medicines you can take. Antidepressants that will help get you through this. We'll make an appointment with Doc Greavey, and you'll be back to your old self in no time."

I withdrew my hand from his. My smile dissolved. The last thing I wanted was to go back to my *old self*. My *old self* was boring and bored. If I had to live another thirty years as my *old self*, I might as well check into the Funny Farm here and now. "This has nothing to do with menopause."

"Now, Connie . . ."

I pushed my chair back and jumped to my feet. "Don't patronize me!"

"I'm not patronizing you. I'm simply saying that what you're going through is normal. There are treatments and therapies."

I heard my voice rising to match my soaring blood pressure. "You have no idea what I'm going through because you still haven't given me a chance to tell you. You're jumping to another conclusion. And treating me like a child who doesn't know her own body *or* her own mind."

The kettle went off like the signal ending a boxing round. I turned my back to Earnest while I made the tea. He kept silent. My hand shook as I poured the boiling water into the mugs, then added a heaping teaspoon of honey to his, just the way he liked it. While I stirred the honey until it dissolved, every nerve in my body continued to scream in response to his condescending attitude. I could keep silent no longer. "Why does everyone and everything always have to conform to your vision of the way life should be?" I asked, forcing my voice not to tremble with rage as I placed his tea in front of him.

His eyes widened. "If you had any idea what I've been going through lately, you'd know that it doesn't."

I leaned my backside against the sink and settled my fists on my hips. "I know all about what's going on back home, Earnest. The holier-than-thou Stedworths are behaving badly. Breaking commandments left and right." I flung my arms in the direction of the far corners of the room. "Stealing. Fornicating. Coveting thy neighbor's wife."

Stepping forward, I placed my palms flat against the tabletop and leaned forward until our foreheads nearly touched. "I've got news for you: *Stedworth* is not a synonym for *saint*. Besides, you're not your brothers' keeper. Their sins aren't a reflection on you. It's not your fault, damn it, and it's certainly not your responsibility. You're the town's mayor, not the morality police."

"Connie!"

"Oh, don't *Connie* me. Life isn't a G-rated Disney movie, no matter how much you'd like it to be so."

His voice took on a pleading quality. "It can be. It once was."

I dropped into the chair with a sigh and shook my head. "Only in shadowy childhood memories that never really existed except in your head."

When Earnest came back from Vietnam, he discovered a country he no longer recognized. So he decided we'd all be better off if we stayed in that saccharine-sweet fiction of the past when Father knew best and Mother spent her days baking apple pies. Out of fear of what the future held, the townspeople at first gave lip service to his dream, but no one ever really bought into it except Earnest. Yes, we were a conservative town, but we didn't live in a vacuum. There were too many daily outside influences chipping away at his fanciful version of Ten Commandments.

"Life was better in my father's and grandfather's days. I wanted what they had for us. For everyone."

"Yes, the *good old days*." I grimaced. He wanted us to

be like the Amish, only with electricity and indoor plumbing. Create our own private utopia to shelter us and our families from the madness of the outside world. He believed if everyone tried hard enough, we could make it happen just as he pictured it.

"Is that so wrong? The world was spiraling out of control. Things were changing, and not for the better. Look what was going on in the rest of the country." He waved his arms at me. "Riots. Drugs. Flag burnings. And it's only gotten worse with time."

"But not in Ten Commandments." We'd never had a race riot or a flag burning. As for drugs, I'm sure they existed, same as they did even in Amish communities.

"That's right. We held fast to what mattered. We kept our family values intact when everyone else was losing theirs." He puffed up his chest and poked at it with his thumb. "Thanks to me."

"Earnest, your ideas are straight out of the black-and-white world of *Pleasantville*. Life isn't *Nick at Nite* reruns. We can't live as spectators, watching the world move on without us."

His expression grew sullen. "The world hasn't moved in a very favorable direction. I didn't want to go along for the ride, and I didn't want my family to, either. Besides, you thought it was a good idea at the time."

Like a good wife, I had agreed with my husband, no matter what the issue. Love, honor, and obey. I had taken a vow. The rest of our generation had ditched "obey" for the more gender-equal "cherish" decades earlier but not the traditionalists of Ten Commandments. To this day, many wedding vows exchanged in Ten Commandments still included "obey." I sighed again and shook my head. "The good old days never existed, Earnest. They weren't better, just different, with their own particular problems."

I took a deep breath. "Face it. Your experiment failed. Look at our daughter. Thanks to you, she now lives halfway across the country because she couldn't live the life she wanted at home." I understood that now. I had begun to feel much the same way. I, too, wanted more of a life than I thought I could have in Ten Commandments.

The muscles in Earnest's face grew tight with anger. Heat rushed back into his cheeks. "You never disagreed with me about Nori. You've always wanted her to become a teacher and marry Eugene. You and Marjorie have been planning the wedding since the two of them were in diapers."

I couldn't disagree. It was the main reason I had come to New York, but since arriving, my eyes had been opened to possibilities that had never dared creep into my consciousness in Ten Commandments. I now understood that I couldn't prescribe Nori's life, no matter how much I'd like her to come home and marry Eugene. I needed Earnest to understand that, too, along with accepting that I could be both a person in my own right and still love him as I always had. One didn't preclude the other. "Things are different now."

"Why? You never complained about your life in Ten Commandments before you came to New York and met that . . . that . . . *man*. What kind of claptrap has he been feeding you?"

A shiver crept up my spine. I grabbed my mug and cupped it between my hands. The warmth penetrated my fingers and seeped up my arms, fighting back both the chill and the memory of Earnest's reaction to that first belly button casting so many years ago. "Hy made me realize my creative potential, something you've always done your damnedest to squelch."

Earnest's brows knit together, deep furrows forming across his forehead. His face reddened from crimson to burgundy and spread from his cheeks to encompass his entire face. His Adam's apple bobbed up and down several times before he sputtered his outrage. "Potential? Potential for what? Making a fool out of yourself and a laughingstock of me with those . . . those belly button things?"

This was not going well at all. How could I explain anything if he continued to be so close-minded? What future did we have if he refused to allow me to grow?

I slipped my hand into the pocket of my suit, withdrew the belly button casting, and placed it in the center of the table between us. "Yes, Earnest. With belly button *castings*."

Chapter Twenty-one

"Sexy boss-man at two o'clock," said Gertie as we entered Bean Around the Block.

As usual, since word had spread about the *Sex and the City* shoot—thanks in part to a mention on *Live with Regis and Kelly*—Bean was packed with dozens of tourists as well as non-locals from trendier sections of the city. You could spot the tourists by their head-to-toe red, white, and blue patriotic garb and their I♥NY paraphernalia. The "slummers" stood out by way of their Prada and Gucci.

"No tables," grumbled Gabe. "For a change."

Reese huffed out an exhalation of annoyance. "I can't wait until Carrie Bradshaw and her cohorts find some new hangout. I want my old coffee shop back."

"Yeah, along with the old prices," added Gabe.

I scanned the crowded tables until I found Mac seated by himself off to the right at the back of the room. He glanced up from his newspaper and grinned, as if he'd heard Gertie's assessment of him, then raised his arm to wave us over.

"This is a pleasant surprise," he said as we crowded around him. Reese settled into one of the two remaining chairs at the table. I took the other.

Gabe flagged down Amber as she passed, carrying a

tray laden with coffee mugs and croissants. "You still keep those folding chairs in the utility closet?"

She nodded toward the narrow corridor that led to the restrooms. "Help yourself, but watch out for the brooms. They have a habit of tumbling out and beaning you when you open the door."

"Well, this *is* Bean," said Gabe.

Amber scrunched up her face, puzzled. Suddenly she giggled. "Oh! Bean. Beaned. I get it."

Gabe offered us a hey-it's-Amber-what-do-you-expect grin and a shrug, then headed for the closet. He stopped after taking a few steps and turned back to us. "Hey, Eugene, how about running defense for me?"

"Um, sure."

"Eugene?" asked Mac as the man in question followed Gabe down the hallway.

"He arrived with my father."

"Your mother plays dirty." He glanced over his shoulder and watched as Eugene and Gabe disappeared around a bend.

"No. It's pure coincidence. He's in town for a morticians' conference."

Mac raised an eyebrow. "You're sure of that?"

"Of the conference?"

"Of the coincidence."

Was my mother that diabolical? I shook my head. "I don't think Mom is capable of the intricate conspiracy theory you're suggesting."

"What puzzles me," continued Mac, taking a swig of his coffee, then scrubbing his jaw, "is how your mother could want *him* to father your babies instead of me. Especially now that I've gotten a look at him."

"Huh?" Reese whipped her head up from Mac's discarded *Post* and the gossip of Page Six that had held her attention since sitting down. "What babies?"

"There are no babies," I assured her. "And no one's fathering any."

"I'm sure somewhere someone's fathering a baby at this very moment," said Mac.

I glared at him.

He retaliated with one of his crooked smiles and a twinkle in both eyes. "No babies?"

"No babies."

"Who's having a baby?" asked Gabe, returning with both chairs under his arms and Eugene in tow. He handed one of the chairs to Eugene. They flipped down the seats and crowded around the table, Gabe scrunching in between Reese and me while Eugene positioned himself on my other side, separating me from Mac.

Mischief played across Mac's face as he scrutinized Eugene. "Nori and Eugene if Mama Stedworth has her way."

"Mac!"

Ignoring my outburst, he extended a hand to Eugene, who was in the process of turning an unappetizing shade of pea green. "Sorry. Just yanking Nori's chain. I'm Mac."

Eugene squirmed in his chair, but he accepted Mac's hand. "You obviously know more about me than I do you."

"Think of me as a rival sperm donor."

I shot Mac another piercing glare. "This is bordering on justifiable homicide. And I have witnesses."

His expression shouted phony innocence. "What? And deprive your child of knowing his father?"

Gabe, Reese, and Eugene stared at me. Three pairs of eyes lowered to my abdomen. Three jaws dropped.

My head told me I should shriek with indignation, but instead, laughter bubbled up. As absurd as the conversation was, I found the idea of having babies with Eugene far more absurd. On the other hand, having babies with Mac had a definite appeal, no matter how much I protested otherwise. "Ignore him," I said between chortles. "The man is certifiable." He had also unleashed a host of flutterbies in my belly.

"Go ahead. Deny you're falling for him. I dare you."

I couldn't, damn it. No matter what my head told me, Gertie and my heart knew otherwise. And no matter how much I tried to deny my heart, I couldn't fool all-seeing, all-knowing, pain-in-my-butt Gertie.

"There you go again, calling me names."

I ignored her. Amber had bounced over to the table while I was knee-deep in Mac fantasy. Her pad and pencil stub poised, she shifted her weight from one purple Nike-clad foot to the other. "The usual, guys?"

Reese, Gabe, and I nodded.

"Ready for another, Mr. Randolph?"

Mac drained his cup. "Sounds good."

She turned her attention to Eugene. "Someone new, huh? Whatcha havin'?"

Eugene glanced across the room at the sign that listed dozens of specialty drinks, a daunting number of choices for someone used to nothing fancier than Maxwell House. "Um . . . I . . ."

Amber's pixie-cut, orange and red streaked blonde head swayed from side to side as she waited, somewhat impatiently, for him to decide.

Eugene never made up his mind about anything in a hurry. He continued to study the selection. Amber snapped her gum and tapped her pencil against her pad.

"Try the mocha cappuccino," offered Gabe.

Eugene considered the suggestion for a moment, then finally agreed. "Sounds good."

"Tall, *grande,* or *venti?*" asked Amber.

Eugene's brows' knit together in puzzlement. Ten Commandments wasn't the only town in America still Starbucks-less, but this was his first trip away from home since attending mortuary school in Nebraska, and the coffee shop craze hadn't hit most of the Midwest back then. I doubted he understood the question.

"Bring him a *grande*," said Gabe, coming to the rescue once again.

Amber finished scribbling the order. "Back in a jiff," she said as she bounced off toward the cappuccino maker.

Eugene smiled in gratitude at Gabe. "Guess my country bumpkiness is showing."

Gabe dismissed the comment with a wave of his hand. "Think nothing of it. You should have seen Nori when she first arrived. Outfitted in gingham, I might add."

"Gingham?" asked Mac.

"Not to mention pigtails," added Reese.

I yanked on one of her long, multicolored cornrows. "You should talk."

"These are *not* pigtails."

"And then there was that white apron and little wicker basket she carried looped over her arm," said Gabe. He smirked at me.

I smirked back. "Very funny."

Mac ducked his head under the table.

"What are you doing?" I asked.

"Checking to see if you're wearing ruby slippers."

"And if I am?"

"I'd chuck them so you can't get back to Kansas."

"Iowa," Eugene and I said in unison.

"And don't worry," I added. "There's no place like home, but trust me, I'm not searching for a way to get back." I deliberately eyed Eugene. "Specifically *because* there's no place like home."

Eugene laughed. "You can say that again."

Gabe turned to him. "You don't care for Ten Commandments, either?"

Eugene shook his head. "It's hard to be yourself in Ten Commandments."

"Then why stay?" asked Gabe.

Eugene grew thoughtful. Why did he stay? I thought he loved the quaintness and old-fashioned character of Ten Commandments, but he had alluded to other feelings during our last telephone conversation. I recalled his words: *Things aren't always what they seem.* Underneath that calm undertaker exterior, Eugene apparently yearned for escape.

"Family responsibilities," he finally said.

"If you live your life according to others' dictates, you'll never be happy," said Gabe.

Eugene stared at him as though Gabe were some Eastern guru imparting the secrets of the universe.

I also stared at Gabe, but I wondered what alien had slithered its way inside his body. Gabe's nature leaned toward the flippant and childish—or churlish, depending on his mood. More often than not, he reminded me of Peter Pan, and I generally don't expect serious philosophical musings to come from the boy who refused to grow up. But he was right. It was the reason I had left Ten Commandments. Maybe Eugene should stand up for himself and leave, too.

Amber delivered our drinks, and we all sat in silence for a few minutes as we sipped. Mac kept glancing over the rim of his coffee cup and smiling at me. Reese noticed. She nudged me under the table and hid a smile behind her mug, but she couldn't keep the mirth from dancing in her eyes.

I smiled back at Mac and began to wonder why I fought the attraction between us.

"*Good question,*" said Gertie. "*Wake up and smell the brewing hormones, girl.*"

Still, he *was* my boss. And I was coming off a bad relationship. My attraction to Mac could be nothing more than rebounditis.

"Bull!"

Reality.

Gertie huffed her annoyance. *"Oh, stop hiding behind excuses and rationalizations."*

Reese drained her cup, set it on the table in front of her, and produced an exaggerated yawn, complete with sound effects and hand gestures. "Oh, excuse me. I'm really beat. Time to call it a night. All I want to do is go home, open a can of Campbell's, and veg out in front of the TV." She rose from the table and yanked Gabe's shoulder. "Share a cab with me. I'm too tired to deal with the subway." Then she turned to Eugene. "Join us. We'll drop you off at your hotel."

No one ever accused Reese of subtlety.

"Um . . . Nori might want me to go back to the apartment with her. Her parents, you know."

"I'm sure they've kissed and made up by now," said Gabe. "And even if they haven't, it's not your problem."

Eugene appeared torn. He was so used to living his life by what was expected of him that he couldn't shake the mantle of responsibility, even when it didn't involve him or his own family.

"Gabe's right," I said. "Besides, even if they're still not speaking to each other, there's nothing you can do about it. Go back to your hotel. I'm sure you have a big day ahead of you tomorrow."

Relief flooded his face. "You're sure you can handle things?"

What was there to handle? Either Mom and Dad had patched things up by now or they hadn't. Either way, it wasn't like I'd have to call over to AWE for a referee. I didn't expect to come home and find my apartment trashed from an all-out brawl. "They're my parents, Eugene. Like Gabe said, my problem, not yours."

He nodded and stood. "If you need me, I'm staying at the Hilton."

"Alone at last," said Mac after Gabe, Reese, and Eugene had left Bean.

I glanced around at the still crowded café. "Hardly."

"Are you suggesting a more intimate venue?"

Was I? I stared at Mac. No, actually I stared at his lips. I wanted those lips pressed against mine again. I wanted to feel his arms around me, taste the salty tang of his tongue as it plunged into my mouth. Once again experience the headiness that had surged through my body when he had first kissed me.

"Go for it," nudged Gertie. *"Take a chance."*

I bit down on my lower lip and nodded.

"Well," said Mac, "under the circumstances, I think your place is out of the question."

I nodded again. "Definitely."

He glanced at his watch. "The library is still open."

I shook my head. "Too crowded."

"The park?"

"Too rainy."

"The Met?"

"Too far."

"Top of the Empire State Building?"

"Too touristy."

He cocked his head and rubbed his chin. "Guess that leaves my apartment."

"Guess so."

"Well, it's about time!"

Maybe it was.

Mac stood and held out his hand. Fingers entwined, we left the coffee shop.

His apartment, it turned out, was halfway between Bean and the radio station, too close to bother with a cab, even if we could flag one down during a rainy rush hour. A quick glance toward the corner revealed that Gabe, Reese, and Eugene still hadn't secured a ride. We waved good-bye before setting off in the opposite direction.

A chilly drizzle fell on us. The temperature had dropped at least ten degrees since I'd left my apartment, and my unlined trench coat provided little warmth from the damp cold. Shivering, I hugged my arms across my chest and ducked my head to keep the rain out of my eyes.

"Cold?" asked Mac.

"Freezing. It feels more like late November than early May."

He wrapped his arm around my shoulders and drew me against the warmth of his body. We quickened our pace from a brisk walk to a slow jog. Still, by the time we arrived at his building, we were both saturated. A misting of droplets sprinkled his hair and lashes, shimmering like crystals in the soft light of the lobby.

As we stood catching our breath and waiting for the elevator, I reached up and brushed aside a shock of hair that had fallen over his forehead. "You're soaked."

He placed his palms on either side of my head and ran his fingers through my damp, tangled hair. "So are you."

My scalp tingled from his touch. "Bad hair day."

"But good for other things." He lowered his head and captured my mouth with his.

I parted my lips, extending an invitation to deepen the kiss. He didn't disappoint. Mac drew me closer. I wrapped my arms around his neck; his hands caressed my cheeks. Our tongues danced and delved and explored. He tasted of coffee and cinnamon. And need. A need that matched the one growing inside me.

The elevator arrived, and we stepped inside, never breaking our hold on each other. Mac reached behind me and pressed the button for his floor. Then, instead of returning his hand to my cheek, his fingers drifted down my spine, his palm settling against my backside, holding me close enough to feel him through the assorted layers of clothing separating us. The ache inside me screamed for release. For Mac.

With an abandon that both surprised and thrilled me, I reached down and stroked him.

He groaned, releasing the pressure on my lips enough to speak. "God, I want you, Nori. I've wanted you from the moment I first saw you." He nibbled my lower lip, his teeth nipping and teasing before he once again captured my mouth, deepening the kiss with his take-no-prisoners, marauding tongue.

I wanted him just as much. To hell with not sleeping with the boss. I'd deal with that problem later. Right now I had other, more pressing matters on my mind— like the one pressing into my belly that I wanted pressing inside me.

The elevator came to a halt. The doors opened, and still lip-locked, we stumbled into the corridor. We continued kissing and fondling our way down the hall, mouths tasting, hands roaming. We unbuttoned and unzipped jackets and tugged at shirttails, desperate to feel flesh against flesh.

By the time we reached his apartment, every nerve in my body ached with anticipation. Mac leaned me up against his door. His tongue plunged deeper into my mouth. With one hand he slipped under my bra and captured a breast; with the other he fished in his pocket for his keys. I moaned at the loss when he broke the kiss to unlock the door.

Three locks later, he swung the door open, and we tumbled inside. Jackets dropped to the floor. As Mac flipped the deadbolts back in place, I unbuckled his belt and tugged at his zipper, eager to expose the bulge hiding behind the thick denim, eager to wrap my mouth around him, to taste him, to feel him plunge between my legs. Again and again until I screamed with pleasure and release.

My heart raced. Clothing flew left and right, leaving a trail as we rushed from the door to the bedroom, the wet soles of our shoes squeaking against the hardwood floors, his apartment flying by in a blur of dark varnished woods and ivory painted plaster. By the time we tumbled onto his down-covered bed, we were both naked, and I was needy beyond reason.

Mac yanked open the nightstand and withdrew a condom. His hands trembled with his own need as he ripped the foil apart. "There's so much I want to do to you, but I don't think I can wait."

"I know I can't." I proved my point by taking the condom from his hand and sheathing him myself.

He laughed. "I guess not." He straddled me. "Ready?"

"More than ready." I wrapped my legs around his waist and thrust my hips toward him.

A moment later I was gasping from the sheer pleasure of having Mac inside me. Frenetic rhythm took hold and drove us to a frenzied height that was over all too soon.

Five minutes later, still catching our breaths, we both craved more. With each subsequent explosion, the craving only grew fiercer. As the evening progressed, we made love to every square inch of each other's bodies. We out-Kama Sutra'd the *Kama Sutra*, creating our own universe of pleasure.

And then, spent but not necessarily sated, we finally rested.

"I could get used to this," said Mac. He drew the quilt up over my bare shoulder and nuzzled my neck.

He smelled of coffee and sex. Of me. I inhaled deeply, imprinting the erotic scent into my memory. A shiver of desire cascaded down my spine and settled between my legs. No man had ever produced such a primal need in me. Dave's lovemaking paled in comparison. "Me, too," I told him, illustrating my continuing need with a bit of body language that left little room for misinterpretation.

Mac shifted his weight, raised himself up on his elbow, and grinned one of those cockeyed grins that melted my insides. "I'm ready if you are," he said. A telltale bad boy twinkle lit up his eyes before he dipped his head and scooted under the quilt.

Chapter Twenty-two

Earnest stared at Nori's belly button casting. His jaw dropped. He pointed an accusing finger at the painted lump of plaster. "That's not what I think it is, is it?"

"It most certainly is."

He pushed away from the table and stood. "Pack your bags, Connie. I'm taking you home."

I refused to budge. "I'm not leaving."

"What do you mean you're not leaving?"

I folded my arms across my chest and leaned back in the chair. "Just what I said. I'm not leaving."

He stared at me, dumbfounded, his eyes bulging in disbelief. "Ever?"

"That depends on you."

"Of all the ridiculous . . . This is *his* doing, isn't it?" He flailed his arms toward the ceiling. "Do you hear yourself? Marjorie was right. You've lost your mind, thanks to that . . . that fruitcake neighbor of Nori's."

I glared at him. "Hy is *not* a fruitcake. He's a genius. And *he* appreciates me."

"Is that so?"

"Yes, that's so."

Earnest pulled out the chair and sat down. He leaned back in the seat and crossed his arms over his chest, mocking my pose. "Well, if you're not leaving, neither am I."

I shrugged. "Suit yourself." I knew Earnest wouldn't leave New York without me. If I had to out-stubborn him to make him appreciate me, then that's what I'd do. I had no idea where this budding career of mine would lead, but I needed to find out, and I couldn't do that back in Ten Commandments. Besides, whether belly button castings became the next mega-rage or not, I now knew I couldn't go back to a life of canning pickled beets.

We barely spoke for the remainder of the evening. While I prepared a salad, Earnest sat at the kitchen table, glaring at Nori's belly button casting. When dinner was ready, I filled two plates and brought them to the table.

"What about Nori?" he asked.

"She's with Eugene and her friends. I'm sure they're eating out."

"What if you're wrong?"

"She's a big girl." I nodded in the direction of the remainder of the beef stew in the crockpot on the counter. "She can help herself to leftovers when she comes home."

Earnest muttered something I couldn't make out, then bowed his head. "Thank you, Lord, for that which we are about to eat." Raising his head, he glanced across the table at me. "And please, Lord, let my dear wife see reason and come to her senses."

I glared at him.

He glared back.

We ate our dinner in total silence, except for the sound of the silverware clinking against Nori's mismatched plates.

Afterwards, Earnest retreated to the living room and switched on the evening news while I cleaned up. Typical. But what did I expect, and whose fault was it, really? This was the way life had always been for us, roles cast in Ozzie and Harriet molds that staunchly defied anything smacking of women's liberation or equality of the sexes.

In Earnest's mind, shared responsibility meant the husband went to work, and the wife stayed home to take care of the house and family. One step removed from barefoot, pregnant, and in the kitchen. Granted, I enjoyed going around without shoes during a hot Iowa summer, but I'd only been pregnant once, and damn it, I was tired of being stuck in the kitchen while my husband got top billing and stole every scene.

However, if I were being honest, I'd have to admit I was equally guilty of perpetrating Earnest's nineteen-fifties stereotype of hearth and home. The hard truth was that I had caused much of my own dissatisfaction with my life by silently remaining typecast in my Harriet Nelson-Donna Reed-June Cleaver-Margaret Anderson role for so many years. Only I never realized the extent of my discontent until I came to New York and Hy unleashed all that suppressed potential I'd kept buried inside me for so long. That's when I finally realized what I had been denying myself for so many years—having a life of my own, being a person in my own right instead of merely an appendage of my husband. I was tired of playing a bit part in Earnest's life. I wanted my own show.

I left the sinkful of dirty dishes, headed for the bedroom, and picked up the phone to call Marjorie. "How do you think Harriet Nelson would have reacted to the women's lib movement?" I asked when she answered on the first ring.

She responded without thinking, as if she had figured out the answer to this question long ago. "Instead of playing bridge, she and the ladies would have sprawled on the living room carpet, pulled down their panties, taken out their compacts, and introduced themselves to their vaginas."

I laughed at the image she had conjured up in my mind—Harriet Nelson, Donna Reed, Margaret Anderson, and June Cleaver with their perfectly permed hairdos, heels, and pearls, their shirtwaists and crinolines gathered at their waists, frolicking in a circle of giddy naughtiness like an updated version of a Matisse painting. "Not before cable."

Marjorie chuckled along but quickly grew sober. "What's going on, Connie?"

A shuddering sigh escaped before I could trap it in my throat. "I love my husband, Marjorie, but I don't want to go back to that phony *Father Knows Best* life he expects me to live."

"Have you spoken to him about it?"

"He hasn't exactly been the most open-minded kernel on the ear since he's arrived."

She huffed a loud, annoyed exhalation. "Well, what do you expect? Thanks to this belly button nonsense of yours, he probably feels like you're kicking him in the balls after the town cut him off at the knees."

"What do you mean?"

"Talk to him, Connie." With that last bit of advice, she hung up on me.

I stared at the receiver. When had Marjorie, the friend who had encouraged me to spread my wings, my childhood compatriot in mischief, switched allegiances? What had happened back in Ten Commandments to make her side with Earnest all of a sudden?

So he had finally opened his eyes to the unsaintly behavior of some of his less-than-saintly relatives. About time, as far as I was concerned. Marjorie and I saw telltale signs of Stedworth shenanigans for years. I'm sure others did, too. Earnest, however, insisted on wearing blinders where life in general—and his family in particular—were concerned. Still, the world hadn't come to an end because one of his brothers was caught with his pants down and the other was on the lam for absconding with the till.

So what *had* happened in Ten Commandments besides what I already knew? I swung open the bedroom door and marched into the living room. It was high time my husband dropped his stalwart protect-the-little-woman image and told me what was going on back home.

Earnest sat hunched in the corner of the sofa, the remote balanced on his knee. His unfocused, glassy-eyed expression stared off in the general direction of the television. I reached for the remote and clicked the anchorman into oblivion mid-sentence.

"Connie! I was watching that."

Doubtful. I tossed the remote onto the sofa, folded my arms across my chest, and jutted out my chin. "Earnest, if I offered you a hundred dollars, I don't think you could tell me who you were watching or what he was talking about."

"I was waiting for the farm report."

"On the *national* news?"

He stared at me blankly.

I sat down next to him and reached for his hand. He stiffened and pulled away from me. I sighed. "We need to talk."

"What's there to talk about? You seem to have made up your mind."

"Not about me. About you."

"There's nothing to talk about."

"Really? I just spoke to Marjorie. I want to know what happened in Ten Commandments after I left."

His face contorted into a grimace, but he continued to stare at the now dark television set rather than turn toward me. "You know what happened," he mumbled.

He wasn't going to make this easy for me, was he? "I'm not talking about the flood along Main Street or

Ezra and Merline or Jonah and Florrie or LeRoy and his topless go-go dancers. I'm talking about you. And don't tell me it's got something to do with my business dealings with Hy. Whatever's going on happened way before you ever knew about Hy and my belly button art."

He remained silent, his lips set in a tight line, his stare never wavering from the dark television screen.

"Damn it!" I punched my fists into the cushions. A cloud of dust—most likely remnants of the plaster disaster—puffed up between us. I batted at the air. "I'm your wife, Earnest. Your partner. Not some china doll that needs protecting from the cold, cruel world."

Heaving a deep sigh, he shifted position to face me and delivered his words in a halting monotone. "The town council held a special session last night. Went past midnight. Packed the Grange Hall to overflowing. Nearly everyone in town showed up."

That explained why I hadn't received any backlash from my appearance on Letterman. Anyone who would have watched was at the Grange. "A special meeting on what?"

"To discuss the petition Leona and Ralph Shakelmeyer are circulating."

"What kind of petition?"

He scowled into his lap. "Demanding my resignation. They claim my mismanagement and lack of leadership led to all the recent problems. If I refuse to resign, they're insisting on a recall vote, followed by a special election to vote in a new mayor."

"They can't do that!"

Earnest bowed his head. "Actually, they can if they get enough signatures."

"That's balderdash."

He shook his head. " 'Fraid not. Says so in the town charter. But that's not the worst of it."

How much worse could it get?

Earnest answered my unasked question. "The majority of the council and a good portion of the town think it might be best if I step aside rather than dealing with the divisiveness a recall vote would create."

I snorted. "Leave it to Leona and Ralph Shakelmeyer to hurl hog slop. You might act lordly at times, Earnest, but believe me, even *you* can't control your relatives' behavior, let alone the rising of the Mississippi. And who do they think could do a better job of running the town than you've done all these years?"

"Ralph."

"Ralph?" I laughed. "Ralph can't break even on his own pig farm without government subsidies." I shook my head. "You have nothing to worry about. No one is going to replace you with Ralph Shakelmeyer. Everyone knows what you've done for Ten Commandments over the years. You've given that town your body and soul."

He reached out and took my hand. The corners of his lips lifted ever so slightly into a rueful smile. "And that's *our* problem, isn't it?"

I nodded. Tears swam in my eyes. He finally got it. But at what price? And where did that leave me? Did I, like a proper Ten Commandments wife, forsake my own dreams to rush home to help save my husband's career? If I didn't grab hold of the opportunities presented to me now, would I ever have another chance at being more than the pickled beets queen of the county fair?

I couldn't believe that the Shakelmeyers presented much of a threat to Earnest. People knew him and knew them. Earnest had spent most of his life helping the citizens of Ten Commandments. Ralph and Leona never did anything that didn't benefit themselves in some way, either directly or indirectly. In my mind, there was no contest.

But what would happen when the town got word of my new life? Pickled beets they could accept, but belly button art? Would my budding career sabotage my husband even more in the eyes of his constituents? Add fuel to the Shakelmeyer fire? Selfishness and guilt battled inside me.

"I don't want Nori to know about any of this. I made Eugene promise not to say anything."

I rose and started pacing across the small expanse of living room floor. "You can't keep trying to protect us from the world, Earnest. Nori left because you . . ." I stopped to correct myself. After all, I was equally to blame for my daughter's flight from Ten Commandments, even though I now understood her need to leave and no longer blamed her for leaving. "*We* wouldn't let her grow up."

"When did we ever keep her from growing up?"

Bad choice of words on my part. I flopped back down onto the sofa. "We didn't allow her to make her own choices. We planned out her life and expected her to go along without so much as a quibble."

"I never wanted anything for her but happiness."

"What you . . . we decided would make her happy, though. Sometimes people need to be allowed to make their own mistakes in order to figure out what they really want, what really makes them happy. She had to run away from us to find herself."

Earnest studied me, his brow puckered in thoughtfulness. "Is that why you came to New York?"

"No . . . Maybe." I winced, then shrugged. "I'm not sure. Marjorie and I cooked up this plan to get Nori and Eugene together. But once I got here . . ." My voice trailed off. I didn't want to bring Hy up again. Not now, but how could I answer Earnest honestly without trying to explain to him how Hyman Perth, trend-spotting entrepreneur, had made me see my own potential?

"Once you got here and met *him*, you mean." He motioned to the ceiling.

"Oh for heaven's sake!" I jumped up, my hands balling into tight fists that I pounded against my thighs. "Stop sounding like a caveman. Hy is no threat to you!"

"No threat? Look at you, Connie. You don't even look like yourself anymore. I hardly recognized you when you walked in earlier. Not to mention this ridiculous belly button stuff. Just what is going on with that?"

So we were back to square one. "That belly button *stuff* has made me famous!"

Trepidation washed across Earnest's face. "What do you mean?"

I took a deep breath and plunged into a ninety-second synopsis of the reincarnation of belly button casting, ending with my appearance on Letterman last night.

Earnest didn't take the news well. I think maybe they heard him shouting all the way back in Ten Commandments. When he finally came up for air and his color subsided from a deep purple to a mottled red, he stared at me as if he were looking at a two-headed polka-dot heifer. He shook his head and spoke in a defeated tone tinged with both sadness and disgust. "I hope your belly button venture is successful, Connie, because once Shakelmeyer gets wind of this, I won't be able to find a job slopping hogs." He grabbed his hat and coat and stormed out of the apartment.

I guess he didn't get it after all.

In thirty years of marriage I'd never seen my husband lose his temper, never heard him raise his voice in anger or hurl accusations at me. Until today. I locked the door behind him, collapsed onto the sofa, and clicked on the TV while I waited for the monster I'd created to cool off, calm down, and return.

I wanted to curl up in bed, pull the quilt over my head, and forget any of this had ever happened. That or click my heels together three times and find myself back home and content to be there, but I couldn't. Not only because I'd never again be content with that life but for another reason as well: Earnest didn't have a key to Nori's apartment.

So I waited.

And waited.

And waited.

Chapter Twenty-three

Nestled in Mac's arms, I woke to the sound of the garbage trucks rumbling down the street. "Hey, sleepyhead." He leaned over and kissed me.

"Hmm." I sank into his kiss. The arousal already stirring within me banished the last vestiges of sleep cobwebs from my brain. My engorged breasts tingled. I shifted my weight and brushed them against the wiry hairs of his chest. They tightened into a pebbled hardness that begged for his lips. As if reading my mind, he bent his head and took one in his mouth, sucking the nub ever harder until the ache shot straight to my womb. His hand stroked my inner thigh, triggering a fiery honey that pooled between my legs and threatened to drive me mad.

An eerie neon glow bathed the room. As Mac turned to remove another condom from the drawer, the numbers of the bedside clock came into focus. "Omigod!" I bolted upright, the air rushing from my lungs, my pulsing heart beating the desire from my body and mind.

"What?"

With a trembling finger, I pointed to the clock. "The time! It's three in the morning." I tossed back the quilt and jumped out of bed, the cool night air jolting me further awake. "I have to get home."

Mac reached for my hand. "No, you don't. Come back to bed."

I hesitated for a moment, staring into his to-die-for bedroom eyes, his lids heavy with desire, his tousled hair dipping rakishly over one eye. I glanced down at the bed, the tangle of sheets warm and inviting. "I can't. How am I going to explain this to my parents?"

Mac cocked his head and chuckled. "I don't know about you, Nori, but I don't generally give my folks a play-by-play on my sex life."

"Are you kidding? My father would have a heart attack if he learned I *have* a sex life." I still couldn't believe that my mother accepted my non-virgin status so matter-of-factly. But then, Mom was full of surprises lately.

He tugged at my hand, urging me back onto the bed. I gave in and fell into his arms. "So why do you have to tell them anything?"

"Because they're staying with me, remember? How am I going to explain being out all night?"

His fingers made lazy circles around my breasts and over my belly. "You're a big girl. You don't owe them any explanations. Besides, now that your father's arrived, where were you supposed to sleep?"

He had a point. I arched my back as his hand dipped lower. "Mom and Dad are probably sound asleep in my bed."

"Leaving you with the sofa." His lips caressed my shoulder; his fingers wandered lower until they found the slick folds of flesh between my legs. I gasped from the torturous pleasure as he found my fiery, throbbing nub and began massaging it.

My body tingled; my brain fought to focus on the conversation. Mac's fingers thrust deeper, quickening the pace and intensity of the massage. My voice cracked as I spoke. "The small, lumpy sofa."

"Or spending the night with a friend."

My body tensed, every nerve anticipating, craving the explosion building inside me. "A friend?"

Mac's hand stilled. "Or a lover." And then those magic fingers returned to their task, rocking my world and driving all thoughts of my parents from my brain.

Chapter Twenty-four

I woke the next morning as the first rays of dawn gave a halfhearted attempt at filtering through Nori's soot-covered, street level window. As I stood and stretched out the kinks, every joint and muscle in my body screamed in protest. Fifty-year-old women have no business falling asleep sitting upright on sofas that passed their prime back during the Eisenhower administration.

It didn't take me long to discover that neither my husband nor my daughter had returned home last night. I wasn't worried about Nori. In truth, I hoped she had spent the night with Eugene. My outlook on life might have taken a seismic shift over the past few weeks, but I hadn't forgotten my initial reason for coming to New York. Nori and Eugene belonged together. Marjorie and I had figured that one out from the time the two of them were in diapers. Maybe outside of Ten Commandments they'd finally come to the same realization. Anyway, that had been our scheme. And no matter what plans Hy had up his sleeve for me, I still wanted those grand-babies. I saw no reason why I couldn't be both a grandmother and the Grande Dame of Crafts.

Earnest, I was worried about, though. My husband was ill-equipped to handle New York City, and I didn't have a clue as to where to start looking for him. In a matter of seconds, every *NYPD Blue* mugging and murder I'd seen on television flashed before my eyes. Should I call the police? Start checking the hospitals?

Somewhere in the back of my mind I remembered something about the police not doing anything about looking for missing persons until the missing person was missing at least twenty-four hours. I glanced at my watch. Earnest had stormed out of the apartment eleven hours and twenty-six minutes ago. I remember because when I turned the television back on, Alex Trebek was introducing the categories for the first round of *Jeopardy*.

I started scouring Nori's bookshelves in a vain attempt to find a telephone book. After searching through every shelf, closet, nook, and cranny that might house books, I turned my efforts to less obvious locations. On hands and knees in the bedroom, I finally found a copy of the *Yellow Pages* propping up the back end of her dresser where the leg was missing.

Still sprawled on the floor, bracing the dresser with my shoulder, I shimmied the phone book out from underneath, lowered the back end of the dresser to the floor, and proceeded to get beaned by one hairbrush, two combs, three bottles of perfume, and a container of deodorant. Luckily, I caught Nori's jewelry box. Unfortunately, I knocked the lid off as I grabbed it. Earrings, necklaces, pins, and bracelets bounced off my head and chest and scattered across the floor, rolling under the radiator, into the closet, under the bed.

Maybe I should have thought to wedge a replacement book under the dresser, but given the circumstances, I wasn't thinking too clearly. My husband was most likely lying in a coma in some hospital, and I needed to find him.

I tucked the massive book under my arm, grabbed the cordless phone from the night table, and headed back to the living room. With the phone book spread across my lap and opened to "Hospitals," I flipped through the pages.

Where to begin? Who would have thought New York had so many hospitals? There were easily more hospitals in Manhattan than there were families in Ten Commandments. It would take me hours to run through them. With a deep breath and a shaky hand, I started at the top of the listing and punched in the first number.

On the second ring someone answered.

"Thank you for calling Abraham Medical Center."

"Yes, I'm . . ."

"Please make your selection from the following list of choices. If this is an emergency, press One. For patient services—"

"It's an emergency!" I pressed One.

"Our staff is currently handling other calls. Please stay on the line. Your call is important to us and will be answered in the order in which it was received."

"Of all the—" A knock at the door stopped me mid-expletive. Without so much as a "Who's there?" I raced across the room, flipped the deadbolts, and swung open the door. "Earnest! Thank God!" I launched myself into his arms and started bawling my eyes out. "I was so worried," I choked out between sobs. "Where were you all night?"

He wrestled out of my grip and stepped into the apartment, closing the door behind him. "I spent the night in the hotel with Eugene. Once he showed up, that is. Most of the evening I paced the lobby, waiting for him to return. He finally strolled in around two in the morning." Earnest rubbed his temples with the heels of both hands, his brows knitting together. "I'm sorry, Connie, but I needed time to cool off and do some thinking. Too much is changing too fast."

He shrugged out of his coat and tossed it on a chair.

Then he turned to me and studied my rumpled hair and wrinkled clothing, the same pantsuit I'd worn yesterday and slept in last night. "I didn't mean to worry you. I should have called, but I was too angry to think straight."

I stared at him, my mouth dropping open. "*You* spent the night with Eugene?"

"Of course. Where else would I go?"

My earlobes began itching like mad. "But if you spent the night with Eugene, where's Nori?"

"She never came home?"

I shook my head as I rubbed both earlobes between my thumbs and index fingers.

"Eugene said she left the coffeehouse early in the evening. With some strange man. Max somebody." He reached for the phone still in my hand. Before I could stop him, he hit 9-1-1.

Even though I hadn't eaten since dinner last night, my stomach suddenly felt like I'd consumed an entire fruitcake—one baked by the culinarily-challenged Leona Shakelmeyer. I grabbed the phone back and disconnected the call. "It's Mac, not Max. And he's not a stranger." I frowned. "Unfortunately."

As I filled Earnest in on the interloper who was undermining my plans for Nori and Eugene, a police car, its lights flashing and siren wailing, screeched to a halt in front of the apartment building. Moments later, we were producing identification and trying to explain the disconnected emergency call to a couple of skeptical policemen.

"Mind if we take a look around, ma'am?" asked the taller of the two, Officer Moorehead, according to the nameplate pinned to his navy shirt.

Earnest switched into mayor-mode. Puffing out his chest, his hands on his hips, he demanded, "Do you have a search warrant?"

"No, sir," said the shorter, squatter officer, "but if we have to, we can get one."

I stepped between my husband and the policemen, placing my palm on Earnest's chest as I spoke to the second officer. For all his businesslike demeanor, he had a kinder-looking face than the first man. Round, with laugh lines at the corners of his eyes and mouth. I glanced at his nameplate. "That won't be necessary, Officer Castellano. Of course you can take a look. We have nothing to hide."

I offered him a smile and a shrug. "It's all a misunderstanding. My husband panicked, thinking our daughter was in danger, but I'm sure I know where she is and with whom." I waved my hand to indicate the general area of the apartment. "Go ahead." Then I added, "Would you gentlemen like a cup of tea or coffee?"

They exchanged an odd look between them, as if my offer were totally unexpected. "No, thank you, ma'am," said Officer Moorehead.

I guess people in New York don't get to know their local police the way we do back in Iowa. I shrugged. "Well, if you change your minds, I was about to make a fresh pot of coffee."

Officer Castellano nodded as the two of them made their way toward the kitchen. Earnest and I followed. After a cursory glance around the small room, they poked their heads into the bathroom, then headed for the bedroom.

"What happened here?" asked Officer Moorehead, indicating the leaning dresser, upended jewelry box, and scattered jewelry.

I winced. The room looked like a battlefield. "I needed the telephone book?"

Three pairs of disbelieving eyes stared at me.

Before I could explain further, I heard Hy shout from the front of the apartment, "Connie? Are you all right?" He hurried into the bedroom, stopping short at the entrance. "What's going on here?"

"How did you get in?" asked Earnest.

"Through the front door."

Earnest glared at me. "He has a key?"

"You left the door open," said Hy. He turned to Officer Moorehead. "What's going on here, Tom?"

I guess New Yorkers do know their local police. But then again, Hy seems to know everyone.

Moorehead scratched his temple. "Not quite sure yet, Mr. Perth. Maybe a missing person. Maybe a domestic abuse situation."

"And maybe nothing," I said. "Which is what it is." I scowled at the officers, waggling a finger under Moorehead's nose. "Don't you gentlemen have terrorists to round up or something?"

Chapter Twenty-five

"I swore I wouldn't sleep with you," I told Mac the next morning after we had showered and dressed, him in fresh clothes, me in the ones I had worn the previous night.

"Why is that?"

"Because you're my boss."

"And you're opposed to workplace romances?"

"Life is complicated enough." I recounted my unsettling confrontation with the no-neck ex-football player host the day before.

Mac waved his hand in dismissal. "J.T. Brown is one of the reasons our ratings were slipping. He's boring. Fewer and fewer listeners are tuning in to hear him."

"Then why do you keep him?"

"His agent brokered a deal that makes it next to impossible for me to get rid of him."

"And you signed it?"

"No, my predecessor did." He grinned. "Which explains why he's the *ex*-station manager. And why J.T.'s history once that contract is up. The guy was a terrific wide receiver, but he sucks as a broadcaster and doesn't have the smarts to coach. This time next year he'll be pumping gas back in Bumblefuck, Mississippi."

"Bumblefuck, huh? Makes Ten Commandments sound like a cultural mecca." I slipped into my coat.

"Still, he made it clear he's looking forward to seeing me fall flat on my ass. I don't want to give him any ammunition for taking pot shots at me."

Mac kissed the tip of my nose. "You won't."

Hand-in-hand, we headed back to my apartment. The rain and chill of last night had given way to a picture perfect May morning in New York, replete with a blazing blue sky accompanied by a cacophony of city melodies—traffic and people abuzz and alive. I inhaled, and my senses were bombarded with a mélange of fresh scents—the sweet and spicy and sharp and pungent aromas of flowers and perfumes and cheese and newly baked bagels—spilling out from the open shop doors we passed.

I raised my face to the sun and basked in its warm glow. For the first time in weeks, I felt empowered. Everything would work out. Mom. Dad. My new job. My budding relationship with Mac.

Even though we had jumped into bed without any preamble, I had no doubt that this was more than a one night stand. Something had simmered between us from the moment we met. Last night that *something* had fired up into a roiling boil that consumed us both.

I'd never before jumped into bed with a guy the way I had with Mac. Good girls from Ten Commandments, Iowa, didn't sleep around. Or so I was brought up to believe. When I finally lost my virginity in graduate school, I spent many a sleepless night wondering if I'd burn in hell for it. My first love affair, born more out of curiosity, rebellion, and lust than love, died a quick death.

Then came Dave. I didn't sleep with him until I had convinced myself I was head-over-heels in love with the prick, and look where that had gotten me.

Maybe it was time to plunge into a relationship just because it felt so good and so right and not worry where it might lead. Last night proved I had cast off the shackles of Ten Commandments as far as sex was concerned. Looking back, I could hardly believe my wanton behavior with Mac, but I felt no guilt or shame over the way I had behaved.

"Amazing what a night of good fucking can do for a girl's spirits."

Crude but true, Gertie.

"So let's give credit where credit's due, okay?"

Meaning?

"Meaning I told you so."

Take all the credit you want, I told her. *I feel too good to argue with you.*

"Especially because I'm right."

She generally was, as much as I hated to admit it. Gertie knew me better than I knew myself. And she wasn't shy about telling me so.

I bounced along on a cloud of euphoria until we rounded the corner and I saw the police car, its lights flashing, parked in front of my apartment.

"Ohmigod!" I stopped dead in my tracks and stared at the small group outside my apartment—my parents, Hy, and two policemen stood on the curb next to the police car.

"What's going on?" asked Mac.

All sorts of scenarios—none of them good—raced through my mind. My father had the world's longest fuse. He never lost control and absolutely never resorted to physical violence. But his world was falling apart before his eyes, both back in Ten Commandments and here in New York. Family meant everything to Dad; Mom meant more than everything to him. Hyman Perth's relationship with Mom might be the catalyst to transform Dad from Mahatma Ghandi to Mike Tyson.

From halfway down the block I couldn't tell if anyone was handcuffed. Couldn't make out blackened eyes, bloodied noses, or dislocated jaws. I craned my neck to see over and around the other pedestrians on the street, but my view kept getting blocked. "Damn! I can't see."

I dashed down the street. Mac grabbed my hand and ran interference as we scrambled our way around strolling tourists, scurrying commuters, and a dog-walker whose assorted brood took up nine-tenths of the sidewalk.

When we stopped short at the group in front of the police car, I quickly scanned my father and Hy for tell-tale signs of battle. No bumps, bruises, or blood on either. And no handcuffs.

"See, I told you she's not missing," said Mom as I gulped in rapid lungfuls of air to catch my breath. She offered the policemen a smug smile. A split second later, that smug smile transformed into an irritated frown directed toward Mac. The irritated frown deepened into a harsh scowl as her gaze zeroed in on our still-joined hands.

"Missing?" Damn! Of course they'd jump to that conclusion when I didn't return home last night. I should have called, but what would I have said?

"How about, 'Hi, Mom and Dad. Don't wait up. Mac and I are going to screw each other's brains out tonight.'"

Not one of Gertie's better suggestions. However, by the way Mom glared at Mac, I didn't need to tell her anything. She already knew. I glanced at Dad. His attention alternately shifted between Mac and Hy, his expression equally severe. What were the chances I could get the police to take me into protective custody until my parents went back to Ten Commandments? Then again, from the looks of things, they'd better take Mac and Hy as well.

"Maybe you could get them to offer a three-for-one deal," suggested Gertie.

When the police were finally assured that all was well on Bedford Street and drove off, my father turned to Mac. "Who are you?"

Mac extricated his hand from mine and offered it to my father. "Mackenzie Randolph, sir."

He turned to Mom. "The doctor boyfriend?"

She shook her head.

Dad stared at the extended hand and responded in much the same way as he had to Hy the day before—with suspicion and a begrudging grunt, no handshake.

Mac withdrew his hand and turned to me. "I have to get to the office."

I nodded. "I'll be in as soon as I freshen up."

Then he bent down and kissed me in full view of my parents. Not an air kiss. Not a peck-on-the-cheek kiss. Not a fleeting touch-of-the-lips kiss. Mac grabbed me in his arms and kissed me in a way that announced exactly who he was and that he didn't give a damn who knew it.

My responding kiss proclaimed a resounding, "Ditto."

My mother gasped.

My father bellowed, "Honora Rachel Stedworth!"

Hy chortled.

Mac and I ignored all three of them. He finally broke the kiss—reluctantly—and strode down the street.

I had no idea where our relationship was heading. From the moment I met Mac, he did things to my body and mind that no man had ever done, and that was before he had touched me with anything more than his eyes. Not that I had *that* much experience with other men, but I did have enough to know something special was unfolding. I decided to live in the moment. I wasn't going to think about tomorrow, much less forever. Besides, I had less than an hour to shower, dress, and get to the studio on time.

"He's ruining everything," I heard my mother mutter under her breath as I headed into my apartment.

I didn't need to ask who *he* was or what *he* was ruining. Mom may have changed her hair and wardrobe and even her outlook on life since arriving in New York, but she'd never give up on the idea of getting Eugene and me together. A fact made apparent when thirty minutes later, I stepped out of the bathroom and found the mortician in question sipping coffee at my kitchen table.

"Good morning, Nori," he said.

I nodded. "Eugene." Then I turned to my parents. "I don't suppose either of you could give me the short version of what disaster took place in my bedroom."

My mother handed me a cup of coffee. "I'm sorry, dear. I'll clean it up later. I needed the phone book."

"The phone book?" Did I even have a phone book? I decided I didn't have time to pursue the subject further. I had to get to work. I held up my hand as she started to launch into an explanation. "Never mind. I don't want to know." I doubted it would make much sense, anyway.

Mom motioned to one of the unoccupied chairs. "Sit down. I'll make you some breakfast."

I took a quick swig of the coffee, then placed the cup on the counter. "Can't. I have to be at work in twenty minutes." I swung my purse over my shoulder and headed for the living room.

Behind me, I heard Mom urging Eugene. "Go. Walk her to work."

"That's not necessary. I know the way," I called over my shoulder as I closed the door behind me.

Halfway down the block, Eugene caught up with me. "Nori, wait."

I expelled a huff of annoyance as I continued taking city strides. "I thought you were here for a conference."

"I am."

I waved him off. "Then go conference."

"Wait, please."

I stopped and turned to face him. He shoved his hands into his pants pockets, hung his head, and shuffled his feet. "Look, um . . . there's something we need to talk about."

He was right. We really needed to put an end to this parental manipulation so we could both get on with our lives. "Okay, but talk and walk. I'm on the air in less than half an hour." I took off again, and Eugene fell in step.

"On the air?"

I told him about the radio show.

"Hey, that's really cool."

"You think so?"

"Sure."

I shrugged. "Just don't spread it around Ten Commandments. I don't think people back home would feel likewise, and my father's got enough trouble right now."

"More than you know."

I stopped short again and spun around. "What now?"

Eugene filled me in on the way the town council had turned against Dad.

"Those ingrates! And after all he's done for that town." Then I thought about the shock Dad received yesterday when confronted with the "new" Mom. And the expression on his face earlier when he looked at Mac and me and put two and two together. A lump the size of Sioux City lodged in my throat. "He must feel like his world is crumbling at his feet."

"It's a hell of a way to get yanked into the twenty-first century."

I chuckled. "Twenty-first century? Dad never made it into the second half of the twentieth century."

"But we have."

"Yes, and I'm sure I don't need to remind you that they don't have arranged marriages in the twenty-first century, at least not in America."

He cocked his closely cropped head and raised one shaggy eyebrow. "So you don't want to marry me?"

"Hell no!" Then I quickly backtracked. My outburst had sounded cruel, and I hadn't meant to hurt Eugene's feelings, only to make it clear that I couldn't and wouldn't marry him. Ever. "I'm sorry, Eugene, I—"

But he didn't let me finish my apology. He placed both hands on my upper arms, grinned, and expelled a happy sigh. "That's a relief, because I don't want to marry you. Never did, in case you hadn't noticed."

We both laughed, then hugged and laughed some more.

A major problem still loomed before us, though. As we resumed walking, I said, "So how do we convince our meddlesome parents to butt out of our lives?" Eugene didn't offer any suggestions. I turned my head to glance in his direction.

He chewed on his lower lip, his brows knit together in pensive concentration. When he noticed me staring, he said, "I suppose I could come out of the closet."

"That's not something to joke about, Eugene."

"I wasn't joking."

For the third time, I stopped short and spun around to confront him. No twinkle sparkled in his eyes. He wasn't fighting to stifle a grin. Eugene's expression was dead serious. "My God! You're not kidding, are you?"

"Queer as they come. Right down to my bunioned and callused toes. You never suspected?"

I shook my head. I doubted anyone in Ten Commandments suspected. I couldn't help laughing. "I suppose it's a good thing I never did fall in love with you."

"Maybe you didn't because deep down you knew."

I thought that over for a moment. "I don't think so.

To me, you were always more like a big brother. Sometimes a pain in the ass, sometimes a pal, but no,"—I shook my head again—"I never thought you were gay."

We continued walking down the street. "Do you think Ten Commandments is ready for a gay undertaker?" I asked.

"I doubt Ten Commandments is ready for a gay anything, but I'm tired of living a double life."

"You don't have to stay there." We had arrived at the station. "This is where I work." I glanced at my watch. I had less than ten minutes before my show aired. "We should talk more later."

He nodded. "Later." Then he bent down and planted a dry big-brother peck on my cheek.

I was still reeling from Eugene's news when, a few minutes later, Mac confronted me in the hallway outside my office. An all-too-serious scowl covered his face. "I like it better when you're smiling," I told him.

The scowl deepened. He clenched and unclenched his left fist as he huffed out a sharp exhale of breath. "I'm afraid I have some bad news."

My body tensed. I didn't want any more news, bad or otherwise. I walked into my office, tossed my coat and bag on the chair, and scowled back at him. "Let me guess. You discovered there's a company policy against the on-air talent sleeping with management."

"Shh!" Mac glanced down the corridor, then followed me inside, closing the door behind him. His scowl softened into the hint of a smile. "No, I made sure I deleted that paragraph from the policy manual before I hired you."

I felt the tension in both my body and the air ease a bit. "That's a relief. So what's the bad news?"

"The suits are flipping somersaults over you. Aside from a few disgruntled jocks whose opinions don't count, everyone loves your show. Especially the sales reps. They've got sponsors standing in line to hand over money."

"So what's the problem?"

"The suits are talking a huge media campaign—print, billboards, TV, the works—with an eye toward eventual syndication. They think you've got what it takes to go national."

"I see." This was a major problem.

"Not that the idea doesn't sound intriguing," said Gertie. *"Admit it. You're tempted."*

True, but what about my parents? I had no doubt once she got used to it, Mom could handle my Gertie persona, especially considering her new direction in life. But Dad? Never. Look at the way he had reacted to Mom's transformation. How could I cause my father more anguish?

"The man is stuck in a make-believe time warp. He needs a swift kick into reality."

Maybe Gertie's harsh assessment was correct, but that kick could destroy him. I may have run away from his controlling attitudes, but I still loved my father. Besides, both Mom and Ten Commandments were kicking him hard enough at present. How could I add to his already bruised ego? I couldn't.

I chewed on the inside of my cheek and mentally counted to ten before reminding Mac of the clause I had insisted on adding to my contract—the clause that kept my identity a secret. The clause he had accepted. "We agreed I wouldn't have to do any publicity other than radio ads."

"I know. That's the problem. They're not real happy with me at the moment."

"Meaning?"

"Meaning if I don't get you to strike that clause, I'm history."

"Crap." I pushed my coat and purse onto the floor

and slumped into my chair. "So I either give my father a heart attack or you lose your job, is that it?"

"In a nutshell." He leaned on the corner of my desk with one hip. Retrieving a sealed envelope from his sport coat pocket, he waved it in front of my face. "Don't worry, Nori. I refuse to place you in that kind of position. I'm on my way upstairs to resign."

"No!" I jumped to my feet. Before he could stop me, I grabbed the envelope from him and tore it in half. Then in half again. And again. I kept tearing until the wad in my hand was too thick to rip. Then I crumpled it up and tossed it in the trash can under my desk.

Mac shrugged. "That solves nothing. I'll simply print another off the computer."

"You will not." Panic seized me. I glanced at the clock. "Look, I'm on in less than five minutes. Don't pull any heroic, sacrificial crap for the next hour. We'll figure something out after my show, okay?"

He shook his head in resignation, his expression determined. "There's nothing to figure out, Nori. You change your mind, or I'm out of here. Simple as that. Black and white. There are no other options. And I'm not going to box you into a corner to save my ass."

With one hand I grabbed the file with today's rant. My other hand reached for Mac. I fought to keep my mounting hysteria from echoing in my voice. "There are always other options, Mac. Promise me you won't do anything until I get back."

When he didn't answer, I squeezed his hand. Hard. Time to call in the big guns. If there was ever a time to employ the ultimate threat, this was it. "Promise me, or I'll never sleep with you again."

He raised both eyebrows and cocked his head. His lips twitched into a smile. "You fight dirty, Stedworth."

"You better believe it." I tightened my grip. "Now promise."

Mac sighed. "Okay. Don't break my fingers. I may need them to dig ditches. I promise."

I released his hand, wrapped my arms around his neck, and kissed him until our tonsils tangoed. When I broke the kiss and stepped back, I raised my chin and fired off one parting shot. "Just a little reminder of what you'll be missing if you break your word."

I opened the door and raced down the hall without so much as a glance back.

Chapter Twenty-six

Earnest and I remained at an impasse twice the size of Cedar Rapids, and although we were both willing to compromise, neither of us would budge enough to suit the other. He remained horrified that I had poured plaster into Mel Gibson's navel on national television and placed all the blame for his wife's fall from grace squarely on the devil incarnate, Hyman Perth.

"At least no one back in Ten Commandments saw you," he said, alternating between heavy sighs and continual head shakes as he pushed cold scrambled eggs and slices of sausage around his plate. "They were all too busy tarring and feathering me at the time."

Why did he think my success had to be another nail in his career's coffin? Why couldn't he be happy for me? I tamped down my anger as best I could, but I'd pretty much reached my limit. After thirty years of marriage, I had used up my allotment of wife-as-a-second-class-citizen patience. "Earnest, I sympathize with your predicament, but don't turn into a drama queen, please."

"What's that supposed to mean?"

"It means it's not the end of the world, even if you do lose an election to Ralph Shakelmeyer, which I doubt very much you will."

"And how do you propose we live if I'm no longer mayor? My great-grandfather's trust pays the mayor's salary, whoever he is, not me. Unless you've planted a money tree in the garden, Connie, I still need to earn a living."

"Why?"

"Why?" He stared at me as if he were seeing that two-headed polka-dot heifer again. "How else are we going to pay our bills? On those . . . those obscene belly button lunacies of yours?"

I bit my tongue before the harangue boiling inside me forced its way out of my mouth. I had become very sensitive and protective of my belly button creations and thanks to Hy, now realized my talent should be treated with respect, not dismissed with ridicule.

Instead of launching into a tirade, I gently placed my fork on my plate and leaned back in my chair. I folded my arms across my chest, offered Earnest a knowing smile, and calmly said, "As a matter of fact, yes."

"Ha!" He slammed his palm on the table, rattling the dishes. "When Shakelmeyer's pigs sprout wings and fly. No one in his right mind will pay for such nonsense."

I raised my eyebrows. "Really?"

"Come on, Connie, get serious. That snake oil salesman has you bamboozled." Then his brow furrowed, his eyes filled with worry, and his jaw grew slack. "You didn't give him any money, did you?"

Widening my smile into a full-fledged smirk, I shook my head as I stood. If Earnest's prediction were correct, at this very moment back in Pottawattamie County, Ralph Shakelmeyer's pigs were taking to the sky. As much as I'd like to see such a phenomenon, I was even more eager to see the expression on my husband's face when I shoved copies of my contracts with Bergdorf Goodman and Tiffany's under his nose. With an extremely confident air, I strode into the bedroom to retrieve the paperwork.

A minute later, my thoroughly confused husband stared with disbelieving eyes at the papers I had spread on the table before him. "All totally legitimate and perfectly legal, Earnest. Not a drop of snake oil in sight. A score of lawyers dotted every 'i' and crossed every 't' before I signed anything. Hyman Perth isn't taking my money. He's making me a very wealthy woman."

Earnest refused to loosen the vise-like grip he held on his closed mind. "Only if someone is fool enough to buy those things. A year from now they'll be overflowing the plastic bins at the Dollar Store."

Scowling at him, I grabbed his plate off the table and began scraping his uneaten eggs and sausage into the trash. "Fine. If that's the way you feel, you may as well go back to Ten Commandments and reclaim your precious reputation. It's all you care about, anyway—what people think."

He pushed his chair back and jumped to his feet. "That's not true, and you know it."

"Do I?" I slammed the plate onto the counter and whirled around to confront him. My eyes welled with tears that spilled onto my cheeks. "I've stood placidly in your shadow for thirty years, Earnest, always supporting you, always playing the role of the perfect wife, going along with your cockamamie Ozzie and Harriet lifestyle without so much as a peep of protest because I loved you and believed in my marriage vows."

I gulped back a huge sob. "Now, finally, something wonderful happens to me. Are you happy for me? Are you proud? Are you supportive? No! You're too worried about what people will think and how it will affect your standing in the community. Well, you know what,

Earnest? If that's all you care about, to hell with you and to hell with Ten Commandments."

"Connie!"

I pushed him aside and ran into the bedroom, slamming the door behind me.

Sprawled on the bed, I spent the next half hour crying my eyes out. For the life of me, I couldn't figure out how I was going to save both my marriage and my *me*. And selfish or not, I wanted both and didn't see why I had to choose one or the other. Somehow, I had to make Earnest see reason.

I laughed between sobs. Wasn't that what he was trying to do to me, make *me* see reason? Only his reasoning and my reasoning were totally unreasonable as far as the other was concerned. We were like two rams in the spring, locking territorial horns. I sighed and reached for a tissue.

Earnest, his face flushed with worry, barged into the bedroom mid-blow. "Connie, hurry!" He grabbed my hand and yanked me off the bed, dragging me back into the kitchen.

"What?"

"Listen." He increased the volume on the radio buried in the corner of the counter behind the drain tray and alongside the toaster.

Welcome back. You're tuned to WBAT-Big Apple Talk Radio, and this is Gertie Gets Even. *Today's topic is "Revolting Male Behavior of a Bodily Nature." For example, why can men scratch their balls in public? If a woman tried to relieve crotch itch with a good scratch, she'd get arrested for lewd and indecent behavior. Who made up this rule? We itch, too, guys. Ever hear of yeast infections?*

I felt the color rise to my cheeks as I stared in horror at the radio. "That's Nori!"

Earnest nodded. "Now do you still believe I was wrong in wanting to protect my daughter?" He paused, his expression intense. "And my wife?"

Pressing my fingertips to my lips, I shuddered. "I knew Nori had taken a job at the radio station, but I'd assumed she was doing office work." I dropped into one of the kitchen chairs and listened to her.

And then there's spitting. What's up with that? Are men incapable of swallowing their own saliva? Maybe there's a genetic deficiency in the Y chromosome that prevents the male esophagus from functioning properly when it comes to spittle. You certainly don't see women walking around expectorating left and right, but try walking through a parking lot or down the street without having to sidestep those gross globs.

I chuckled.

Earnest glared at me. "What's so funny?"

"She does have a point. On both counts."

He harrumphed as he flipped off the radio. "That's totally beside the point."

"Is it? She's talking about the age-old, male-female double standard. What's fine for men is taboo for women. Why? Why can't I spit in public but you can? Why are you allowed to scratch certain body parts and I'm not? Why can you walk around bare-chested in the heat of August but I have to wear a bra and blouse?"

"Really, Connie. Don't be ridiculous."

"I'm not being ridiculous. Stop patronizing me. This isn't about spitting or scratching. It's about us. Why can't I be a *me* and you can?"

From the expression on his face, I had to assume the two-headed polka-dot heifer had returned. "A what?"

"A *me*. A person in my own right."

Earnest shook his head. "You're not making any sense, Connie."

I sighed. "I'm making perfect sense, but you're too close-minded to understand."

We could have debated this topic until the cows came home and probably would have if the doorbell hadn't rung. "It's probably your Svengali," said Earnest, his mouth dipping into a scowl as he headed for the front door.

But it wasn't Hy. It was Eugene. "There's something I need to tell the two of you," he said, following Earnest into the kitchen. He appeared nervous and uncomfortable as he settled his long, lanky frame into a chair at the table. My earlobes began itching like mad.

"We certainly do need to talk," said Earnest.

But neither of us expected the bombshell Eugene proceeded to drop in Nori's kitchen.

"Homosexual?" cried Earnest. "You can't be a homosexual."

"Can and am," Eugene assured him.

"Since when?"

"Since always."

"But what about Nori?" I asked.

"She knows I'm gay."

"This doesn't make any sense," I said. "You and Nori are supposed to get married. We've planned it for years."

Eugene smiled. "But no one ever consulted Nori and me about it. Besides, Nori's going to marry Mac."

"Don't be ridiculous," I said, my hand batting at the traitorous words hovering in the air between us. "She hardly knows him."

"True, but I've rarely seen two people as crazy about each other. Except for my mom and dad. And the two of you."

I glanced at Earnest. He stared back at me, not the two-headed polka-dot heifer stare of earlier but staring in that way he used to stare at me across the room when we were first married. His face had softened. He reached across the table for my hand and squeezed it. "I'm sorry, Connie."

I could tell he didn't only mean he was sorry about the death of my dreams for Eugene and Nori. Somehow Eugene's admission had put everything into perspective for both of us. Earnest hadn't been the only person trying to create a make-believe world for us to live in. Marjorie and I had been equally as guilty. I squeezed back. "Me, too. We've both been pigheaded fools, Earnest. For a long time."

He took a deep breath; his brows knit together. "I suppose I'm going to have to get used to a lot of changes."

Finally, he got it. And was willing to accept it. I was sure of it this time. I felt my eyes welling up with tears again, and swallowed hard to force back the sob that had lodged in my throat. "I'm not about to lose you, Earnest. We'll work it out, all of it. Together."

"What about Nori?"

I shrugged. "It's her life. We have to let her live it her way." I glanced over at Eugene and sighed. I suppose I'd have to get used to that Mac person. If Eugene was correct, he'd be hanging around for some time to come. As long as he made my daughter happy, I suppose I could learn to like him. "Even if we don't always agree with her choices," I added. And at least she had ditched the fancy-schmancy Parker Avenue skin doctor who made my earlobes itch from halfway across the country.

Earnest nodded in agreement. I knew he was taking a huge leap of faith that everything would work out for the best, and I admired him for having the courage to do so. My poor husband's world had been turned upside down and inside out over the past few days. A lesser man wouldn't have the will and strength of character to deal with the colossal changes, let alone accept them.

Maybe that was one of the reasons I loved him so. Deep in my heart, even during my blackest despair, I had clung to the hope that everything would work out for the best. And it would. I knew that now. You don't invest thirty years of your life in a marriage without knowing your spouse will come through for you in the end. Besides, I suspected now that Earnest was finally on his way to coming to terms with the present, he'd really enjoy the future. Our future.

Meanwhile, we both owed Nori a huge apology.

Chapter Twenty-seven

"Face it, Nori, it's time you stood up to your parents."

Didn't I do that when I left Iowa for New York?

"No, that was running away from the problem, not confronting it."

Gertie was right. For a change. Instead of screwing up my courage and demanding they allow me to live my own life, I had dealt with my parents' controlling attitudes by tucking tail and skulking out of town. Ever since I left Ten Commandments, we've danced around the topic, each of us afraid to address it. My parents have waited me out, expecting I'd eventually come to my senses and return home—to them and Eugene.

"They're going to have to give up on the Eugene part."

I'll say. Eugene gay? I still kept shaking my head in disbelief. He certainly masked his sexual orientation well, at least in Ten Commandments, but I suppose he'd had to in order to survive in such a conservative environment.

None of this musing helped me solve my immediate problem, though. I couldn't let Mac resign. When my segment ended, I returned to my office and our unresolved dilemma. To my dismay, he had reprinted the resignation letter.

"If I let you talk me out of resigning, you'll grow to resent me, maybe even hate me, and I couldn't live with that," he said, giving one of his crooked smiles. "After all, I'm a firm believer in a kid's parents living under the same roof and being on speaking terms with one another."

"Please don't joke, Mac. This is serious."

He took both of my hands in his. Stubborn determination settled across his face. "I'm not joking. I know how much you love your family. All the cracks about Ten Commandments and your parents' old-fashioned attitudes aside, they mean the world to you. Don't deny it."

He was beginning to sound like Gertie. "Your point?"

"We both know your father will never accept what you're doing. Maybe your mother could handle it. After all, any woman who can diddle with Mel Gibson's belly button on national television is capable of accepting anything. But not your father. Not from what you've told me about him."

I pulled my hands away from his and paced the small confines of the room. "Dad always worries how everything will impact his reputation and standing in the community. He's got to be this exemplary pillar of virtue and morality, always setting the proper example, and his family has to fall in line behind him." I laughed. "I guess I'm more like him than I realized."

Mac's expression grew skeptical. He raised one eyebrow; his eyes twinkled with devilment. "You a pillar of virtue and morality?"

My cheeks flushed with heat as visions of last night flashed across my brain. "Not that." I landed a soft punch on his bicep. "He's always worrying about what people back in Ten Commandments will think of him, and here I am worrying what he'll think of me."

Mac folded his arms across his chest and stared down at me as if I were a child caught stealing candy. "I won't buy into any rationalizations, Stedworth."

"I'm not rationalizing. I really want to strike the clause, Mac. I love doing the show, and I want the recognition that comes with it. Maybe that's my mother's influence on me. I now understand her excitement over Hy 'discovering' her."

"That still doesn't solve the problem of your father, though."

I sighed. "Back to square one, huh? You're right about my mother. She's not the person I thought she was. She's proved that in spades since her arrival. But my father?" I shook my head. "He'll never change."

"Don't be so sure, young lady."

I spun around. Mom, Dad, and Eugene stood in the open doorway. Monica hovered behind them. "I didn't think you'd mind," she said, waving as she headed back to her reception desk.

"Dad, I—"

He cut me off. "Interesting show, Nori. Looks like I'm going to have two famous women in the family."

"You know?" I glared at Eugene.

He held his hands up. "Don't look at me. I didn't tell them."

"We heard you on the radio," said my mother.

I looked from my mother to my father. "And you're not upset?"

Dad shrugged. "I'll get used to it."

I glanced over at Mac in time to see him dropping the letter of resignation into my trash can.

Epilogue

To borrow a cliché from the Bard, "All's well that ends well"—thanks in good part to me.

Nori continues to rant on radio and receive raves. She's writing a book, a collection of the best of Gertie Gets Even. You'll also find her popping up frequently on Good Morning America, where she dishes out commentary on the male/female tug-of-war du jour.

Her success became Mac's success. He climbed the corporate ladder at WBAT with breakneck speed, canning the no-talent jocks and hiring real talent to replace them.

As for their relationship, they were both pretty sure they were madly in love with each other, but Nori had learned her lesson with Dave. She insisted on taking things slowly—well, at least in all areas other than sex. That part of their relationship continued to be as explosive and mind-blowing as the first time. And believe me, as someone who was there, I can tell you it was definitely explosive and mind-blowing that first time. And every time since. For both of them.

Mac didn't mind Nori's live-for-the-moment attitude. He was enjoying himself too much. Besides, he knew down the road they'd be giving Connie those grandbabies she wanted.

Earnest finally dropped his paranoia and came to accept

302

Hy as Connie's business partner and nothing more. He loves his wife and has no intention of losing her, so he had no choice but to accept the "new" Connie and everything that came with her. Eventually, he learned to love the "new" Connie as much as he loved the "old" Connie.

As for Connie, she had never stopped loving her husband. The love she and Earnest had for each other enabled them to reach a compromise concerning her career.

Earnest couldn't argue with success, and he had to admit, his wife had become an overnight success—with belly button portraits, of all things. However, he was ecstatic when the belly button craze died down and Connie moved on to a less radical craft. The belly button art had established her as the "New Martha," though, so anything Connie came up with after belly buttons achieved instant "must-have" status.

Earnest was able to convince Connie to build her budding empire back in Ten Commandments. He took over day-to-day operations while she managed the creative end of the business. Hy handled manufacturing, imports, and marketing from New York. They even built a television studio so *The Connie Stedworth Craft and Home Hour* could be taped in Ten Commandments.

The recall vote went through, and the town replaced Earnest with Ralph Shakelmeyer, but lived to regret it. Within weeks they were begging Earnest to resume his post as mayor. Earnest declined. He no longer had the time nor inclination to run the town, not after the way everyone had turned against him.

Besides, he had come to accept that he wasn't the guardian of his ancestors' legacy. Ten Commandments and its citizens, including his extended family, were welcome to live their lives as they saw fit, and if that meant acting like fornicating, embezzling low-lives . . . well, it was their lives and their reputations, not his.

Several times a year Earnest and Connie flew back to New York to develop new projects and product lines for Connie Stedworth Enterprises. Hyman Perth even made the occasional trip out to Ten Commandments and actually fell in love with the bucolic town. Rumor has it he's thinking of purchasing a vacation home off Main Street. He's been seen squiring Aunt Irma around town. He even took her all the way to Des Moines for Sunday dinner last week.

Irma was Uncle Ezra's wife. She filed for divorce the day after the Illinois State Police picked up Ezra and Merline Tibble outside Chicago. They're now both doing twenty years in separate state penitentiaries.

Although Earnest and Connie have accepted Mac and no longer yearn for a Stedworth-Draymore union, Marjorie still hasn't come to terms with Eugene's lifestyle. She's trying, though. The rest of Ten Commandments doesn't know about Eugene yet, and Marjorie hopes to keep it that way, at least for as long as possible. She's sworn her husband, Eugene, and the Stedworths to secrecy—not that any of them would say anything, but Marjorie wants to make sure. After all, you never know how people will react, especially people in Ten Commandments. They might even decide to take their funereal needs ten miles down the road to Badger Bluffs.

Meanwhile, Eugene has followed Nori's lead and moved to New York, where he's set up housekeeping with Gabe. The two of them opened the first exclusively gay and lesbian funeral parlor in Manhattan. Reese went back to school for a cosmetology license and now spends her days making the corpses look beautiful. She's seriously considering Eugene and Gabe's request that she become an egg donor and surrogate so they can have a baby.

Marjorie doesn't know anything about this yet, but since it's the only way she'll ever become a grandmother, Eugene thinks she'll eventually be thrilled—if the shock doesn't kill her first.

As for me, I'm going back into lurk mode, but I'll be keeping an eye on everyone and popping up from time to time whenever I'm needed.

CONNIE'S PAPER NAPKIN DECOUPAGE

Nori might not think too highly of her mother's penchant for paper napkin decoupage, but it's an easy project for even the most craft-challenged. And Nori's disparaging *Iowa hick* comment to the contrary, paper napkin decoupage can produce some very sophisticated results, depending on your choice of surface and napkin pattern.

Although Connie enjoys decoupaging on straw accessories, decoupage will work on just about any surface—straw, glass, wood, plastic, metal, ceramic, clay, terra cotta, slate, leather, plastic foam, paper, and fabric. To begin, clean the item you want to decoupage. Wood should be smooth and dust free. Wipe down glass surfaces with rubbing alcohol or vinegar. Metal surfaces must be coated with rust-resistant sealer.

Choose a napkin pattern. Carefully cut the desired image from the napkin. Peel off the top printed layer of the napkin. Discard the bottom layer. Using a foam brush, apply Modge Podge® to the item. Position the napkin design on the surface. Smooth to eliminate wrinkles. Allow to dry. Apply a second coat over entire surface. When dry, apply clear acrylic sealer to eliminate tackiness.

KATHLEEN BACUS

CALAMITY JAYNE

Tressa Jayne Turner has had it up to *here* with the never-ending string of dumb-blonde jokes and her long-time nickname. Crowned "Calamity Jayne" by Iowa Department of Natural Resources officer Rick Townsend, Tressa's out to gain a little hometown respect—or die trying. She's just been handed the perfect opportunity to get "Ranger Rick" to finally take her seriously. How? By solving a murder no one else believes happened.... No one, that is, except the killer.

Yup, Calamity Jayne is in it up to her hot pink snakeskin cowgirl boots. Tressa would tell you her momma never raised no dummies, but the jury's still out on that one.

JENNIE KLASSEL

IT HAPPENED IN SOUTH BEACH

If she's a beauteous, bodacious babe, gettin' down, gettin' it on, gettin' her man, she's definitely *not* good old Tilly Snapp. So what's the safe, sensible twenty-six-year-old Bostonian doing in Miami's ultra-hip, super-chic South Beach?

She's on the trail of the fabled Pillow Box of Win Win Poo—the most valuable collection of antique erotic "accessories" in the world. And she's after the fiend who murdered her eccentric Aunt Ginger. And while Tilly might not know the difference between a velvet tickle pickle and a kosher dill, with the assistance of the sexy yet unhelpful Special Agent Will Maitland, she's about to get a crash course in sex-ed.

Meet the new Tilly Snapp, Sex Detective.

South Beach ain't seen nothin' yet.

Love, Lies and a Double Shot of Deception

LOIS WINSTON

Logan Crawford is gorgeous, charming, and his kisses make Emma feel like she's the only woman in the world. Oh, plus he's a billionaire. Not that Emma needs the money. As Philadelphia's most beloved heiress, she has it all: the grand estate, flashy sports car, high-society connections. But the haunted widow also has dark secrets, and someone out there doesn't want to let Emma forget her past quite so easily. Trouble is brewing darker than a double espresso for Emma and her newfound love. Now if only she can keep from getting burned....

ISBN 10: 0-505-52719-7
ISBN 13: 978-0-505-52719-6 $6.99 US/$8.99 CAN

Unlucky

JANA DeLEON

Everyone in Royal Flush, Louisiana, knows Mallory Devereaux is a walking disaster. At least now she's found a way to take advantage of her chronic bad luck: by "cooling" cards on her uncle's casino boat. As long as the crooks invited to his special poker tournament don't win their money back, she'll get a cut of the profit.

But Mal isn't the only one working some major mojo. There's a dark-eyed dealer sending her looks steamier than the bayou in August. Turns out he's an undercover agent named Jake Randoll, and for a Yank, he's pretty darn smart. Smart enough to enlist her help to catch a money launderer. As they race to untangle a web of decades-old lies and secrets amid a gathering of criminals, Mallory can't help hoping her luck's about to change....

ISBN 10: 0-505-52729-4
ISBN 13: 978-0-505-52729-5

Available November 2007